Stigma from the Past

Anuli Ausbeth-Ajagu

Strategic Book Publishing and Rights Co.

Strategic Book Publishing and Rights Co.
12620 FM 1960, Suite A4-507
Houston, TX 77065
www.sbpra.com

ISBN: 978-1-61204-792-8

Book Design: Suzanne Kelly

Dedication

To my beloved mother, Mrs. Ebele Grace Ufodike, who encapsulates the true essence of motherhood: a beautiful heart, kind and generous spirit, long suffering and enduring, inspiring and committed, compassionate and caring, merciful and gracious, loving, forgiving and practical in support. You are a beautiful mother and a real inspiration to your world.

Contents

Prologue

It was raining heavily when the band of hoodlums filed out of the scene. They sauntered into the jalopy parked outside, their heads swirling, all seven of them falling into the truck, boozed and satiated. The driver hopped behind the wheel and ignited the engine, drove a few meters, and suddenly he started gyrating. All he could see were pictures running in duplicates. Possibly, it was the aftereffect of overindulgence in the bottles. Otherwise, how would one explain the faintness of his sight? Sadly though, his vision continued faltering, culminating in a complete loss of concentration. Suddenly, the vehicle made a leap off the road and started descending a cliff. His attempt at maneuvering was poor . . . and alas! Too late!

Meanwhile, their gang leader remained glued to the defilement spot. He was in no hurry to leave as he viewed, with utmost satisfaction, the helpless figure lying on the floor. Instinctively jolting out of introspection, an eerie feeling engulfed him. What were the likely consequences of the act? What if there was a scandal? The possibility couldn't be ruled out completely, going by the way the victim vehemently resisted their assault. A lot could be at stake for him, particularly his sustenance. It wasn't as though he particularly appreciated his present calling. Matter of fact, it was becoming a drag . . . except, of course, with his recent boorish feat.

Slowly and steadily, he pulled himself together, took a last long look at the victim and quietly made his way out of the room. He walked with quick strides, not minding the thundering and downpour, until he arrived at his flat located a few blocks away. Without thinking, he fished out a bag from his scanty wardrobe and started packing. As he threw in his possessions, his mind was everywhere, roaming and wondering. The thought of leaving abruptly was really no concern at all. After all, he had often lived as a tramp. His problem and major concern was how to escape the possible arms of the law. Instinctively, he felt his dreadlocks. Certainly, that identity could easily betray him. Ironically, his victim shared the same, only hers were neatly bound to suit her femininity. Dada, that was his name and hers too, the traditional name in Nigeria for children born with natural dreadlocks.

Such irony, such similarity, yet they had always trod different paths. But alas, the time had come for a change—Dada Salako's physical alteration, his own deliberate change, a change of identity.

A total disguise will surely do him good, so he pulled open his drawer and reached out for a pair of scissors. Without thinking, he started chopping off the long tangled mass on his head. In a matter of minutes, the pile lay scattered on the floor. He couldn't believe his eyes when he looked at himself in the mirror. The haircut had dramatically transformed his appearance. Still, Dada Salako was not satisfied. He was not one to leave any traits for a clue, so he reached for his shaver and started shaving. How he managed to give himself a clean hair shave remained a mystery even to him.

By the time he gazed into the mirror to appraise his new look, it was clear he'd succeeded in disguising totally. To make his new look complete, he made up his mind to start growing a moustache . . .

There was more thundering, just as his roaring laughter echoed in the walls. He was happy . . . satisfied . . . contented with his new identity. Nobody will recognize him. Not even the victim. A thought struck him. The new man would certainly not be complete without a new name. "A new name?" he wondered. "Hmm . . . a change of name wouldn't be a bad idea." He certainly could do with a complete change of scene, a change of environment. As he racked his brain for a solution, the answer hit him like a thunderbolt. He couldn't believe his luck. What on earth could be better than the substantive offer he got earlier in the year? It was still valid for a couple of weeks so he needn't search further. That sorted, his mind again began to wander, this time to the girl. "Will she survive the ordeal?" he wondered. Without further delay, he threw the remaining items into the bag, packed the mass of hair he'd just chopped off, took a last look around the empty room and stepped into the dark.

Fortunately, the rain had finally stopped so he had no problem hurrying to the main gate. Meanwhile, his mind flashed to his cohorts—the idle hoodlums he'd contacted to join in desecrating his victim. They'd done an excellent job and deserved his commendation, so he chose their hideout as his first point of call. By the time he arrived at their place, there was no sign of them. He lit a cigarette and decided to wait patiently for their arrival . . . they never made it back. He was to discover a few days later that their vehicle had skidded off the road and somersaulted into the lagoon. Some of their mangled bodies were recovered. Others were hungrily devoured by ravenous crocodiles. Dada was shocked but counted himself very lucky. Very lucky indeed because the deed was done and nothing, absolutely nothing, could ever expose him. Now to the present: He was set for a long journey, a very long journey into another phase in his already eventful life.

CHAPTER ONE

It was a cold, wet, and windy night in June. The fierceness of the thundering and the terrifying downpour kept most residents of the National Foundation for Young Mothers and Kids indoors, away from their usual weekend barbecue night. The philanthropic institution, under the aegis of a munificent mission, was established for the primary aim of giving shelter, counsel, and hope to abandoned and underprivileged young mothers in Ghana. Located in Tamale, in the northern region of Ghana, the highly reputable institution had liaison offices in major cities like Accra, Kumasi, and Takoradi. The charity was considered the leading lifesaving organization in the country because of their proactive crusade against abortion and child abuse. Various activities were in progress to mark their twentieth anniversary. Their target for the year was to raise sufficient funds for the orphanage, which needed expansion and sponsorship for the increasing number of children in their care. Mercy, as head of the organizing committee, was laden with the responsibility of making necessary contacts with generous and good-spirited individuals who could donate in cash and kind to their laudable mission. Her mind was preoccupied with the planning as she lay in bed under the warmth of a thick woolly blanket, appreciating the serenity of the quietened weather.

Besides the intermittent sound of ceasing raindrops, everywhere was tranquil. The atmosphere looked heavenly, with stars glistening in the sky, the moon disappearing in the horizon, and the freshness of the earth filling the air. It was indeed a shivery night, and cool as it was, nature's refreshing allure could not pass by unappreciated. She could have remained lost in her reverie but for the sudden thrust at her door. Esi entered to announce that Mercy was urgently required by the reverend mother. Their training and calling as nuns required prompt response at any time of the day to emergency calls to duty. She immediately sprang to her feet, threw on her robe and in a matter of minutes was descending several corridors that led to Mother Araba's office.

There was a stranger in her company; a very unusual one at that. Extremely pretty, very ostentatious, elegant, and stately, she looked every inch like royalty. Her perfectly manicured fingers were adorned with dainty gold rings, while her glittering necklace and earrings were made of fine diamonds. The sweet fragrance of her Elizabeth Arden perfume filled the air, and her elaborate coiffure was a classic African design adorned with silver beads. Underneath the glamorous appearance, however, was the saddest, loneliest figure of a woman in dire need of help.

"Meet Mrs. Tisco," Mother Araba introduced briefly. "She'll like to see you privately."

"Certainly, Mother," Mercy responded with a bow before facing the visitor. "You'll please come with me," she stated, leading the way into an adjoining office.

"Welcome madam," Mercy greeted as they settled on their seats. The office was sparsely furnished, with a conference table, six chairs, and a chest of drawers.

"I've come a very long way," Elizabeth Tisco began the moment they were seated. "I have been informed by the reverend mother that you are in charge of the orphanage."

"Yes I am, though we work together as a team."

"Can I trust you?" she probed, her eyes gazing intently at Mercy, who was thrown off balance by the question. "Can I trust you?" she reiterated, unmindful of the former's quizzical expression.

"Well, *em*, trust in the Lord with all thy heart . . . but you can count on me," Mercy responded simply.

"I hear you are in charge of adoption procedure."

The former replied in the affirmative before the stranger spoke almost in a whisper.

"I need a baby. I'll prefer a male . . . dark in complexion, oval face, dark hair, and AA genotype. O-positive blood group, and please, this is strictly confidential."

Mercy wore a perplexed expression as she listened to the woman. It seemed she'd taken no notice of the nun's bewilderment because she quickly added, "How much?"

"I beg your pardon, ma'am?"

"How much will I pay you to give me a baby?" She asked, bringing out a checkbook from her handbag. She made to endorse one when the nun's voice stopped her in her tracks.

"It appears you have gotten things mixed up. Adoption certainly isn't a buying and selling trade. Moreover, specific physical criteria are difficult to meet. Hair color, blood group, et cetera have hardly been of any consideration for fosterage. Besides, we don't get such an avalanche of children to pick from."

"Now we are talking. Let's say you have about nine months from now to do the planning. I'm counting on you to give me a baby . . . my baby," she stated in a doleful tone. "I'm desperate. If I don't get this baby, my life will be ruined. Oh sister, promise you will give me a baby," she pleaded, tears dripping from her eyes.

"You don't have to cry, please," Mercy said, moved by her sentiments. She offered her a paper napkin and squeezed her hand reassuringly before speaking. "Let's start from the beginning. Why do you want this baby in the first place?"

"I have to give my husband an heir, or else he'll remarry. Or rather, his callous mother will impose another wife on him."

"Permit me to ask you some personal questions. Your husband, does he love you?"

"Yes . . . I can swear Nick loves me."

"For how long have you been married?"

"Three years."

"Three years?"

"Yes"

"Only three years and you're already desperate?"

"His mother has been watching my stomach since we got married. By the fifth month into our marriage and with no signs of pregnancy, she's been on my neck—our neck, pressuring her son, calling me horrible names. She'll regret this . . . I swear she will."

"Thou shall not swear," cautioned Mercy, before questioning further. "But why the anxiety? She should exercise some patience."

"She hates me. She hates me because Nick married me against her wish. She's prejudiced, egocentric, and malicious."

Mercy took a deep breath and pondered for a while before speaking.

"You live here in Tamale?"

"No. I came in from Nigeria."

"You—you came all the way from Nigeria?"

Elizabeth nodded her head, and observed the nun's bewilderment.

"Aren't there—I mean, surely there are orphanages there in Nigeria. Why come all the way just to adopt a child?"

"Don't you understand? Don't you understand that nobody's to know the child isn't mine? I'll be a laughing stock if I'm ever discovered. Nobody's to know the baby isn't mine. Not even . . . not even my husband."

Mercy wore a disapproving expression before Elizabeth quickly added.

"I hate to do this to Nick . . . but I have to. I can't stand losing him."

"You should tell him. I mean, if he loves you, surely he will understand. Besides, you need his consent for things to work out."

"You don't understand, sister. You don't understand the nightmare I've been through. My mother-in-law will broadcast the news that I didn't bear the child."

"You might end up complicating things, ma'am. I mean, how do you prove that the baby's yours when your husband knows you aren't pregnant?"

"I'll think of something. I'll pretend I'm pregnant . . . I'll take a long vacation. I'll . . . oh please, sister, just get me the baby. I'll sort myself out somehow," she spluttered, suddenly feeling odd and jittery.

"I know this means a lot to you, but I insist you think seriously before acting," Mercy pressed.

"I don't think you're getting me right. I don't think you understand what I am going through. Do you know what it's like to be taunted because you don't have a child? Do you know just what it feels like being labeled a barren witch? I thought this out seriously before coming all the way. There is nothing more to think about. I need a baby, okay? I said I need a baby!" Elizabeth thundered, reaching out for the handkerchief in her bag. Her tears trickled and burst into a downpour.

Mercy watched in awe, unable to speak. She'd never seen such display of sentiments. "Not even that night," she thought with a shiver; her memory betraying her. She quickly brushed aside the intellection and faced the woman.

"I—madam, please don't cry. I only needed to be sure you won't regret your decision in the future."

"There can never be regrets. This is the only solution; otherwise, my marriage will crumble."

"But this is surprising," Mercy put in. "I mean, if your husband truly loves you, he should speak to his mother to stop pushing."

"What hasn't Nick done to pacify her? What hasn't my poor Nick done to have her back off? But no, never will she give up. She's bent on ruining us. She's obsessed with her son. She thinks she knows what's best for him."

"It's amazing," Mercy whispered. "Such is life. It beats my imagination, man's unkindness to his fellow man. Yet God created us all in His image and likeness. Male or female, black or white, Hausa, Igbo, Yoruba, Efik, Chinese, Indian, American, British, or Spanish, once married, every human being has a right to live without harassment."

"Not my mother-in-law. She hates me, and I swear, I hate her too."

"Please don't swear. Don't hate her either. Pray for her. Ask God to show her mercy," Mercy said softly. "That way, you will be obeying the golden rule: do unto others, as you will have them do unto you."

Elizabeth sat up in her chair. She shook her head before speaking. "No, no, sister. I believe an eye for an eye, a tooth for a tooth. After all, it's not my fault things turned out this way. She hates me, and I assure you I hate her with a double measure. The feeling of animosity is mutual," Elizabeth asserted with a lingering baleful expression.

Mercy took a deep breath and watched the other woman. She could empathize with her situation, having experienced severe hurt herself. Her mind flashed back to that fateful day, and she immediately shook herself out of the unpleasant reverie.

"When do I get the baby?" Elizabeth asked, gazing intently at the reverend sister.

"We'll give you a baby," Mercy said, breathing hard. "There are about three young girls who'll be due for confinement in a couple of months."

Elizabeth listened with rapt attention as the reverend sister flipped through the huge diary on the table.

"The first girl will be due in about seven months, the other six, and the third says approximately five months from now. Let's keep our fingers crossed, Mrs. Tisco."

"Thank you, sister, thank you. Please call me Liz. Elizabeth if you prefer. I will forever be indebted to you."

"No problem. Just remember, we don't sell babies here. The important thing is having a healthy family environment to raise the child. Other procedure and documentation follow with ease."

"Once again, I appreciate this," Elizabeth uttered, before handing her a check. "For your foundation's anniversary."

"Thank you. We are most grateful," Mercy responded, examining the check. It was appropriately written in the name of the foundation, payable in cedis. It was the equivalent of USD $10,000.

Elizabeth smiled back and for the first time, noticed the pretty, youthful face belying the plain convent clothes. Indeed, Mercy was a beautiful woman. With an average height of about five feet six inches, a smooth dark skin, hers could have been a face for modeling and magazine covers if she hadn't chosen the way of seclusion. Her slim figure would have been any photographer's delight, going by her innate elegance. Her calling, however, easily concealed the allure of the reverend sister's natural endowment.

"You're a beautiful woman, sister," Elizabeth said, almost in a whisper.

Mercy was numb for a moment. The word beautiful felt odd to qualify her. She was used to such connotations as reverend, holy, chaste, humble . . . but certainly not beautiful.

"Tell me, sister Mercy, what does it feel like to be a nun? What does it feel like to live without love?" Elizabeth probed, unaware of the nun's inner turmoil. "Life is all about love, and I can't imagine not loving Nick, or not having him love me in return."

"I—well, people are made different," Mercy managed to say, clearing her head of its many conflicts. "We have different callings in life. Mine is a life of service," she avowed.

"Thanks for everything," Elizabeth said finally, rising to her feet. "Yours is a life of service—a life of helping others. I'm counting on you to give me my baby," she stated decisively, reaching out for the other woman. She embraced her, squeezed her shoulders, before concluding, "Here's my call card. If you ever need my help, do not hesitate to call, and please keep me updated on the happenings."

"I certainly will keep in touch," the nun responded, rising to her feet as her visitor made to leave.

"Good night, sister Mercy."

"Good night ma'am," Mercy replied, watching the woman make a brisk exit and disappear into the dark. There and then, the reverend sister made up her mind not to disappoint the woman.

Day in, day out, Mercy prayed earnestly for a baby that would suit Elizabeth's imagery and description. Months rolled by and nothing significant happened, except for the birth of a premature baby boy to one of the girls. Unfortunately though, the baby died. Mercy was dispirited, particularly when the second girl delivered a set of twin girls. Elizabeth didn't want a girl. She wanted a son, one that would be heir apparent to her husband. There was just one more to go, and if things didn't work out as planned, the woman would be devastated. She'd been in close contact with the foundation since her last visit.

"Something positive better happen," the compassionate nun often recited as she travailed night and day for the woman. She'd made a promise, and she needed to fulfill it.

CHAPTER TWO

"Sister Mercy . . . Sister Mercy!"

Mercy turned in the direction of the caller. It was Esi.

"Hi," she responded, getting up from the lonely spot in the garden where she'd been sitting, meditating for the past hour.

The girl Efua insists you come now. She is in labor."

Mercy stared at her, a bit stupefied, before scrambling to her feet and heading in the direction of the obstetrics unit.

"Sister Mercy, Sister Mercy . . . I need Mercy . . . help!" Efua cried the moment the compassionate nun appeared in the delivery room.

"Easy dear," Mercy comforted, holding the girl's clenched fist. Despite the midwife's efforts at calming Efua, Mercy had to intervene.

"Now remember your Lamaze exercise. Take a deep breath in, out . . . in, out. You can make it," Mercy enthused.

"No I can't—the pain—ouch! It's excruciating!"

"Oh yes you can, be positive, you can make it. You're doing just great, my dear . . ."

It wasn't long before the piercing cry of the newborn filled the room with welcome cheers.

"Congratulations! It's a boy. An adorable boy," Mercy said as the midwife held him up for them to see.

"I don't want to see him, please . . . can I go home now?" The teenager asked, relieved of the unwelcome burden. She certainly wasn't going to mother the child. "Thanks to the orphanage," she thought, glad that the sisters were going to put the baby away for adoption. She suddenly felt free—free as the birds of the air.

Moments later, she was transferred to another room where she showered and sat to a meal in Mercy's company. She ate in

silence, reminiscing over the past months of her life. The pregnancy had been a disaster and a major setback to her academics,
as she was unable to take her final secondary school exams as
a result. Now she'll have to put bits of her life together again. It
all seemed like a jigsaw puzzle.

"How do you feel, my dear?" Mercy asked, jolting her out
of introspection.

"Great and relieved. Can I go home tonight? Please?"

"First things first. Now finish your meal and get some rest
before anything," Mercy stated firmly.

"But I feel very normal now," she protested, gesturing dramatically with her hands. "I feel fresh as the morning."

"Not to worry, I'm sure we won't keep you for too long.
Besides, you still have a few counseling classes to attend."

"Oh please, sister, I've heard all the advice I can possibly get
for a lifetime. It was a mistake, I admit. Now the ordeal is over,
thank God. I want to resume normal life immediately."

"You would, my dear, but the counseling is very important.
There's still so much for you to learn."

"I know everything already. Thou shall not fornicate, thou
shall not defile the temple of God . . . sex before marriage is sin
. . . abstinence is the key . . . what else? I already know all that.
In fact, I know enough to make me become a nun like you. But
. . . I don't want to become one."

Mercy took a deep breath before speaking. "We cannot keep
you here against your wish. We are at least thankful that you
gave us that precious little one by keeping it alive and giving it
an opportunity to see the world."

"Please don't talk like that, sister, you'll make me feel guilty.
I should be the one thanking you and the entire foundation for
your kindness and understanding."

"That's okay, it's a fair deal. We are grateful to you, and you
are thankful to us. Nobody loses, no victor, no vanquished," she
put in wittily.

The youngster laughed delightedly and as usual, felt very
relaxed in the empathetic woman's company.

"What are your plans for the future?" Mercy asked, airily.

"I'll go back to senior secondary school, graduate and proceed to the University. I want to be a medical doctor."

"Really?"

"Yes, I've got great plans to build a hospital. In fact, the hospital will be a world-class hospital located in the capital city, Accra. You know that thing doctors wear . . . *em* . . ."

"Stethoscope? It's the instrument for listening to the sounds generated inside the body," Mercy offered.

"Yes, stethoscope, I like it."

"Great. That is a good dream you've got. Medicine is a very good profession, but it calls for hard work, dedication, and selfless service to humanity."

"That's no problem. I could be very serious and studious. I can spend long hours reading. I know doctors constantly bury themselves in medical books and journals, and I am willing to pay the price."

"Smart girl," Mercy commented, enjoying the company of the optimistic sixteen-year-old.

They chatted for a while longer, before a nurse came in to do the routine post-parturition checkup.

Several days passed by, and Efua left the foundation feeling rejuvenated, invigorated, exhilarated. The youngster had gotten impregnated by her school boyfriend, a seventeen-year-old boy who had disappeared from her life since the day she announced the pregnancy. Efua, who got severely reprimanded by the boy's mother, had been thrown out of her family house by her mother and stepfather, who disowned her and swore to have nothing to do with her. It was then the girl sought help from the charity organization, and the nuns intervened. Her family, after much intervention and pleas from the Reverend Mother Araba and Sister Mercy, agreed to take her back. They insisted that it would be possible only after she had gotten rid of the baby, as they were not interested in raising her bastard, as they'd labeled the unborn child. Efua was then taken in by the nuns, and now that she had done away with the baby, her family was ready to reintegrate her. The teenage mum's experience with her unwanted pregnancy had taught her some hard lessons about life. She vowed to pursue her studies, make up for the setback and make the most of her career life, whilst being wary of teenage sex. Sadly, her lover boy was gone with the wind, as his parents had sent him off to another school outside the shores of Ghana, where he will be away from her seduction, as they had labeled it.

After several futile attempts to reach Elizabeth Tisco for the adoption of the newborn, Mercy received the bombshell.

"Elizabeth Tisco is dead!"

"What?" The reverend sister screamed in disbelief. "What happened? I mean—how? When?"

"She is dead! Dead!" And then the phone went dead.

Mercy looked around in confusion, unable to make much sense of the news.

How could the woman be dead? Elizabeth Tisco, so vibrant, young, and full of life. Despite her cares and worries, life seemed very promising for her. It seemed ridiculous that she could be cut off prematurely in her prime. More ironical was the fact that her dream child was set for adoption. The boy vividly replicated the late woman's physical description of how her dream baby should look.

Mercy wailed and mourned the demise of the woman who had left a remarkable impression on her. There was something about Elizabeth. Her passion, her life, and her hazy future seemed to bear witness with the nun's heart. Something about Elizabeth elicited Mercy's curiosity and interest. There was a magnet about her fervor. It was as though a new reality was birthed, the dawn of a new era with the realization that life was full of uncertainties. It was necessary to make hay while the sun shines, to redeem time and work with the leading of one's heart. Something in Mercy suddenly cried out for exhalation. Further delay might mean further denial, but how was she to explain? And who will understand? If she dared voice her thoughts, she may suffer eternal castigation.

With these gloomy thoughts, her mind was in battle for several days, then weeks, and months. Her confusion and depression were taking their toll on her and especially evident in her mien. Life became a miserable routine. She was cheerless, despondent, and severely mortified. The more she ignored the thoughts, the more the pressure came on her. It wasn't long before Mother Araba became concerned. She decided it best to invite her colleague for a chat.

"What's bothering you, Sister Mercy?" she began, the moment the younger nun arrived at her office that sunny afternoon.

Mercy was surprised but remained quiet as the reverend mother spoke.

"Remember we are here for each other, to share and to care. Whatever the problem may be, there must be a solution."

Mercy managed a smile but chose to remain mute.

"Talk to me, Mercy, we are sisters, remember."

"It's nothing, Mother, I'm fine. Thanks anyway for your concern."

"There is a problem. I've been watching you, and it's very glaring that you are in distress. Over the months, you have become more and more withdrawn. Nothing on earth can convince me otherwise. Let's share your burden."

"Oh Mother, there is nothing to talk about—or rather, how do I explain?"

"Start from somewhere."

"I feel unfulfilled. I . . . feel empty. I feel a vacuum in my heart."

Mother Araba looked perplexed as she listened to the younger woman.

"Am I making any sense, Mother? I need to exhale. That's the problem."

Araba shook her head disapprovingly and cogitated for a while.

"Do you need a vacation? A retreat? A time away from the hustle and bustle around here? Poor child! I know you've been under pressure lately. You never really get time to relax, do you? I insist you take a break."

"No . . . not that," Mercy protested before she was interrupted.

"Oh yes, I insist. You need a holiday, Mercy. Take two weeks off, dear; with that, you shall be refreshed and revitalized again."

CHAPTER THREE

L ectures had just ended for the week at the Institute for French Education, Accra, as students and teachers noisily packed their paraphernalia in excitement for another weekend. It had indeed been a very busy week at the lingual institution, where the National Conference of Linguistics had just been hosted. Seminars, essay contests, and debates were some high-lights of the highly successful event. Chants of "thank God it's Friday" filled the air, a popular slogan amongst the students and lecturers who toiled night and day to ensure they maintained the institution's high academic standards.

Alexander Moyo, one of the popular male teachers, stood in front of the staff-room, his slim neck outstretched expectantly as he anxiously awaited his colleague's arrival. It wasn't long before he sighted her, the pretty, dark-skinned lady who'd been causing him sleepless nights lately.

"Hello, Dorothy," he greeted, his heart thumping hard in excitement.

"Hi, you wanted to see me?"

"Hmm, yes. Can we go somewhere private and talk?"

"Sure, why not?" she asked before taking his hand, unmindful of the lanky fellow's astonishment.

"I must say I was impressed by your speech on bilateral communication," she commented as they walked towards a comfortable shade away from the hustle.

"I'm flattered, your highness," Alexander replied, taking extra care with his mannerism as she relaxed on the luxuriant lawn. The landscaping was a horticultural splendor, another plus for the institution, which prided itself not only in academic excellence but also in environmental friendliness. Their school management had been inspired by Kenyan Wangari Maathai's

Green Belt Movement and her tree-planting program geared at environmental conservation.

"This is no flattery, Mr. Moyo; it's a statement of fact. I've always admired your brilliance and eloquence. Tell me, which college did you attend?"

"A very unpopular one, Dorothy," he replied, wearing a broad smile, "my pedigree may not be impressive, but I certainly know my onions. I must also commend your intelligence. Of all the female lecturers in this institution, your astuteness is legendary. You are also very pretty. I bet you were born on a Sunday," he continued.

Dorothy laughed. "See what I mean? You are a wizard. I was born on a Sunday."

"Aha! So you are Akosua—born on Sunday. I guessed as much. Born on the day reserved for special beings. Tell me something, Dorothy, you are from the Ashanti region, true?"

"Have you been prying into my pedigree?" she probed.

"Not at all, but the historic strength of your ancestors runs in your blood. You have such a strong, forceful personality," he proffered.

"I look like a warrior, don't I? Go on and say it. People tell me I'm an Amazon; I really don't care. Yes, I am of the Ashanti region, and I am proud of it."

Alexander watched her with bewilderment. "I didn't mean to be offensive, ma'am. I intended complimenting your phenomenal quality."

"What did you want to see me about anyway?" she queried, ignoring his explanation.

"*Em* . . . well."

"Go on, I'm listening."

"I . . . I, *em*, wanted to tell you that I . . . like you a lot. What do you say about you and me becoming friends?"

Dorothy burst out laughing. Alexander watched her quizzically, feeling perplexed by her reaction.

"What's the joke?" he asked.

"You," she responded, yawning and stretching out tiredly.

"I don't understand."

"What sort of friendship do you want from me, Alexander?"

"Well, *em*, male female . . . I mean boyfriend, girlfriend . . . or maybe intimate. You know, something long lasting and enduring, Akosua."

Dorothy again burst out laughing, while he watched her with greater perplexity.

"May I share your joke?"

"Oh certainly, darling," she replied in a sarcastic tone. "First, point of correction . . . I may have been born on Sunday, but my parents did not name me Akosua, so please don't rename me. People who change their names have something to hide or something they are running away from. Call me Dorothy."

"Absolutely ma'am—Dorothy. But permit me to dwell a little on the issue of names. Yeah, I agree that a stigma from the past may taunt one into changing a name in order to have a new identity. But I also think that on a positive note, names can also be adopted as a symbol of a rediscovered identity. For you, my dear, with royalty in your blood, I cannot simply refer to you as Dorothy. Perhaps Princess Dorothy will suffice, or probably Her Majesty Queen Dorothy."

"Flattery won't get you into my heart, mister," she said, grinning from ear to ear. "Furthermore, it is either I am getting old fashioned or civilization has taken its toll on the romantic instincts of twenty-first-century men." Alexander was agape as she spoke. "I remember once a boy told me he was in love with me. He was down on his knees with a rose flower as he sang the most romantic song I ever heard. I found it very funny. I would have preferred a love letter; accompanied by an emotional card and a complimenting gift. That was my preference then. With the benefit of hindsight, he was an absolute romantic. Here you are today, proposing under a guava tree, lush lawns, surrounded by classrooms. Whatever happened to those exotic restaurants with beautiful scenery and candlelight? What do you take me for, Alexander?"

"I'm terribly sorry, Princess Dorothy. I didn't realize . . ."

"Save your breath! Your explanation wouldn't make a difference. Consider yourself lucky to have met me in my good mood. For your information, I obliged your invitation because I like you too. Your rusty approach will be overlooked because I like you," she echoed.

"I, *em*—I'm truly elated, darling . . . you've simply blown my mind. As for the candlelight dinner and exotic setting, I swear I'll tour the world with you in my arms. You'd wake up to delicious breakfast in bed, exotic cruises, saunas, and massage in the best aromatic oils. Darling Dorothy, if you give me your heart, I'll build you a palace where I'll worship you forever and even the goddess of love will grow green with envy. Be my girl, baby, and I'll be forever yours," he concluded, down on his knees as Dorothy shut her eyes in ecstasy.

CHAPTER FOUR

Dorothy put finishing touches to her hair and makeup before taking time to admire herself in the mirror. She looked smashing, having spent time preparing for the dinner date ahead. Her ebony skin glowed with the finishing touches of her Mary Kay foundation and powder. Her berry sparkle lip gloss glittered, and her freshly braided twist cascaded elegantly on her shoulders. She wore a sparkling white blouse atop a frilly rainbow-colored skirt. Alexander was expected shortly, and thoughts of him filled her heart with joyful feelings. For once in her life, it seemed she had met the right guy.

Once, she had discovered that her date was already married to two women, and she was completely miffed by the discovery. Another time, she was embarrassed when he confessed he was bisexual. Since then, it was difficult to make a choice or even entrust her heart to any man. Alexander, however, looked different from the lot. Sensitive, caring, intelligent, poetic, unpredictably romantic, he appeared to be her knight with shining armor. Since the day he proposed a relationship under the guava tree weeks back, they had enjoyed a whirlwind romance, and things were getting rosier by the day.

The doorbell rang, and she scurried out of her sparsely furnished but neat bedroom into her equally sparsely furnished living room. Her residence was in the staff quarters of the institution of learning, something she considered a great benefit and convenience for a spinster like her. Her wages did not have to go into settlement of house rents, so she could save for other things, like household gadgets and kitchen utensils, which she would purchase for her new home once the wedding bells rang. "Wedding bells" was her favorite phrase recently, as she was eager to settle down with her newly discovered heartthrob. She gasped for breath in anticipation as she flung the front door open, eyes shut, waiting to be caught in the warm embrace of Mr. Right.

"Good evening, ma," the intruder greeted, as Dorothy opened her eyes in utmost displeasure.

"Can I help you?" she queried, visibly disappointed. The door was ajar, but she wasn't willing to move an inch.

"May I come in please?" The girl asked, putting a foot forward.

"How can I help you, young woman? And just where do you think you are going?" Dorothy asked, blocking the entrance.

"This is private, urgent, and it has to do with Mr. Alexander Moyo. Please, we need to talk."

At the mention of his name, Dorothy became apprehensive. "What could be the problem with Alexander?" she wondered as she let the young lady into her simply furnished apartment. She did not fail to notice how dark, plain faced, unattractive, and frumpy the lady, who must have been about twenty-three-years-old, looked.

"Yes, what about Alexander?" Dorothy asked the moment they were seated.

"Ma, I . . . I."

"You're what?"

"My name is Adorkor; I . . . I don't know how you'll take this."

"Look, I'm losing my patience, out with it!"

"Miss Dorothy, I know this is none of my business, but I care for you because you are a very nice lady. You are also my favorite lecturer."

"So?"

"I . . . I hear you are planning to wed Mr. Alexander," she blurted out.

Dorothy couldn't believe her ears.

"I'm sorry . . . maybe I'm not making myself clear," Adorkor continued.

"What's your business with me, young woman? And what's your business with my private life?" Dorothy interposed angrily.

"Pardon me, Miss Dorothy; I have evidence to prove that Mr. Alexander is vile. He is abusive and nothing short of an opportunist. He constantly harasses us—his students. I also suspect he is a rapist. I chose not to fall victim to his wantonness, and for that reason, my career is being threatened. My ambition is to become an international writer and poet. I want to be a source of pride to the African continent. Names like Buchi Emecheta, Chinua Achebe, Wole Soyinka, Ngugi wa Thiong'o have inspired my writings. I am paying the price to ensure I succeed, and nobody, not even Alexander Moyo, will stop that dream from becoming reality. Please, Miss Dorothy, you are the head of the disciplinary committee of this college, and I know you are in a position to expose his illicit activities. We have suffered for too long. We want justice, we want liberation, we want . . ."

"Enough!" Dorothy barked, pointing at the reporter. "Has the girl lost her mind?" she wondered.

"I know it sounds stranger than fiction, but believe you me, this is not a fairy-tale narrative. It is real life, and I have more than enough proof." Her words cut through Dorothy's thoughts.

"Who sent you? My enemies, ay? Killjoys who don't wish me well are at it again. So it has come to this? Defamation is now a game for young females? You are a liar!" Dorothy thundered.

"Ma, I have nothing to gain from slander. You are a woman like me. I respect you; that is why I have come to expose Alexander's atrocities."

Dorothy took a long disdainful look at the figure before her. The girl's outrageously big nose was moist with sweat. Her fingers looked worn out with manual labor. Her feet were fat, with scattered toes, each facing a different direction. She was by no means attractive, the sort of lady that even a chronic philanderer wouldn't want to spare a second look. How on earth could she claim that her lover boy, her articulate and suave Alexander as much as gave her a thought, not to talk of having an amorous conversation! The disdain and scorn on Dorothy's face was riveting. Adorkor shifted uncomfortably on her seat. The attractive and older woman's thoughts, though unspoken, appeared written in bold characters on the icy silence.

"Alexander chased you? I mean . . . he actually flirted with you?" Dorothy slurred, breaking the silence.

"I may not be attractive, madam, but at least I've got mammary glands and a heavy backside. The African woman is endowed in various ways. An ugly duckling can capture a man's heart if she knows his weak points . . ."

"You flatter yourself, young lady; in fact, you insult me . . . you insult my man and his masculine instincts," Dorothy spat.

"Ma, I am not interested in your man. I am a woman with a vision. What I may not have physically going for me, I am making up intellectually. When the time is right, I know what to do to catch the attention of the man of my desires, and that man certainly would not be a despicable fellow like Alexander Moyo. I must say that I did not come here to trade words with you . . . you are far too refined and beautiful for such. I admire and respect you a great deal, so my coming here is to solicit your cooperation," Adorkor offered, suppressing her voice in deference.

"What do you want from me?" Dorothy asked, totally deflated.

"If we allow Alexander Moyo's misdemeanor to continue, our gender will be the worse for it. Men like him should face the law and be tamed," came Adorkor's response.

"How am I to believe that my man is vile? How?" Dorothy sobbed. "If by any chance you are lying . . . if by any chance you fabricated this . . . I swear you'll regret it."

"No madam . . . I have evidence, witnesses. Mr. Alexander himself cannot deny it."

Just then, the bell rang. The door opened, and Alexander walked in with a swagger, looking dashing in a neatly cut caftan made with Kente fabric. His mien vacillated from enthusiasm to surprise and suspicion and fear. His eyes roved the room. First to Dorothy, then to the girl, and back to Dorothy. Shivers ran down his spine, and he became crestfallen. The guilt in his eyes was glaring as he put up a front.

"Set for the evening, darling?"

Dorothy stared at him like a stranger. The atmosphere in the room was heating up, the tension intensifying.

"I beg to excuse myself," the reporter voiced, looking at Alexander with scornful eyes.

"Stop right there!" Dorothy commanded in a stern voice that startled her date. "Now repeat all that you told me," she said, pointing at the younger woman. "And to you, Alexander, do you know this girl?" she shrieked in quick succession, giving neither of them space to respond. Alexander was surprised at her tone. He'd never seen her so irate.

"I asked a question, Alexander; do you know this lady?"

"Why? What if I know her? Obviously she's my student."

"Your student? Is she just your student? How many of your students have you harassed sexually? How many young ladies have you assaulted?"

"Cool your temper, darling. I can't believe you'll easily swallow such cock-and-bull story by disgruntled elements. She's . . . she's not my class."

"Tell me it's not true, Alexander, tell me she is lying," Dorothy said, breaking into tears.

"Go on and answer her, Mr. Moyo. Your intrigues have been discovered. Miss Dorothy certainly deserves much better than a despicable, infamous wolf for a husband!"

"You must be out of your mind!" Alexander barked, surging at his accuser with a warning finger.

"You can't shut me up with your threats. Nemesis has finally caught up with you, mister."

"You still haven't answered me, Alexander," Dorothy said, in between sobs.

"It's a pity, Dorothy, that you choose to believe this deranged desperado's tales."

"You are the desperado, Mr. Moyo! What defenses have you got? Go on and disabuse her mind. Confess your folly. You shameless licentious lewd lecturer!"

"I've heard enough please!" Dorothy blurted out in despair. Her head was swirling as she spoke. "It seems to me there is a problem here and we must get to its roots," she cried, gazing intently; expectantly at Alexander, hoping he would refute the allegations, desperately awaiting his soothing words to assuage her fears that he might not be her Mr. Perfect after all . . .

"Believe her fables, Dorothy, okay? She's obviously fed you with a truckload of lies, and you fell for it. I am certainly not going to stand here and listen to this bullshit!"

"Stop blabbing, sir! I have unequivocal evidence of your ignominy!" the lady interjected emphatically, bringing out three photographs from her bag.

She dumped them on the side stool beside Dorothy. All the photographs were obscene, the first showing Alexander, underpants down, pleading with a frightened young lady who looked distressed. In the second picture, Alexander was stark naked, tearing the girl's blouse in what looked like attempted rape, and in the third picture, he wore a surprised expression as he shamefacedly covered his penis with both hands, his victim running out ahead of him.

"I hope these pictures speak volumes . . ." Adorkor said with a gloat. "That was your attempt to rape my friend after you had harassed me, threatened to victimize me and foolhardily went ahead to assault my friend. But you were intercepted by our timely intervention and banging on your door that day, myself and two other students you had equally tried pressuring for sex. Shame on you!"

With that, the lady Adorkor looked pitifully at Dorothy, despicably at Alexander before stepping out. Dorothy was horrified at the sight of the pictures. Alexander was placid. He ransacked his brain for an alibi . . .

"I can explain . . . it's not what you think. I swear it was a setup . . . those girls are insane! They set me up . . ."

Dorothy screamed and rushed at Alexander in a rage, throwing hard punches on his stomach. He made to speak, but a slap hit his face.

"To hell with you! Damn you!" he screeched, shoving her aside and storming off.

Inside his apartment, heavy rock music blared at its highest pitch. Curse words, swear words, and f . . . words reeled out of the lyrics of the music. All his adult life, Alexander enjoyed and filled his mind with lewd lyrics. The friends he fraternized with had congenial tastes, mainly guys whose preoccupation was watching raunchy movies, getting drunk in strip clubs, flirting and philandering with the opposite sex, indulging in sex orgies and generally living life to the hilt of their sensual cravings. With this unexpected development, it appeared there was nobody to call up for advice. Who amongst his circle could offer a word of counsel to soothe his intense anxiety? "They are all probably caught in the embrace of some daughter of Eve now," he thought, "the same seductive beings for which I got into his present dilemma," he continued, racking his brain; cogitating for an action plan.

In less than thirty minutes, he finished a pack of cigarette, several wraps of marijuana, and a bottle of dry gin. His head was in a whirlwind, his senses high on substance when he eventually sailed out of the premises, clad in a pair of torn jeans, a sleeveless polo shirt, and a pair of heavy black boots. For him, it was good-bye to the Institute for French Education, Accra, Ghana. He'd been discovered, and no doubt, the scandal would soon be full blown. It was more honorable leaving before he suffered ignominy. As for his friends, there was no point telling them about his intentions. There wasn't a single one of them he could trust anyway, so what was the point? Asking them for recommendations on what to do would be silly, he figured, since none of them had any reasonable sense of judgment, except on issues concerning the assessment of the female anatomy. For a split second, he felt a wave of pity for himself and his pathetic affinity. "That is why I am a man," he rationalized, pushing the thought aside and feeling justified for his proclivity. Certainly, wherever the tides threw him, it wouldn't be difficult finding and blending with new congenial company. His destination? Time will tell, but top on his list of options was none other than the country from where he migrated some years ago.

CHAPTER FIVE

A few days after Araba declared Mercy's compulsory vacation, they were back on the drawing board in the reverend
mother's office. The younger nun apparently had something else
coming, certainly not a holiday request nor even a break from
work. Her problem was far from the perception of ordinary eyes.

"I can't make sense of what you are saying, Mercy," Mother
Araba stated, hoping her ears were deceiving her.

"Believe me, mother, I have lost touch with the vision. I
can't continue living like a hypocrite."

"Remember you are under oath. A commitment to serve, a
high calling which cannot be revoked."

"But I feel choked. My potentials are wasting away. I need
to reach out to the people. I have a burden to heal and inspire
the brokenhearted, but I cannot do that within the four walls of
a convent."

"No! No! No!" Araba's voice was harsh and resolute. "Don't
ever say that again. You are a reverend sister, and a reverend
sister you shall remain!"

"I want to be free. I want to breathe normal air. I want to be
me. Mercy Treasure Dakova. That's the real me."

"No man puts his hands to the plow and looks back," Araba
replied. "You cannot leave; you are bound for life! Do not be
entangled with the carnal things of life, my dear. Do not be
lured by the deceitfulness of pleasures. Yours is a high calling.
The highest spiritual calling to be a nun. For the sake of the
kingdom, Mercy, you chose to be a nun."

"No . . . no . . . I'm guilty. I confess I didn't do it for the sake
of the kingdom . . . I did it for myself, for myself, Mother. A guilt
. . . a guilt which remains sore in my heart. A stigma from the
past pushed me to the nunnery. It was too painful to bear . . ."

Mercy's eyes were tear filled, and Araba watched in awe as she spoke. "I know the Lord understands my plight. Please, Mother, try to see reason."

"I don't understand you. I thought you were happy here. I thought you had the heart of a nun. What has come over you, Mercy? Think deeply about this before you make a big mistake."

"My mind is already made up. I will forever be grateful for the discipline and knowledge I've received here. Mine is a life of service. A life of sacrifice, nothing can change that fact, but it has to be outside the walls of this cloister."

Mother Araba shut her eyes. Perhaps she was in the middle of a dream, or even a movie. Was this an excerpt from the 1965 musical film directed by Robert Wise and starring Julie Andrews as Maria? Was this a scene from *The Sound of Music*? "Maria's not an answer to the abbey." No way! That was just make-believe. Such things don't happen in real life.

As if by intuition, Mercy spoke softly, soberly: "I do not have a place in the abbey; Mother, I must leave now. God bless you, Mother."

With that, she was out of the reverend mother's office, heading towards her bedroom, the room she had lived in for the last couple of years.

Packing for her was an easy affair since she had little or no personal belongings. Surprisingly though, she remained calm, despite the thumping of her heart and occasional dread of the decision she'd just made.

Walking out of the convent was something she'd never anticipated or contemplated in the past, particularly since her life in seclusion had been quite a fulfilling experience. It was the lifestyle void of innate human selfishness and adventure, a focused life of absolute service to mankind. Over the years too, she'd built an intimate and enduring relationship with her Creator. She could feel His omnipresence and omnipotence at every point in time. It was akin to the relationship between a Father and an only child, a father who empathized with the travails of his precious child. Hers had been a gradual transition from grass to grace, from a life of utter condemnation to a life of purity and holiness.

Absolute purity of the soul and body was what she'd experienced in her fifteen years of full-time service in the work of God. And now, was she about to relinquish all that because of feeble sentiments based on probable fleeting emotions? What if she quits and later regrets the decision? "It will be no different from the case of a foolish dog returning to its vomit," she thought, as her heart missed a beat. Suddenly, she felt all alone in the world. If anything went wrong with her plans, she'd be out on the streets with no one to turn to. The only enduring relationship she had was with her Lord and Maker. That was one relationship she couldn't trade for anything in the world, and perhaps, that was the reason she brushed aside the dreary thoughts and concentrated on her immediate plans.

Finally, she was done with packing just as a tap on the door jerked her out of her reverie. It was Esi, the one and only reverend sister she'd closely interacted with over the years. Esi was such a dear. She was one person Mercy never ceased to admire. Her compassion, gentleness, passion, clarity of focus, humility, and cheer were qualities that endeared her to Mercy.

"Esi?" Mercy called with an inquiring eye, the moment the former entered the room.

"You didn't tell me you were leaving," Esi stated calmly.

"I meant to tell you, Esi," Mercy said, quickly adding, "It's all happening so suddenly. I didn't plan on leaving."

"You're off to another mission, I believe?" Esi stated before adding, "Where exactly are you going to? Mother Araba spoke in very hazy terms."

Mercy watched her friend for a while, sighed and sat beside her on the bed.

"I'm leaving for good, Esi. Perhaps I will no longer be revered. I will no longer be Sister Mercy. I'm going to face the world as it is with all the challenges and uncertainties."

"What are you saying?" Esi asked in confusion.

"I'm quitting the convent. I will no longer be a nun."

"You must be kidding!" Esi cried in shock, staring at her in disbelief. "It's never happened here before. Tell me it's not true, Mercy, tell me this is a joke . . ." she cried, falling on her knees and weeping uncontrollably.

"I'm afraid it is true . . ."

"No . . . It can't be . . .you're making a big mistake. You're not fashioned for that kind of life," Esi insisted in between sobs.

"Esi, I know what I am doing. I'm not about abandoning my faith in God. I remain a believer for as long as I have breath. But I must leave this place. I must be free. I must be me."

"What are you talking about, dear sister?" Esi questioned. "Christ has set you free. There's no other liberty but that which God gives."

"You're missing the point, Sister Esi. I am talking about physical and emotional emancipation. The spirit remains the same, but the body is crying out for exhalation," Mercy stated firmly.

Esi wore a perplexed look before quietly replying, "You want to get married? Is that it? You want to gratify the desires of the flesh? You want to feel natural and feminine? You want a man's physical touch . . . you want romance . . ."

"Stop it please!" Mercy interposed. "You're missing the point. You are missing the point, Esi. I'm not Maria from *The Sound of Music*. I'm not an actress, Esi. I know it will be difficult for you or anyone else to understand. I'm talking about freedom of expression. I'm talking about taking responsibility for my actions. I'm talking about being able to reach out without reservation. Can't you understand? That's the freedom I'm referring to."

"Many saints lived and died with a vision like yours, but they never contemplated life outside seclusion. Mercy, you can be all you want to be and still remain a nun."

"I am Mercy Treasure Dakova. I'm different. I was born different. I was born . . ."

"You were born what, Mercy?" Esi asked, unable to comprehend Mercy's sudden loss of speech.

"I . . . I'm different," Mercy voiced slowly, swallowing hard. "I'm different, believe me."

"Of course you're different," Esi said. "We all are different in personality and characteristics."

"What I mean is, I have a calling outside the convent. Remaining here will be hypocritical. I am not a hypocrite. I have to leave by all means."

"You surprise me, Mercy. I would never have imagined in my wildest dreams that this day will come. Life outside the convent is very unpredictable, full of uncertainties, aches and pains. It's a wicked world out there . . . you'll get your heart shattered, broken to pieces. It's not the kind of life you want, Mercy. You are making a big mistake."

"Don't judge me, please. Don't be a stumbling block either. My mind is already made up," Mercy stated decisively. "The least you can do is to wish me good luck," she continued.

Esi sighed and sat in exasperation, unable to find any more convincing words. Trying to dissuade Mercy was like trying to move the Rock of Gibraltar.

"I appreciate your concern, Sister Esi," Mercy said, placing a hand on her shoulder. "I truly appreciate, but believe me, I know what I am doing. My heart tells me I'm doing the right thing. I have a guiding conscience, remember, and even more importantly, I have God, and I'm convinced that this is what He'll have me do."

Esi sighed and watched her with tenderness. "I'll miss you Mercy," she said with sobriety.

"I'll miss you too, Esi," Mercy said, embracing her. "I have to keep my vision alive. That's why I'm doing this, so that at the end of my sojourn on earth, I will have fulfilled my purpose."

"I wish you luck," Esi said finally, with an outburst of tears.

Mercy watched with tender eyes and embraced her friend. She forced back her tears and put up a courageous face. "I'll be in touch. I promise I'll never forget you or this wonderful foundation."

Thirty minutes later, she was the cynosure of all eyes as Mother Araba conducted a brief impromptu farewell service for her. It was very solemn, like a funeral mass, as emotions took the better part of the ceremony. Mercy's decision had dealt them a heavy blow. Everyone appeared forlorn. Some of the nuns even looked devastated. Sister Esi sobbed all through the ceremony. Mother Araba looked particularly worried as she didn't fully comprehend Mercy's decision. However, there was nothing she or anyone else could do. Mercy had made up her mind, and they could only bid her farewell. Eventually, it was time for her to leave. She walked the length of the corridors carrying her bag and baggage, with her heart heavy with mixed feelings.

CHAPTER SIX

The journey from Tamale to Accra was very uneventful. It was a ten-hour bus ride on an STC bus. Mercy had several motivational and inspirational books to keep her busy during the journey, so she wasn't bored. Reading was a habit she had developed over the years, as it kept her positively occupied in her spare time. She also realized that learning kept her mentally alert, informed, and confident.

The lady was also in the habit of listening to inspirational and personal development tapes, a habit that had been of tremendous help in keeping her enthusiastic and progressive. She therefore had her Walkman and a few tapes with her, which she listened to in the course of the journey. One of them was an inspiring talk titled "Dream Seeds" by Mike Murdock. It made her understand that there is a seed of greatness in everyone and dreams take a process to become reality. She also had a Kenneth Hagin series on faith, which she found quite challenging. It made her feel like she could conquer the world if she had the basic ingredient of faith.

A few hours later she was dozing. She slept peacefully like a baby and woke up to use the restroom and eat her midday meal when the bus made a stopover at a fuel station. For the rest of the journey her mind wandered to and fro, thinking of the future, cracking her head for guidelines on what the action plan should be for the next phase of her life.

On arrival at the capital city Accra, Mercy decided to spend the night at a cheap hostel near the bus park. The place had no bed, and occupants had to lie down on a huge blanket spread on the floor for sleeping. The room was an open space with enough room for twelve adults to sleep on the floor and a wooden cabinet for placing luggage. The bathroom was shared by all residents of the hostel, and each had to queue up for their turn to use the dilapidated facility. There was no water in the tap, and they had to fetch a half bucket of water from a drum that was rationed by the facility's supervisor. Anyone desiring more than the recommended quantity had to pay a fee for it.

Mercy took her bath that evening after standing for almost two hours on the queue to get her turn. The night was also quite uncomfortable because the room was cramped with eleven obese women who took up all the available space, leaving her squeezed to the wall with no space to turn or roll over for comfort. Apparently, they were all relatives from the same clan who had come for a wedding in Accra.

There was one small window for ventilation, and there was no netting, so mosquitoes feasted on their bodies all night. Mercy was fortunate to have a dose of anti-malaria medicine she gulped before settling down to sleep. Having wasted time that night on the queue before getting her turn, she planned better to beat the queue the following day. She therefore had to wake up by three the following morning to enable her get an early space in the bathroom. Thereafter she checked out by 5:30 a.m. to go to the park at Tudu Station Makola to board a vehicle.

Alexander Moyo had also arrived at the park and was set for his journey home. They paid their fare and took their seats inside the 504 saloon car. While her mind was preoccupied with her experience in the country, his was blank. Occasionally he wondered if he'd made the right decision to leave. The country he considered his own probably had very little prospects for him. "So why return there?" he wondered. "But fifteen years is long enough to obliterate the past," he continued in his train of thoughts.

As the vehicle thrust forward, Mercy reminisced over her peaceful stay in the country. It had been a very interesting period, particularly her familiarization with the environment. Her vocation had taken her around all the regions; she could even speak Akan fluently. The hospitality she enjoyed amongst the people was one that really beat her imagination. It was as though all the people she met were specially ordained to love and appreciate her—just for who she was. She found their warmth quite consoling, giving her a sense of belonging and true love "unlike those . . ." She snapped out of the eerie thoughts and focused on the scenery.

Tears escaped her eyes as they drove past the Centre for National Culture, popularly referred to as the Cultural Centre. Next in her consciousness was the view of the Accra Stadium, then the National Theatre. She sighted the Children's Park, the 37 Hospital, and before long they were on the airport road, heading towards the Tema Motorway. Ghana, which became an independent nation on the sixth of March 1967, was quite a hospitable country. Mercy had enjoyed every bit of her stay there and had even thought that she could one day naturalize as a Ghanaian. With her recent decision to return homewards to the land of her birth, those aspirations were no longer feasible.

Slowly and gradually she drifted from her reverie . . . to a slumber. Alexander, on the other hand, was busy with the bottles. He'd already consumed several shots of brandy since the journey began, and it appeared he still had space for more. Mercy stirred and opened her eyes. The stench of alcohol oozing from her co-passenger was very discomforting. Worse still, he kept puffing like his life depended on fags. For a second, she thought he looked familiar when he turned to ask if she cared for a cigarette.

"I don't smoke, thank you," came her blunt response before she shut her eyes, despairing and praying silently that the nine-hour journey, riddled with intermittent border checks, will suddenly come to an end.

Alexander also had a *Playboy* magazine that he flipped through; relishing the nude and semi-nude pictures of women in it. Suddenly he had a strong urge to watch pornography. It was his favorite pastime to watch X-rated movies and put to practice the sexual acts he saw in them.

Alexander groaned as he felt a flush in his groin. He began to shift uncomfortably on his seat then shook more vigorously, to the chagrin of his co-passenger. He tapped her shoulder, winked at her but met a stern, hostile look. Mercy was very uncomfortable and getting irritated by his behavior. However, she was unable to summon courage to challenge the fellow. He unbuttoned his shirt and from the corner of her eyes, she caught a glimpse of his exposed hairy chest. "Lord, have mercy!" she exclaimed inwardly, quite embarrassed by what she considered his indecent exposure. Desperately in search of better scenery and unpolluted breeze, she shifted closer to the wound-down window, ducking her head out to inhale fresh air.

If she was to put up with him for the rest of the journey, she certainly needed patience, and hers was fast running out. She prayed silently that the Lord would give her the grace to cope with the fellow's excesses. What a way to launch into life afresh, sitting closely with one with such unholy appearance. In a bid to put aside her immediate concerns, her mind again began to wander. It all looked like yesterday, when she left her homeland fifteen years back.

Now a full-grown thirty-three-year-old, she'd certainly matured a lot and was ready to face life as it was. Her immediate plans included registering for the external General Certificate examination. Next would be to pursue a part-time degree in psychology. Afterwards, she'd practice full-time in the profession. For the rest of the journey, she daydreamed about her future plans and goals. A sanguine attitude was all she needed, and she never allowed one minute of gloom to dampen her optimism.

CHAPTER SEVEN

Homecoming wasn't a very exciting affair. To start with, she hadn't any formal family she could call her own. Home for her was the orphanage where she had been raised. Although the orphanage in Badagry, Lagos, still held good memories for her, Mercy was not interested in going there, as she had nothing material to offer them, and right now, she was in dire need of help herself.

A very bright and astute kid she was when she gained full scholarship into one of the highbrow colleges. It was a boarding school renowned for high academic standards. The matron of the abandoned children's home where Mercy was raised was so delighted about the girl's academic feat that she pasted her profile and photograph on the notice board. She wanted to motivate other children in the orphanage to aspire for meritorious scholarships and excellent performance. Her motto for the children became "if she can, you can too!"

It was whilst Mercy was in her fifth form and at the point of completing the West African school certificate examination that the hideous assault occurred. That was the worst day of her life, the day she experienced a terrible dose of man's inhumanity to man. The greatest miracle of her existence so far was her resilient survival of the nightmare. She shuddered at the recapitulation of the obnoxious experience. Not wanting to dwell on the unpleasant reverie, Mercy alighted from the cab that had just made its final stop at the boisterous Mile-Two bus stop in Lagos, Nigeria.

In spite of her raging hunger, her immediate priority was to locate an old friend who had been in touch with her during her self-exile years. Having converted the few cedis left in her purse to Naira, she proceeded to the Festac 23 Road abode of her friend. It wasn't difficult locating the house, which was a two-bedroom apartment in a block of flats on K Close.

"Good grief! What a surprise!" Mairo exclaimed on seeing her.

"Good to see you, dear friend," Mercy responded as they embraced each other warmly.

"You are the last person I was expecting. So what good wind brings you here, Sister Mercy?"

"Home fever. It's been such a long time," Mercy said, making herself comfortable on the sofa at the same time, appreciating her friend's sleek taste.

The living room was posh, compact, and very appealing. There was a deliberate color blend between the peach and lilac curtains, black leather seats adorned with peach and lilac throw pillows made with Aso Oke fabric, and the richly padded rug adorned by a matching miniature Persian rug. The split air-conditioning unit kept the room cool, while the sweet fragrance of vanilla air freshener filled the air.

"You finally decided to visit," Mairo remarked, placing a tray of assorted biscuits and a glass of juice on the stool beside her.

"I'm back for good, Mairo," Mercy said, taking a deep breath and watching to see her friend's reaction.

"You're on transfer to Nigeria?"

"No, Mairo, I quit the nunnery."

For a moment, Mairo stared at her in disbelief. "You can't be serious," she uttered in amazement.

Mercy sipped some of the chilled pineapple juice and relaxed as she spoke. "It's a long story, friend, but to cut it short, I suddenly realized the nunnery wasn't the place for me. Don't get me wrong—it was good while it lasted, but now I feel I need a change."

"I always knew it!" Mairo exclaimed delightedly. "Oh Mercy, I am so glad you finally realized that the nunnery isn't the right place for you. There's so much that life has to offer outside the four walls of the convent."

Mercy smiled and deliberately avoided further comments on the subject. "Obviously you look very well and comfortable. Good taste you've got too," she commented.

"Thanks for the compliment. These are the fruits of hard work and diligence. You know the economy is bad, but a few of us are able to stay afloat despite the depression," Mairo added airily.

"You are still your usual confident self. You haven't changed one bit," Mercy remarked.

"You can say that again, except of course, I no longer fight the way I used to," Mairo put in.

"You were such a strong, agile girl. Nobody could bully you," Mercy added jovially.

They laughed at the recollection of their secondary school days.

"Mairo," Mercy called.

"Yes dear, my dear ex-reverend sister."

"Can I ask you a favor?"

"Sure," Mairo responded. "I'm all ears."

"I don't know anybody I can turn to at this time. My life needs some reorganization, and for a start, I need a roof over my head."

"Well, Mercy, you've got yourself a house. You can stay here for as long as you wish. I've got a spare room and it's all yours. Only do me one favor."

"What?"

"Feel free and comfortable. This is your home."

"Oh thank you, Mairo," Mercy voiced, overwhelmed by the kind gesture. "How can I thank you enough?"

"Come off it. What are friends for?"

"I appreciate it."

"My pleasure," Mairo said, gladly leading the way to the guestroom.

"By the way, Mercy, you never really told me why you chose to change your name from Dada Iseoluwa to Mercy Treasure Dakova. It's like you went to Ghana for an image makeover,"

Mairo began, as she helped her friend settle into the posh bedroom.

Mercy was taken aback. However, she immediately harnessed her thoughts.

"Inquisitive now, aren't you?" Mercy stated, folding her arms as she leaned against the floral pink wallpaper. "Hope you don't mind my being an African to the core," she continued, wearing a smile.

"Certainly not, why?" Mairo probed.

"Because I am about to answer your question with a question."

"I'm all ears, Mercy," Mairo responded, sinking into the comfortable bed.

"Well, Mairo, do I look like the same girl you used to know in school?"

"That is a little complex, you know," Mairo answered, toying with her index finger on her chin. "You're somewhat a mystery to me, Mercy. Rather complex and unpredictable."

"Me?" Mercy quizzed, bursting forth with laughter. "Those are rather strong terms to qualify me."

"But you should know that . . ." Mairo continued. "One day you're in college, the next you decide you've been called to the nunnery. Fifteen years later, you quit. Don't you think this is rather complicated?"

Mercy continued smiling as she took slow strides towards the bed where Mairo sat.

"I know . . . I can just imagine what you think of me. Capricious and inconsistent, perhaps, but really, I have been treading the path of destiny. Let's start with this simple logical explanation. I'm older now, more mature, and entitled to whatever name I choose."

"That's true. Maybe I should also change my name to something like . . . Queen Elizabeth," Mairo joked.

"Stop kidding," Mercy put in jauntily.

"But quite seriously, Mercy, you've changed over the years. That scrawny plain-Jane teenage look with natural dreadlocks has given way to a svelte elegance."

"That's very flattering," Mercy said with amusement.

"It's the truth, even though for fifteen years you failed to realize it. You chose rather to waste away in a convent."

"I didn't waste away," Mercy interposed. "I went there for a purpose, and when I fulfilled it, I left." she explained.

"Well then, I'll watch and see what you have in stock for this new era," Mairo stated.

"It really is a new era for me, and I'm looking forward to it with all my heart," Mercy responded, giggling like an excited child. She stood by the dressing mirror and felt her short, plaited natural hair.

"For one, I'll do away with these," she said, fiddling with the hair. "I'll go for easy perm as soon as I can afford it," she added airily.

"What do you know about hair and looks, Mercy?" Mairo asked sardonically.

"Not much perhaps but I have a picture in my mind. Neat, presentable, but certainly not loud," she announced, as Mairo burst out laughing.

"We'll see to that," Mairo commented finally, winking at her mischievously.

Mairo left Mercy alone to settle into her room. The erstwhile nun fell into the bed, pulling the luxuriant quilt over her head. It had been a long day, starting with the long drive from Ghana, the immigration checks at all the West African borders on their axis, the smoky passenger on the ride with her, the mental turmoil of beginning a brand new life; she was exhausted. For the first time in years, she did not have the strength to shower before going to bed. As a matter of fact, she did not even know when she dozed off.

It was a very refreshing night sleeping in the cozy bedroom, enjoying the cool air-conditioning under comfortable blankets and a duvet. The only problem was that she jumped out of sleep at about 3:00 a.m. following a vivid nightmare that got her on her knees in serious prayers that lasted till about 5:00 a.m. She recollected clearly how the co-passenger in the taxi had tried strangling her, claiming he was the stigma from her past, destined to hound her to the grave. Mercy rejected the evil declaration and fervently prayed against tormenting spirits and evil omens.

She went back to sleep after using the restroom and slept until 9:00 a.m., when Mairo tapped at the door to announce that she was going out. She left five thousand Naira cash on the dressing table for Mercy in case she needed anything. She also announced that there was sufficient food in the refrigerator, groceries and fruits in the kitchen. Mercy expressed appreciation and saw her off to the door before returning to shower, eat a heavy breakfast and begin her day in earnest.

The returnee took a walk down the road to buy newspapers. She bought the *Guardian*, *Vanguard*, and *Daily Times* newspapers and spent time looking out for vacancy adverts. Most of the opportunities were for graduates and school leavers, a not too encouraging scenario for her since she hadn't any certificate or formal qualifications. After scanning the dailies, she felt a little low in spirits but became revitalized when she read an article by Helen Ovbiagele of the *Vanguard* newspaper. Ovbiagele's inspiring article on womanhood was deeply encouraging and strengthened her resolve to be resolute and resilient no matter the challenge.

Later that evening after Mairo returned home, Mercy decided to seek her hostess's opinion about job-hunting strategies.

"You see, Mercy, being under-qualified has little to do with your gaining meaningful employment and earning money in Lagos," Mairo began, when the issue was raised over dinner. "The important thing is, are you willing to pay the price?"

She scooped some food into her mouth before proceeding. They were having steamed white rice, peppery chicken stew, fried plantain, and steamed green vegetables for dinner.

"The truth is that jobs are hard to find. Even if you are qualified, the competition is stiff. Just imagine five thousand people clamoring for one job. The chances become very slim. Coupled with poor wages and remuneration, it's not worth the trouble at the end of the day," Mairo said decisively.

"What then do you suggest?"

"I must be honest with you. The only way out is, use what you have to get what you want."

"What do you mean?"

"You're a mature woman, Mercy, and attractive too. It shouldn't be difficult for you to mix with the society's cream. Several options are available to choose from: get yourself a rich boyfriend or better still, join the flourishing team of . . . society big girls. Once you are in the circle, your money concerns will be over. It calls for a lot of hard work, a few risks, but it certainly pays off in the long run. What are condoms there for anyway? If I contract an STD, I know how to fix it."

Mercy almost choked. She gratefully drained the glass of water Mairo offered her and finished her meal in silence. A long stillness engulfed the dining room afterwards. Neither of them spoke until Mercy excused herself to her bedroom. She lay in bed, musing over their discussion. Mairo gently tapped on the door and entered.

"Mercy," she called in a soft tone.

"Yes?"

"I . . . I guess I shouldn't have been so blunt."

"It's okay, Mairo, you were only giving me suggestions."

"I know how you feel, especially since you just quit the nunnery."

"Please, Mairo, don't say anymore."

"You make me feel bad. I was only trying to help."

"But have I said anything? After all, I'm in no position to condemn your lifestyle," Mercy added sarcastically.

"Look, this should not dampen our spirits. I have my life to live, and you have your life to live. I have my own convictions; you have your own convictions. As long as we don't get in each other's way, there shouldn't be a problem."

"I guess so," Mercy said, sitting up and managing a smile. "You know, I really admire your independence, but is it really worth it? I mean, there must be a better alternative to earning a living. Besides, think of yourself, your dignity, your honor, and of course, your virtue. You're a woman, Mairo, a vessel fit for divine purpose."

"Are we in the middle of a sermon or something?" Mairo queried cynically. "I thought you left behind your old-fashioned ideas in the abbey. Spare me further preaching, please."

"All right, no further talks on that, but remember, AIDS is real, and it's gradually taking root in Africa."

"You . . . you reverend sister talking about AIDS?" Mairo sneered. "Wonders will never end. Anyway, AIDS for your information is not for us Africans. It is a white man's disease."

"Believe me, Mairo, AIDS is real," Mercy reiterated. "In the course of my mission work, I came across many cases of HIV/AIDS. The media haven't been effective in reporting the reality of AIDS in Africa, but believe me, it's as real as the air we breathe. This is 1990, and I assure you before the turn of the millennium, the disease will be widespread."

"Stop boring me, Mercy, okay? I own my body, and I can do anything with it. Besides, are you a prophet of doom?"

"No, but I want you to know that you are a beautiful woman. You don't have to cheapen yourself to make ends meet," Mercy put in.

"That's the point." Mairo spat, flicking her long human-hair weave back, as if in sudden realization of her good looks.

She was one of those women endowed with natural African beauty. Mairo was very shapely, the kind of contour described as figure eight, with full hips, bursting pointed breast, height towering a little above five feet nine inches, and a natural glowing light skin. She had the features of a Hausa Fulani woman. However, Mairo wasn't Fulani. She was from the eastern part of Nigeria, Onitsha to be precise, even though she was born and raised in Sokoto state in northern Nigeria. She, however, had her secondary school education in Lagos.

"The point is, a beautiful woman needs to maintain her beauty," she stated definitively. "It costs money to look good," she re-emphasized.

"I know . . . I understand what you're saying," Mercy replied. "But you don't have to trade your femininity. There is dignity in decent labor, Mairo. Dignity in working with your hands, earning a living the legitimate way."

"Okay! Enough! Saint Mercy, Virgin Mary. Save your sermon for someone else. I hate to watch you swim in your cloak of hypocritical piety. What gives you the right to judge me anyway? I despise your holier-than-thou attitude to say the least!" Mairo snarled in defiance.

Mercy watched with surprise.

"I'm beginning to realize your reason for chastity. Tell me, Mercy, your reason for joining the convent was to cover your guilt, isn't it? You wanted to cloak your filthiness!" Mairo spat, as Mercy's expression transited from surprise to shock. "I am no fool, Mercy! It's been fifteen years, but I haven't forgotten that night when you walked into the dormitory drenched in rain, staggering like someone who had just been raped."

"Mairo . . . I," Mercy yelped, cringing back in horror.

"I haven't finished!" Mairo interposed. "The way you carried yourself—I could see you were in pain—you walked like someone who had just experienced a wild orgy."

"My God! Stop!" Mercy yelled, cupping her face with her hands. It was as if a nail had just pierced her head.

"You lied to me, Mercy. I'm your friend, but you lied to me. You told me you fell into a ditch and got yourself hurt. But remember when I helped you to the clinic, you were almost in a coma. The doctor asked you what really happened, and you couldn't even talk. You were visibly shaken. You were in pain. You were afraid, like a band of robbers were chasing after you. I'm not trying to judge you. I don't know exactly what happened to you that night, but I believe you have something to hide. I'm sick and tired of your holy acts. After all, right now you're living off my hard-earned undignified money," Mairo yelled, storming out of the room.

Mercy was drenched in sweat. The heat in the room felt so intense despite the coolness of the air conditioning unit. She couldn't utter a word. Her eyes were sore and bloodshot, as though an unidentified flying object had just pierced through her iris. Was this a nightmare or what?

"Why on earth would Mairo react in such a brutish manner?" she wondered, gazing confusedly into space, just as Mairo returned to continue her tirade.

"You see, Mercy," she began, pacing the room, her voice brash and unflinching. "Life is like a game of chess. You either win, or you lose. Winners are people who face challenges, like I'm doing. Not people who flinch from reality like you. A woman needs to be bold, to be confident; to use her charm and femininity to her advantage. Mercy, you've got to face reality. For how long do you think you'll be under my roof, eating free food and enjoying all the benefits of my hard-earned money? Tell me, for how long?" she queried.

Mercy was agape for a few moments before summoning courage.

"I'm sorry, Mairo," she said when she finally found her voice. "I didn't know . . . I mean, I didn't . . ."

"Go on, don't be modest. Say it to my hearing!" Mairo snarled. "You didn't know I'm a prostitute, eh? You didn't know that I am a piece of trash used and funded by men. Well, I am . . . big deal. At least I'm using my brains to earn myself a living," she said with a prolonged hiss.

"Mairo . . . I'm sorry. I'm sorry I've offended you. I appreciate your generosity. I appreciate your hosting me and giving me a roof over my head. How can I ever repay your generosity? Oh Mairo, I didn't mean to upset you in any way . . . but I will never compromise the truth," Mercy concluded, her gaze fixated, before she pulled herself together and quietly made for the restroom. Shortly after, she returned, opened the wardrobe and put all her stuff into her bag.

"I'm leaving. I'll keep in touch as soon as I am sorted out. Just remember you have a friend in me," Mercy said, watching Mairo turn red.

"I . . . you don't have to leave," Mairo stuttered with unease, feeling very awkward. "I . . . I'm not chasing you away please," she managed to say in a croaky voice. "I mean, you've only spent a night here . . . there's no hurry."

"You're not chasing me away, my dear friend. I'm the one that opted for the easy way, the convenient way. I think I should gallantly face the challenges ahead of me. Good-bye, Mairo,"

Mercy said, making for the door. She stopped in her tracks and turned to face Mairo, who stood frozen on the spot.

"Thanks again for everything," Mercy said finally and disappeared through the door.

CHAPTER EIGHT

It was past forty-eight hours, and Mercy remained homeless. The day she left Mairo's house she'd spent the night in a decrepit inn located in the heart of Ajegunle, where accommodation was relatively cheap. The room was a direct contrast to Mairo's guest room. To start with, there was little or no ventilation, and the six-spring bed on which she lay was so rickety that in the middle of the night she had to pour sachet water on her body to reduce the heat and refresh herself. To worsen matters, the cockroaches and rats in the closet were such a nuisance that she had to jerk out of sleep several times in discomfort. She spent the greater part of the night fighting to keep away the unwelcome pests. Eventually, when she heard the first sign of cockcrow, she was up on her feet and ready to embark on an aggressive job hunt.

Her first point of call was at a fashion house across the street. A blackboard inscription in front of the shanty shop read: "Vacancy. Apply within." On further inquiry, however, she was bluntly informed that they needed a qualified tailor to fill the position. Still undaunted and determined to find herself employment, Mercy walked the length of the street, stopping at almost every corner shop to inquire for any vacant position. By midday, she hadn't accomplished much, except for the rigorous exercising of her feet that were by now wobbling. She was hungry and fatigued as she slumped into a seat at a roadside cafeteria. The money she had could only pay for a bowlful of rice and a pinch of stew, without meat. Hungrily, she consumed the food and thankfully drained the cup of water she was offered.

The next couple of hours were spent roaming the town, trekking as far as her feet could carry. It was surprising how many kilometers she covered on foot that day. At the first sign of dusk, she became dispirited. With no money and no resting place, she had to pray for a miracle. She stood at the busy Masha junction of Surulere, confused and agitated. It was already getting dark, and she watched in panic as several motorists sped past and the hustle-bustle of the city increased as several commuters dropped off the commercial buses they boarded. At a point, it appeared the whole city's dwellers were cloistering around her. Ironically, none took notice of her as they hurriedly made their way past, all in eagerness to get home or wherever their destinations were.

"Hey sweetie, how far are you going?"

Mercy looked up in confusion. She didn't even realize she'd left the busy scenario and was now walking down the adjoining street.

"Care for a ride?" continued the gentleman seated inside the black Mercedes Benz jeep, which had stopped beside her.

"Do I know you from somewhere?" she asked in confusion.

The coarse laughter from the stranger in the car put her on alert.

"Sure, you know me from somewhere, sweetie," came the man's response as he turned down the volume of his blaring radio. "Hop in and we can talk about how or where we met."

Mercy watched him with a frown, made to say something but was unable to find the right word.

"How much?" he questioned, stroking his chin. Mercy was agape.

"Come on, how much will it cost for a night out with you?" he continued, throwing open the door for her.

"You must be a joker," Mercy said finally with a hiss before turning in the opposite direction, hurrying as far as her feet could carry. She continued walking, this time with quick, unsteady strides, with no destination, no direction, until she arrived at the front of a wooden kiosk at the end of the road. It was deserted and without thinking or reasoning, she slumped into it.

The sound of hooting vehicles got her up very early the following day. She couldn't believe she'd slept peacefully inside the shanty kiosk. To her utmost surprise, however, her bag was gone. She looked around in confusion, not believing her eyes.

Her shoes were also gone and so was her wristwatch. At that point, she sat up in fear. She'd been robbed without her knowing it. She jumped up in confusion and then slumped to the floor crying. Her tears stopped suddenly as she dried her eyes.

"Thank you, Lord, for sparing my life. Weeping may endure for the night, but joy comes in the morning. I will never compromise my values. I'll rather die," she pronounced, a flood of tears breaking from her eyes again. She cried a little longer and rose to her feet, ready to traverse the town. Finally by midday, she got lucky.

"You've got the job," a stout middle-aged man announced. Mercy had just undergone a brief impromptu interview.

"I've got the job?" She asked in surprise before letting out a delighted cry. No formal interview, only a few questions and she got the job. It certainly was her lucky day.

"Thank you sir. When can I start work?" she asked effervescently.

"Immediately if you like," the man announced, peering into her face as if he was searching for something. "The housekeeper will give you a pair of uniforms and sandals," he said, emphasizing the last word with eyes fixed on her bare feet. "You really are desperate for this job, aren't you?" he quizzed sardonically, depressing a button on his table.

A neatly dressed lady appeared immediately and was given further instructions on the new employee's scope of duties.

"Take her to John and tell him that she should amongst other things, see to the cleaning of all the toilets, including mine," the manager concluded, turning to face the new employee.

"I've arranged for you to squat in the boy's quarters with Miss Ekaete, the cook. It's important you live in the premises as you can be called upon any time to discharge your duties," the manager explained, wearing a wry smile. "When I say any time, I mean any time. Is that clear?"

"Yes sir. I pledge to discharge my duties efficiently."

"Good. You may leave now," he said, dismissing the two. "By the way, I'm Mr. Shino," he said, winking as he stopped her in her tracks. Mercy acknowledged with a nod and followed the lady out. By evening of that day, the ex-nun was already quite familiar with the environment and her new job.

Without looking back, she sank her time and energy into the very hectic schedule of her job as a cleaner in the two-star hotel located on Herbert Macaulay Way in Yaba. Days turned into weeks, and she visited Mairo to inform her of her new situation. Her friend was not impressed at all by what she tagged Mercy's degradation of womanhood. As far as she was concerned, working as a cleaner in the hotel was akin to self-enslavement. She went further to apologize for her utterances that according to her, led to Mercy's desperate acceptance of the menial means of sustenance.

"Mairo, you are my friend, and my friend you shall remain. Thanks for your concern, but I'm quite satisfied with my job. I cannot despise my humble beginning because I believe that God will someday promote me," Mercy had explained.

"Amen O," Mairo replied pitifully, shaking her head in disapproval. "I don't envy you one bit. I just hope you don't come to your senses by the time it's too late," Mairo continued in derision. "A beautiful woman like you shouldn't waste away with a menial job like that. There are valid alternatives that you have turned down. Anyway, I can see you are destined to suffer, so who am I to dissuade you? I can only wish you good luck," she concluded.

"Thanks," Mercy replied, getting up. "I have to leave now. It's my day off, so let me go and get some rest."

"All right, take care," Mairo said, seeing her off to the door.

That same day when Mercy returned to the hotel, she was informed that the manager had urgent need to see her. Despite the fact that it was her official day-off duty, she scrambled to her feet and went straight to Mr. Shino's office. She was met by his secretary who handed her a note dropped by the manager. It read:

The toilet in room 401 is filthy and needs to be cleaned immediately.

Signed, Shino.

Mercy read the note several times, frowned and turned to the secretary.

"It's my day off today; besides I'm not in charge of room 401. John the male housekeeper is," she said, containing her irritation.

That was not the first time she'd received such instructions from her boss, and she wondered why on earth he derived pleasure in assigning her colleague's duties to her, particularly on her off days.

"I have work to do, Miss Mercy; you can complain to the manager when you see him," the secretary replied, resuming her work on the computer.

Mercy sighed and left the office. She made straight for room 401, and within minutes the toilet was cleaned out and smelling quite fresh. She always had a way of painstakingly discharging her duties.

"Good job, Mercy, I'm impressed," Mr. Shino said, entering the room just as she finished cleaning.

Mercy muttered a polite greeting and made to leave the room.

"Just a minute, my dear," Shino said, stopping her in her tracks. "The guest in room 402 just checked out, and I want you to fix the room immediately," he said, grinning from ear to ear.

"Sir, please, it's my day off today. I'll clean it out first thing tomorrow morning, or better still, let me call John. He's on duty today," Mercy explained.

"Since when did you start refusing my orders?" Shino questioned, his nose getting moist with annoyance.

"I don't mean to refuse your order, sir; it's just that I need a little rest. I work for eighteen hours every day round the week with only one day off. I think I deserve to observe my day off," she replied.

"You must be out of your mind. You must be very stupid to tell me such rubbish. Do you remember I clearly stated that you could be called upon any day, any time to do your job?" He barked.

"I didn't know that included my off days, sir," Mercy argued, getting agitated by his reasoning.

"You wretched slut! You came in here ready to die for the job. You didn't even have a pair of shoes. I gave you a job, gave you accommodation; I pay your salary, and you dare to challenge my order? You may wish to know that I am the reason you're employed here. I pitied you. Get that into your godforsaken skull. I pitied you and gave you this job, okay?"

"I'm sorry, sir," Mercy said in confusion. She didn't know what else to say as she watched him snarl.

"Bitch! Come here," Mr. Shino ordered, wiping his sweat off his face with his bare hands.

Mercy wasn't sure she'd heard him right.

"I said come here, bitch," he reiterated, unbuckling his belt.

"I beg your pardon sir!" Mercy exclaimed, watching him in shock and horror.

"I've been dying to have you, bitch. I've been dying for this moment when you and I will become one in flesh."

Mercy was out of shock in a moment as she dashed to the door.

"Hell!" Shino yelled, raging at her. "Where the hell do you think you're going?"

"Please sir, I beg to leave," Mercy stuttered, shaking in fear.

"I can change your life, Mercy, I can give you honor and dignity. You only need to cooperate with me. Your suffering shall be a thing of the past. Come, let me feel you," he recited lustfully, salivating and drooling; surging at her with all his energy. Mercy screamed and kicked him hard in the groin.

"Bitch! Bitch! You're fired!" Shino roared, groaning in pain as he fell to the floor.

"I quit! I quit sir!" Mercy said tearfully, storming out of the room.

Suffice it to say that Mercy threw in the towel. She dropped her resignation letter at the reception that night and left the hotel premises before Shino could make her termination official.

Luck was destined to shine on her when a few days later she landed a job at a fast-food joint on Ahmadu Bello Way, Victoria

Island in Lagos. Fortunately, she had free accommodations and worked two shifts as a waitress and as a cashier. This availed her the opportunity to start saving in earnest for weekend tutorials. Within a short period, she registered for the external General Certificate examination. As with her previous employment, she'd informed Mairo of her new job. Mairo was not impressed with Mercy's commitment to low-paying jobs, but Mercy was bent on proving her mettle at work, so her friend let her be. However, each time they got together she never ceased rebuking Mercy and trying to persuade her to try something more profitable. Mercy on her own part was resolute; unmoved, undeterred, and unwavering in her principles.

Her fighting spirit was evident, her maturity at warding off contrary views amazing. Her convictions were deep rooted, and she was not in a hurry to get rich quick, so despite challenges that cropped up from time to time, she gallantly sailed through victoriously. Her perception of daily problems was that they were an opportunity for learning and growth, as well as stepping-stones to greater opportunities. She lived an extremely frugal life, devoid of waste, and she was able to scrimp and save to make ends meet, particularly with regards to funding her part-time education. Whenever failure stared her in the face, she remembered and recited the Mary Kay slogan, "failing forward to succeed."

One evening towards the close of work, she had a visitor. It was Mairo in the company of a handsome, lanky, six-foot-tall Lebanese chap.

"It's been ages. You don't even ask after me," Mairo complained the moment they exchanged pleasantries.

"Forgive me friend, you know how it is at work. I am so busy, and even on weekends I'm occupied with my G.C.E. classes."

"Busy bee. Even the first lady, Maryam Babangida, is not as busy as you."

"I'm guilty as charged, but I'll make up some time very soon . . . I promise."

"Ever heard about giving flowers to a dead man?" Mairo quoted.

"What's that supposed to mean? A promise is a promise," Mercy put in.

"Not when it is coming very late," Mairo quipped before adding, "Anyway, have I introduced Razman to you?"

"No . . ." Mercy replied, facing the stranger.

"Razman, meet Mercy. Mercy, Razman."

"Nice meeting you," they both offered.

"I came to inform you that I won the American Visa lottery. My application has been processed and approved, and my interview was successful," Mairo explained jauntily. "My destination is Houston, Texas," she added.

"Wow! Congratulations!" Mercy exclaimed.

"You know I've always wanted to settle abroad, but I was waiting for the right opportunity."

"I am glad you finally got your heart's desire," Mercy said delightedly.

"Thank you. Now the second part of the news is, I am getting married."

"You? Getting married?"

"Yes. Razman and I will be tying the knots at the Ikoyi Registry tomorrow. We'll be leaving together for the U.S. afterwards."

"This calls for celebration. Congratulations," Mercy said, giving her friend a big hug.

"Will you be our guest tomorrow?" Mairo asked, glad that Mercy rejoiced over her recent fortune.

"I . . . have to be there. I mean, I just have to be there. Hurray! My friend is getting married!"

Mairo smiled blissfully, quite surprised at Mercy's exuberance.

"You know what, Mercy?"

"What?"

"You're a friend indeed," Mairo pronounced.

"Am I?"

"A friend is somebody who speaks the truth in love, someone who admonishes and inspires integrity. You have been all of that and more to me."

"I'm lost; what have I done to deserve the encomiums?" Mercy quizzed.

"You are a woman of virtue, a woman of dignity, a woman of substance. Continue to uplift the cause of womanhood, and I assure you the reward will be great."

"I am flattered, thank you very much . . . it's encouraging to hear that, but really I'm still lost."

"Must I spell it to you in black and white? Well, if I must, very few women can adopt your 'no compromise' philosophy, especially when faced with life's difficulties. Just look at you . . . so determined . . . undaunted despite all odds," Mairo declared.

"Come on, I'm only doing what I should as a human being," Mercy was saying when her friend interposed.

"I like your modesty. Well, I certainly want to be remembered in heaven. At least if I have your recommendation, I may be considered in the kingdom of God."

Mercy smiled and looked from Mairo to Razman. She wondered what point her friend was driving at.

"Can I see you privately for a minute?" Mairo asked, pulling her aside as Razman stepped back.

"You see, Mercy, the truth is often bitter, but I've learnt the hard way."

"What are you talking about?" Mercy asked, rather puzzled by her utterances.

"All these years, I've been defiling my body with all kinds of men. I traded my dignity for material gain. But I recently realized it is all vanity."

Mercy's brows were raised as she listened with surprise at the turn of their discussion.

"I lost my best friend and business partner of many years, Ngozi."

"Ngozi is dead?" Mercy asked with surprise. She had met the lady twice in Mairo's house.

"She contracted this deadly venereal disease and despite all efforts to cure her, it degenerated until the doctors eventually recommended evacuation of her womb. It got complicated; she became anemic, hemorrhaged, and she died. She died, Mercy! She didn't survive. You know, it could have been me," Mairo stammered, repressing her tears. "Ngozi who was full of life died just like that. Her money couldn't save her."

"I am sorry, Mairo; I didn't have the slightest inkling of her death."

"Well, I decided to quit messing around, but I'm so scared my past will come haunting me. I want to change for good. I want to be a good wife to Razman, but I feel I need divine help to see me through."

Mercy watched with surprise, then tenderness, and then affection, as her friend spoke unreservedly.

"I need you to remember me in your prayers, Mercy. I mean it. I want to turn a new leaf."

"I . . . I don't know what to say. It's overwhelming to hear you say all this," Mercy said with excitement. "Oh Mairo, I assure you the Lord will give you the grace to live a new life. All you need do is to ask for His forgiveness and invite Jesus into your life as personal Lord and Savior. That is the starting point to divine empowerment."

"I want to do that right away," Mairo said with eagerness. "Razman," she called excitedly. "Razman, come please," she beckoned with urgency.

Razman joined the ladies and was surprised when Mairo asked Mercy to pray for them.

"What's this all about?" Razman questioned, feeling quite embarrassed.

"Let's pray, Razman," Mairo said with urgency.

"We're in public, for goodness sake," Razman protested, looking flabbergasted.

"Please, Razman, if you truly love me, you'll do this with me," Mairo pleaded.

Reluctantly, Razman joined them as Mercy led them to a quiet spot and led the brief prayer, asking God to intervene, forgive and take total control of their lives.

"Thank you, Mercy," Mairo said in excitement when they finished. "Thank you so much. I feel relieved," she announced, embracing Mercy.

"Thanks, Raz darling," Mairo added, planting a kiss on his cheek. "Give us a few more minutes, will you?" she said as Razman again stepped aside.

"I'm grateful to you, Mercy. Thank you so much."

"Oh come on, what have I done?" Mercy asked, grinning from ear to ear.

"Don't be infernally modest!" Mairo said heartily, nudging her playfully. "I'll be eternally grateful to you."

"Thank God," Mercy said with contentment. "So how did you meet Razman?" She inquired curiously.

"It's a long story, but in summary, we met at the cemetery shortly after Ngozi's funeral. He'd gone there to pay respect to his late brother."

"Really? What an odd place to meet your spouse," Mercy said. "So from there he vowed to marry you?" She added jokingly.

"Gush! I didn't realize you had a sense of humor," Mairo said with roaring laughter. "Anyway, Mercy, you are not far from the truth. Razman and I have known each other for barely six weeks, and it's all happening like a dream."

"Six weeks?" Mercy exclaimed. "Are you sure you are not rushing things?"

"I know what I am doing; Raz is my soul mate. Please just wish me well, okay?"

"Okay, I'm happy for you, Mairo," Mercy said as they walked together towards Razman, who had placed an order for pizza and was already munching away.

"Care for some?" he asked, gulping some orange juice.

"Sorry for keeping you waiting," Mairo apologized, taking a seat beside him.

"No problem. I'm quite busy with this," Razman replied.

"One more thing, Mercy," Mairo put in, searching out a bunch of keys from her handbag. "Here . . . for you as my farewell gift," she added, placing the keys on her palm.

Mercy looked at the keys. "I don't understand . . ."

"They are her car keys. Please accept," Razman put in.

For a moment, Mercy was speechless. "But Mairo, you don't have to . . . I can't accept this, please."

"You'll break my heart if you refuse," Mairo said pleadingly. "Please, Mercy, I want you to have it. The car is parked outside, and it's all yours. Thanks for accepting my little gift."

"Thank you, Mairo. How can I thank you enough? But I think you should sell the car and use the proceeds for yourself," Mercy argued. "Honestly, I'll feel guilty accepting this."

Mercy returned the keys and to her utmost shock, Mairo rose to her feet in tears.

"You hate me, don't you? You haven't forgiven me for those nasty things I said to you in my house. I thought you said we'll be friends forever."

Mercy was even more surprised. She watched in confusion as Razman offered Mairo a handkerchief to dab her eyes.

"You're hurting her," Razman said, looking Mercy straight in the face.

"She made me believe you're the only true friend she has. Her greatest joy will be for you to have the car. Please don't refuse it," Razman added, soothing his fiancée whose sentiments were causing a bit of attention from other tables.

"Mercy, I'm begging you again to forgive me. I didn't mean to throw you out of my apartment. I didn't mean to hurt you either. Let bygones be bygones. I want to leave this country in peace, knowing that I still have your hand of friendship," Mairo voiced throatily.

"Oh Mairo, you don't have to say all that," Mercy said, hugging her reassuringly. "I honestly don't hold any grudge against you. I'm only concerned that you could need the extra cash if you sell the car."

"I am going to the United States to work. I'm going to labor with my hands. I'll do legitimate work and earn a living. You're doing just that, and I intend to follow in your stride," Mairo declared.

"Thank you. It's such a blessing hearing you say that. God will be with you. He'll never fail you," Mercy pronounced, hugging her again before finally accepting the keys.

Mairo and Razman decided to wait until Mercy closed from work. The trio proceeded to dinner at an exclusive Chinese restaurant along Ozumba Mbadiwe Street in Victoria Island. Mairo was an addict of Chinese food, and they all enjoyed the meal. Mercy ate with great relish, particularly the savory jumbo prawns in chili sauce.

They parted and reassembled the following day at the registry. Mercy was happy that the registry wedding fell on her day off work, so there was no need to seek official permission to be away from her duty post. It was a very private wedding with just a handful of family members in attendance as witnesses. The charming newlyweds smiled all the way, while Mercy shared their joy and laughter amidst farewell tears and sentiments at the end of the day.

CHAPTER NINE

It was a bright, beautiful morning as the sun shone brilliantly in the sky and birds chirruped the dawn of a new day. Cassandra had just woken up from a long, peaceful night rest. The lithe, muscular, and ruggedly handsome fellow lying beside her was still fast asleep and snoring quite loudly. She smiled contentedly and spent a few moments observing the sleeping chap whom she adored greatly. He had brought sunshine into her life, flowers, romance, and superlative passion. He'd never wearied pampering her, and she never got tired of reciprocating his affection. She yawned and sprawled tiredly on the massive waterbed before drifting off to sleep again. By the time she finally awoke, her eyes were fully cleared of sleep as she observed the wall clock ticking. It was a few minutes past nine.

"Alexander! Alexander!" she called, tapping her bedmate gently on the shoulder.

He responded sleepily and turned to the other side.

"Wake up, Alexander," she persisted, nudging his side.

"What is it, darling?"

"You were snoring."

"Oh please, Sandra, let me get some sleep."

"It's already past nine."

"Nine? So what? It's a public holiday," he mumbled.

"Remember my daughter is coming home today. You should freshen up before she arrives."

"You win," Alexander said, stretching his limbs before pulling her to himself.

"Did you have a good night rest, darling?" he asked.

"You bet I did."

"Did you dream of me?" he continued, feeling his clean-shaven head.

"Well . . . em, let me think about that."

"Naughty girl," he said, planting a kiss on her lips. "I spent the whole night dreaming of you," he remarked, stroking her eighteen-inch human hair.

"And what was I doing in your dream?"

"You were laughing and giggling and full of exuberance."

"You make me so happy, Alexander," she muttered, snuggling closer to him.

"And you are my precious jewel, Cassandra. Will you make me your man forever?"

Cassandra laughed aloud before rolling out of bed.

"You didn't answer my question," her lover boy said.

"Well, everything depends on you," Cassandra replied.

"What do you mean?"

"If you are a good boy, Alexander, you've got me for as long as you wish. If not . . ."

"Sandra, have I ever given you reason to doubt my loyalty?" he questioned in a solemn tone.

"No, but one can never be too sure with you men. You often change like the weather."

"Change for the better," he put in, jumping out of bed. "You know how I feel about you, Sandra."

She was quiet as he pulled her into his arms. "I can't see any reason why this flame of love should ever quench. We are destined to be. Besides, no right-thinking man will have you and ever desire another. Baby, you are all I've ever dreamt of and more . . ."

"I believe you. Let's hope it lasts forever," she said, feeling his jaw and moustache with her palm.

With that, he swung her into his arms, planting kisses all over her face and gliding with her towards the adjoining door.

"What are you doing?" she queried, giggling in excitement.

"I'm going to give you a warm bath."

"Oh please, darling, put me down," she protested, wriggling free. "I'll go order our breakfast while you go take a bath," she said, gradually receding.

"Your wish is my command, darling." Alexander whistled, sailing into the luxurious bathroom.

He entered the Jacuzzi, relaxed in the warm water and tuned the radio. As he enjoyed his bath, Cassandra placed an order for their breakfast over the intercom.

"Toasted bread, bacon, sausages, cheese, boiled eggs, omelette, fries, coffee, milk, oats, and fresh fruit juice. Also include boiled white yam with kidney sauce. Make it snappy," she concluded, before slotting in a blues CD.

Breakfast was served shortly by Akpan. He was Cassandra's chef, a stout man from Calabar who was very good with churning out various delicacies—English, continental, and Nigerian, without much ado.

Cassandra was a plain-faced, light-skinned, buxom woman. A longtime divorcee, she was a renowned journalist as well as a politician. Her meeting the gigolo was fortuitous. She'd gone shopping for groceries when she suddenly realized at the paying counter that she had run out of cash. Alexander was on hand to offer loose change to the elegant personality, who in turn was instantly drawn to his rugged masculinity and was eager to repay his kindness.

From there, they got chatting; she offered him lunch; he obliged and zestfully accompanied her home afterwards. They hit it off immediately, and since then it was bliss all the way. For Alexander, homecoming wasn't a bad idea after all. His fortunes changed for the better as he fraternized with the vivacious society woman. It was a glamorous lifestyle, partying with society's cream, dining and shopping at exotic spots, romantic escapades and adventure, plus an overflow of legal tender to spend.

"Life couldn't be better," he thought, settling to breakfast beside her in her bedroom dining area. He was wearing his boxers, having just finished taking his bath. They joked and chatted as they busied themselves with their meal.

"Mum, I'm home," a youthful voice called from outside.

"Tobi is here," Cassandra whispered, rising to her feet and throwing a bathrobe to Alexander, who immediately threw it on.

The door flung open, and the youngster flew into her mother's arms.

"Welcome home, darling, I missed you," Cassandra said.

"I missed you too, Mum."

"You look very well. I see you're enjoying school."

"School is stressful. I'm glad the session is over. At least I will get to rest for a couple of weeks."

Cassandra laughed and led her daughter towards their squatter.

"Hello Tobi, welcome home," Alexander said, getting up to welcome the attractive young lady. Tobi was five feet eight inches tall, spotlessly light skinned, with deep brown eyes, healthy brown hair, sparkling white dentition, and an amazing panache. With little makeup, she was drop-dead gorgeous.

"Meet Alexander Moyo, dear," Cassandra introduced.

"Hello," Tobi greeted, taking his outstretched hand. The two were transfixed for a moment.

"Join us for breakfast, love," Cassandra offered, pulling a chair for her daughter.

"Thanks, mum, but food is the least of my priorities now. I'll go change, get some rest and then settle to a sumptuous lunch."

"What would you like for lunch?" Cassandra asked.

"How about fresh fish with spicy jollof rice, peppered snails, and fried plantains?"

"Right, I'll tell Mr. Akpan."

"Thanks, mum, see you later."

"Cheerio," Cassandra said, watching her daughter breeze out of the room.

"She's such a cheerful kid," Alexander commented the moment she was gone.

"She makes me so happy," Cassandra stated smugly.

"How old is she?"

"Seventeen."

"Really? She looks like a twenty-five-year-old."

Cassandra laughed and gulped some juice. "She matured. Anyway, most undergraduates look older than their age."

"It's amazing what the four walls of a university can do," Alexander commented.

"These days, age is a thing of the mind. You are as old as you feel. The young feel older, the old feel younger," Cassandra put in.

"Such irony. Little wonder you look younger and more radiant every day. Nobody will believe you gave birth to her," he commented.

"I am flattered."

"You shouldn't be. It's a statement of fact," Alexander uttered, eating the rest of his meal in silence.

The meal, which he was earlier on enjoying, suddenly tasted like sawdust in his mouth. His mind was in disarray, preoccupied with thoughts of Tobi. Certainly he couldn't have fallen so easily for the teenager? "Tread softly, Alexander," his instinct warned. He quickly brushed aside the lustful thoughts and concentrated on the woman beside him.

"I love you, Sandra," he pronounced before smothering her face with kisses.

The following day the trio went picnicking at Lekki Beach. Sandwiches, barbecue chicken, beef kebabs, assorted cookies and cakes, chocolates, ice cream, and chilled drinks were amongst the variety of things to choose from. Alexander Moyo carefully avoided the girl's eyes. He could feel her gaze from beneath her thick spectacles. Cassandra's loquacity depressed the company as she went on chattering while the other two were preoccupied with their individual thoughts. As they rode homewards at sundown, her babble continued. She rattled on about subjects her company found boring. They were almost sleeping on her until she turned to ask if they were listening and they both responded in the affirmative. Now fully attentive, they gave her undivided attention as she spoke.

"So like I was saying, I'm glad you two get along well. I want us to live peacefully like a family. What do you say, Alex?"

"You have my word, baby."

"And you, Tobi?"

"You can count on me, mum. We'll live as one happy family."

"Good! I have a business meeting in London, and I'll be travelling tomorrow night to return after one week. When I get back, we can all plan a vacation together."

"Fantastic, mum, I need a change of scene," Tobi chipped in enthusiastically.

"Where would you prefer, my dear?" her mother asked.

"Hmm . . . how about South Africa?"

"You're kidding. I don't want to get caught in their racial riots," Alexander put in jokingly. "I would have preferred somewhere in the coast like Greece, Venice, or the Bahamas."

"This is 1994; apartheid is over. Who knows, I might be lucky to see Nelson Mandela, then I'll get his autograph," Tobi put in.

"Fantasy," Alexander uttered. "The best you'll see will probably be the derelict Soweto."

"Never mind him, dear. After all, there's nothing wrong with you dreaming of meeting Madiba, the freedom fighter," Cassandra teased.

"Yeah, I know Madiba is Nelson Mandela's Xhosa clan name. But, sweetheart, a vacation to me should be a fun trip, not a depressing historical tour," Alexander put in with seriousness. "Yeah, I also know that Mandela won the Nobel Peace Prize last year. Kudos! He is no doubt a living legend, but when it comes to fun, I don't mix with antiquity."

"Seriously, mum, let us plan to be there for Mandela's swearing in as the first black president of South Africa. He'll be inaugurated on May 10th, this year 1994. Please, mum, can we be there live to witness the historic event?" she pressed, ignoring Alexander's comment.

"You've got a point there, my dear," her mother said, thoughtfully.

"No no . . . let's not get partisan here. I thought we are planning a vacation, not a political tour," Alexander put in emphatically. "Nobody seems to be considering my argument."

"That's a point too . . . besides, we can follow the events on CNN. Let's leave a South African vacation for another time when the post-apartheid political situation will have stabilized," Cassandra added, winking at Tobi convincingly.

They all agreed and continued chatting until the car came to a halt in front of the house. Dinner for them was an elaborate affair outside by the pool. They had a la carte seafood, and for dessert, all settled for fresh fruit salad and cream. By the time they were done and ready for bed, they were thoroughly exhausted. Cassandra fell asleep immediately, while Tobi spent a restless night alone in her bedroom. For the gigolo, his mistress's trip couldn't have had better timing. He counted the hours, minutes, and seconds until the time came for her to head for immigration checks and security screening. They had gone to the airport together, and the five minutes Cassandra spent at the check-in counter seemed like eternity to her boyfriend, who could not wait for her to get out of the way.

Cassandra's flight was scheduled to depart by 10:00 p.m., and the time was now about 8:00 p.m. She was flying first class, so she had about two hours to be at the first-class lounge before boarding. Alexander heaved a sigh of relief as Cassandra hugged, kissed and bade them good-bye.

"Tobi," Alexander called as they drove homewards.

"Yes?"

"I . . .I, em."

"You what?" she asked.

"Well, your mum's traveled."

"So?"

"What I mean is . . ."

"What do you mean, Alexander?"

"Well, I was just wondering if we could get extra groceries from the store. We could do with some in her absence."

"That shouldn't be a problem. The chef and housekeeper already have instructions on that!" she bluntly replied.

"I sound stupid, don't I?"

"I didn't say so. Anyway, don't bother yourself about trivialities. Mum always ensures the house is fully stocked, especially when she's traveling."

"Ah . . . mummy's girl. You both seem very fond of each other," he remarked.

"I love my mother . . . she's all I've got."

Alexander kept quiet and started humming a tune. After a few minutes, he stopped and turned to face her.

"I've often wondered about so many things," he began.

"Such as?"

"Well, em . . . I don't know," he dismissed.

"Go on, what's on your mind?"

"Hmm . . . you and your mother have a very strong bond."

"Obviously . . . that's expected of mother and child, isn't it?"

"I guess you're right," he responded with a shrug.

"What exactly do you have in mind, Alex?"

"Me? What do you think I have on my mind?"

"I wonder. Anyway, whatever the case, my mother and I are indivisible. The bond between us can never be broken!" she announced with a harsh air of finality.

The man gaped in surprise. He remained quiet for the rest of their drive home. From that moment onwards, Alexander and Tobi rarely spoke, except when they managed to exchange routine monosyllables. It appeared Cassandra's absence from home created an unusually tense atmosphere between them. Minutes soon rolled into hours and hours into days. The first few days of Cassandra's trip elapsed uneventfully. She'd called several times daily on the land line to ensure that all was well.

"Mum, I can't wait for you to get back," Tobi said for the umpteenth time during their recent conversations. Alexander sat beside her, listening to the drollery between mother and child. His brows were raised in derision as he waited patiently for his turn to exchange pleasantries with the woman. Finally, Tobi gave him the receiver, which he accepted, albeit with a long, inquiring glance before uttering his well-versed declaration of love.

"What was that about?" Tobi quizzed when he finally went off the line.

"What?"

"You looked displeased when I was chatting with mum. Are you jealous?" she questioned.

"What? You're crazy!"

"I hope I am 'cos it'll be ridiculous if you expect by any means to come between mum and I."

"Why are you always on the defensive, Tobi? I have no doubts about your strong allegiance to your mother. Must you always spell it out?"

"Of course I should, especially when she's dealing with a scum like you!"

Alexander was aghast. It took just a few moments for him to overcome the shock. Tobi looked at him, hissed and stormed out of the living room. She didn't care a hoot if the man felt insulted or offended. As far as she was concerned, his feelings were inconsequential, and she was glad to give him a piece of her mind. For the rest of the day, she lay in bed cogitating. One thing that often bothered her was the issue of her mother dating. She had never liked any of her mother's boyfriends, as she often saw them as tramps and opportunists.

Oftentimes, she felt lonely; and at such moments, questions and depressing thoughts about her paternity cropped up. She had no memory of her father. She'd never seen his picture. She hadn't any idea what he looked like, and it was a source of frustration trying to paint mental images of the man.

Tobi felt resentful about her lack of paternal love and care, despite her mother's unequalled devotion to her. Every man in her mother's life was a potential enemy, and she saw no reason for their interfering in her cherished maternal relationship. "Alexander will be no exception," she swore under her breath, feeling uneasy and confused.

"I hate him. I swear I hate him," she echoed before switching off the lights. For a while she couldn't sleep. She kept thinking, very deep thoughts that eventually led her into a restless, troubled sleep. In her dream, Alexander was the main actor. By morning when she woke up, she was even more troubled. Her dream was so detailed, yet she couldn't make much sense of it.

She couldn't even remember what happened except for the fact that Alexander was the principal player there.

Meanwhile, Alexander had equally dreamt of her all through the night. He woke up with a contented smile. He was happy. Something in him told him that their paths will cross . . . for the better.

"I'm in love," he sang as he lay in bed, lazing with lustful thoughts of the girl. By midday when he finally stepped out of the bedroom, Tobi was nowhere to be seen. She'd left the house very early to Ikoyi Club with her friends. It was obvious she was avoiding any contact with him.

"I know how to tackle her type," Alexander thought, plotting and calculating his next line of action.

It wasn't until 8:00 p.m. that she eventually returned home. Alexander was at the door to receive her.

"Hello, Tobi," he offered, wearing a broad smile. "How did your day go?" he continued, shutting the door after her. Tobi looked at him a bit confusedly. She opened her mouth to speak and suddenly decided against it. Without sparing him a second glance, she walked straight towards her bedroom, leaving the man in a state of abashment.

The following morning, Alexander was up very early. He was at the breakfast table at the basement where the girl often had her meals. She didn't show up for the three hours he sat there waiting, despite Alexander's persistent instructions to the chef to invite her down. Just when he was about to give up, the door opened. Tobi stepped in looking radiant in a pair of bright pink shorts and a black boob tube. She was surprised to see Alexander, and against her better wish, she decided to settle to her breakfast.

Alexander gently took his seat opposite her and watched her eat. She appeared unmoved by his gaze. Suddenly, she dropped her coffee mug and squealed.

"Can't you leave me alone, for goodness sake? Leave me alone! Just leave me alone!" she shrieked.

Alexander remained calm, watching with delight at her outburst. She was irked by his countenance, ready to squawk when he said:

"Oluwatobi Majekodunmi." He pronounced each word with a deliberate drawl. "Tobi, my dear, my sweet little girl. I'm not your enemy. I'm just Alexander, the guy who's dying to have your hand of friendship. I want us to be one, to have a good rapport, to relate cordially. What exactly have I done wrong? Why do you despise the sight of me? Tell me please, I swear I'll do just anything to make amends."

"I just want you to leave me alone, okay?" Tobi said, wiping her mouth with a napkin. "I can never be impressed no matter how hard you try."

She sprang to her feet. Alexander followed suit.

"Listen, Tobi, there's no need to wage war against an innocent fellow like me. I don't mean any harm . . . I swear I'm a good guy. Your mother's even aware."

Tobi's face creased into a frown when he mentioned her mother.

"Hey, I'm just Alexander, okay? A jolly good fellow . . . and I think you look prettier without that scowl."

Tobi watched with mistrust, pondered for a while and said, "Leave my mother out of this . . . you've obviously deceived her with flattering words."

"Tobi! I take exception to that innuendo. What I feel for you and Cassandra is real."

"And what might that be, deceiver?"

"True friendship, a strong bond of enduring and selfless friendship . . . I truly care."

"You never give up, do you?" she asked, taking a deep breath.

"Not when I'm dealing with a tough nut like you," Alexander remarked.

Tobi wore a wry smile. It lingered on as silence engulfed the room. Suddenly, she burst out laughing. Alexander watched with surprise, wondering if his eyes were failing him. When it was apparent her laughter was genuine, he joined and they both continued laughing until Tobi sank into her seat.

"I . . . I don't even know why I'm laughing," she stated flatly when she finally found her voice. "What's wrong with me? Am I going crazy or something?" she asked no one in particular.

Alexander was there with her, but she seemed oblivious of his presence as she went on soliloquizing.

"Oluwatobi Majekodunmi, you must be out of your mind," she stated with an air of finality.

Alexander watched her keenly, his face somewhat amused by her actions. Neither of them spoke for a while until she finally broke the silence.

"I'm sorry, Alexander."

Alexander looked at her in utmost disbelief.

"I don't know what's come over me these past few days," she continued with a sigh. "I've been rude and uncouth, haven't I?" she asked, looking for the first time in his direction since her vituperations.

"I . . . I'm sorry. I'm not always like this, honestly. It's just that I'm always so scared . . . especially . . . never mind," she quickly dismissed, rising to her feet.

"Especially what, Tobi?" Alexander prodded, stopping her in her tracks.

"It's nothing really," she quickly dismissed.

"I don't mean to pry, dear young lady, but we've come a long way. I mean, you're like my own kid sister. You should feel free to talk to me."

Tobi kept quiet. She felt uneasy. She retraced her steps to her seat and pondered for a while before saying:

"It's nothing, honestly. I . . ."

"You make a lousy liar, Tobi. Come on, feel free . . . just imagine you're talking to your big brother, your favorite big brother for that matter," he said, placing a hand on her shoulder. "You're like my own sister, trust me," he pressed, watching her gradually melt away every resistance.

"It's stupid . . . I mean, how do I explain?" she started off, quite unsure of herself.

"Nothing is stupid, especially if it's strong enough to bother your mind. Go on and talk please . . . kid sister."

Tobi smiled and watched him inquisitively. Perhaps he wasn't like all the others—out to date her mother just for pleasure and selfish gains.

"Do you like my mother, Alex?" she asked suddenly. Alexander stared at her. What should be his response to the question? He certainly had to tread softly with his words.

"I . . .yes. Of course, your mother's a very nice woman."

"I mean, do you love her?" The girl quizzed.

Alexander was numb; he couldn't find an immediate response to the question. If he answered in the affirmative, it could ruin his plans. On the other hand, if his response was negative, who knows what she had in mind asking the question in the first instance?

"I hope I'm not pressing," she quickly put in, watching his blank expression with an inquiring eye.

"Em . . . well, no. What can I say? I wasn't really expecting that question, least of all from you," he stuttered.

"Anyway, please don't break my mother's heart. How old are you by the way?"

"Me?"

"Yes, you."

"What does my age have to do with us?"

"Oh come on, tell me. I'm just curious," she pleaded.

"How old do you think I am?"

"Fifty?"

"You're crazy. Do I really look that old?"

"Well then, tell me."

"Forty-seven."

"Really? And you look at least ten years younger," Tobi said.

"Don't flatter me."

"I'm serious. Anyway, age is in the mind. I'm glad that you're at least two years older than mum. Perhaps one day you two will . . . I mean . . . perhaps, maybe get married."

Alexander gaped at her. He'd never been more shocked in his entire life. Could the girl really be nursing such thoughts or was she just pulling his legs? It had to be the latter, or else how could he explain that look in her eyes? Those moments . . . when he literally felt the chemistry rising between them.

"She must be joking," he thought, her words cutting through his riotous mind.

"I've always wanted mum to settle into a decent relationship," Tobi uttered, unaware of Alexander's inner war. "I've always dreamed that someday mum will remarry. I think she deserves a good man who will love and respect her . . . unlike my father."

Alexander's lips drooped. Their discussion was taking an unpredictable turn, and he was the one to experience all the shocking waves.

"My father wanted a slave for a wife. He wanted her to idolize him. He wanted her to worship him. He almost succeeded, except that she revolted. He couldn't suppress her vigor and strength."

"So what happened?" Alexander offered when it appeared she'd run out of words or perhaps, a focused narrative direction.

"They got divorced, and since then mum vowed never to marry again. She always speaks of him with much distaste."

"But you . . . what's your opinion of your father?" he asked, watching her expectantly.

Tobi remained quiet.

"Are you okay, Tobi?" he asked, when it became apparent she wasn't forthcoming with an immediate response.

"I don't know. I . . . I don't know him. I don't know my father," she said, breaking into tears. Alexander was petrified for a moment.

"You don't know your dad?" he voiced suddenly. He seemed to have run out of words as he simply peered into her face, watching her clouded eyes release tension in torrents.

"He died. He died shortly after their divorce. I was just about two years old then," she said, trying without luck to fight back the tears.

"I'm so sorry. I didn't realize your father's late. I'm sorry, Tobi," he cooed, gently taking her in his arms. "It's okay, baby," he comforted, soothing her with his gentle words, calming her, reassuring her, revitalizing her.

"Thank you," she said, breaking away briefly before reaching out for another warm embrace.

"I feel . . . I feel like I got myself a new dad," she said when they eventually separated.

"If that's what you chose to call me . . . the pleasure will be mine."

"Are you serious? Oh Alexander, thank you. I beg your pardon, dad," she said, reviewing him with new eyes and a novel affection.

"You know what, Tobi?"

"What?"

"We have something in common."

"And what can that be?" she inquired.

"I never knew my dad too. I was raised an orphan. All my life I've been on my own. No family ties, no brother, no sister."

"Are you serious?" she asked, watching him with perplexity.

"Oh yes, I am. So you see, I do understand how you feel. It can be frustrating for a child to live in a world without a clearly defined pedigree. Other kids taunt you, some adults take advantage of you; generally speaking, there are times your emotions are in disarray. I understand those feelings, and really, sometimes I wish I had a family, I mean, people I could have looked up to, especially in my youth. But all that is in the past. I really don't care anymore."

"That is serious!" Tobi exclaimed. "But tell me, how did you survive? I mean, without anyone to care for you? At least I have my mother's love," she added.

"I was a very brilliant kid and very luckily gained scholarships through college and the university. I spent my first few years in an orphanage though."

"I doubt if I can ever gain a scholarship. I'm not as brilliant as you."

"You're wrong, Tobi. I think you're a smart kid. Very apt too."

"Thanks, dad. It's good to hear you say that."

"I . . . I don't know what to say to all this, Tobi. You're making me your dad? Is that what this means?"

"If you'll accept . . . yes. And if you'll accept mum, we'll be forever one happy family. My dream of family will become real. Father, mother, child, this is what I've wanted all my life," she confessed. "And maybe we . . . we can also make up for your lost childhood," she stuttered. "For me, it is often frustrating trying to figure out what a father's love would have been," she said, sobbing quietly.

Alexander watched her sentiments, and suddenly something roared within him. He suddenly had a craving for marijuana, but he forcefully repressed the feeling. This was one of those times when his head went crazy, and he felt the urge for narcotics use. Since his relationship with Cassandra got deep, he had willfully subdued the use of hard drugs because there were times in the past he lost control, went uncontrollably wild with bad behavior that landed him into the police net or the rehabilitation center for drug users. He cherished his relationship with Cassandra too much to want to get into her bad books with antisocial behavior. As a matter of fact, she was the publisher of a wellness and lifestyle magazine at the fore of exposing drug abuse and the effects on people and the society. Thus, he had deliberately kept a distance from drugs. And now . . . this Tobi girl was pushing him. She was awakening a repressed demon. Who the hell did the girl think he was? An empathetic comforter or what? Surely she didn't expect him to play mediator in their family while he suffered unfulfilled carnal craving. Not with her mother—no! With her? Yes! Certainly, she was the one he wanted. She was the one he'd been dying to attract, and here she was with sloppy tales of her family memorial, begging to be his foster child and worse still, asking him to marry her mother. Well, as long as she was willing to play gullible, he'll dance along her naivety . . . until the time is ripe and nothing . . . nothing will stop him from executing his plans.

CHAPTER TEN

Cassandra had since returned from her trip, and life continued as usual for the trio. She was surprised, albeit happy
that her daughter was excited at the possible prospects between
her and Alexander. The man, however, had other plans. His
days were preoccupied with lustful thoughts of Tobi. He continued to repress the feelings—to suppress it—pending the right
opportunity.

That fateful day after breakfast, Cassandra announced that
she'd be traveling outside the country again. Her trip was due to
last a few days, after which she'd promised they could finally
take a two-week vacation, a boat cruise from Hawaii to the
Bahamas before the new school semester resumed for Tobi. As
with her last trip, they'd seen her off to the airport, and farewells
concluded, Alexander and Tobi walked back to the parking lot.

"Tobi," Alexander called the moment they were seated
inside the car.

"Yes, dad."

"I . . . I wonder if we can go out to dinner somewhere."

"Sure, dad."

They settled for an exclusive Indian restaurant overlooking
the lagoon.

"Enjoying the meal?" Alexander asked, watching her eat in
silence.

"Yes, thank you."

"Spicy and nice?" he asked, scooping a spoonful of chicken
masala into his mouth as she nodded in the affirmative. "That
makes it two of us," he added, gazing into her face admiringly.

Tobi smiled and continued in silence with her meal.

"I think we should celebrate tonight," Alexander said, order-
ing a bottle of champagne.

"Why, daddy? It's not your birthday, is it?"

"I wish she'd stop this daddy nonsense!" he thought, managing to conceal his irritation before he proceeded: "My dear, our merriment is a perennial affair."

"Oh yeah?"

"Certainly, and you bet, when your mama comes back, we're going to have a real family party before our vacation cruise."

"Oh dad, you can be so sweet."

"Anything for you, daughter, and even more for my darling Cassandra."

"Hmm, I'm glad you love her so much," Tobi commented innocently.

Their drink arrived, and Alexander poured a full glass for her. She consumed the first glass and watched as he refilled it.

"Don't you think this is a little too much?" she asked, her head swirling after she'd consumed a few glasses. "Mum never lets me take more than one little glass," she explained.

"Mum! Mum! That's all I ever get to hear. Hey, you're with daddy, remember? Let me spoil you a little," he blurted out, pouring her another glass. Tobi consumed it as Alexander continued, "Cassandra is a connoisseur of wines, and as a society big girl your mother knows that taking a bit of alcohol is a regular part of our high profile lifestyle. My darling Tobi, like your mother you need to be initiated into the club of the big girls," he pressed. "A beautiful babe like you needs to measure up," he added.

"Dad, excessive consumption of alcohol is dangerous to the organs. I don't want to have kidney or liver failure," she argued.

"Like hell, you won't! It's the same message they preach about cigarettes, but I haven't had lung cancer, despite smoking for decades," he defended.

"But many smokers suffer from cancer, and the surgeon general even warns that cigarette smoking is dangerous to health. Maybe you've just been lucky, dad," she put in with a shrug.

"Like hell I have! I've got healthy genes and so have you. An occasional indulgence wouldn't kill, would it? Besides, somebody must die of some disease someday, anyway," he argued with emphasis.

Tobi looked at him with perplexity, wondering why he was bent on pushing. He sounded irked and desperate, and she didn't have the energy for argument. Besides, she was feeling tipsy and dizzy.

I have to visit the loo," she announced, getting up from her seat.

Alexander immediately swung into action. He felt his pocket for the stuff, poured a generous portion into her drink and waited patiently for her arrival. She returned shortly and took her seat.

"I feel sick," Tobi announced, feeling her forehead.

"Sorry, baby . . . why not finish your drink and let's go home."

"No, dad . . . I've had too much already."

"Come on, daughter, an extra glass will do you no harm. Let's not waste this expensive wine."

Tobi reluctantly gulped the remains of her drink and rose to her feet. She could hardly support herself, and Alexander had to carry her all the way into the car. He drove at top speed, jamming on the brake only when they arrived at the front of the house. Once inside, he headed for Cassandra's bedroom, and in a matter of minutes, he undressed the girl.

His eyes feasted on her bare skin, and for a few seconds, he was transfixed . . . enthralled by the beauty of her youth.

"Oluwatobi Majekodunmi. I love you. I swear I'll give my life for you," he recited in euphoria, falling on his knees beside her. "I love you, Tobi, with all my heart . . . all my soul . . . all my being. I adore you," he pronounced, raising his head in ecstasy.

Without thinking or wasting further time, he started undoing his shirt buttons. One, two, three, then the fourth one got stuck. He squawked and yanked the shirt apart. Then it was time to unzip his trousers. His patience was fast running out, and he was already sweating when the stiff zipper finally gave way.

Alas, he was relieved and ready to gratify his burning passion. But first he had to switch on the air-conditioning unit. His eyes caught a glimpse of the compact disc player, and he rushed at it, slotted in his favorite blues CD, heaved a final sigh of relief and sailed towards the sleeping girl. Just as he was about to pull off his boxer shorts, he heard a voice. For a moment, his heartbeat stopped. Surely his imagination was betraying him, but not so. His bulging eyes turned in the direction of the door, awestricken, shocked to the marrow as Cassandra stepped in.

"My God! Alexander!" Cassandra squealed in utter shock and disbelief.

"Cassandra . . . you didn't travel?" Alexander stuttered, bashful and petrified, his mind in total disarray.

"Alex! Oluwatobi! Cassandra shrieked, cupping her head in her hands. Her head felt heavy; like a rock just crashed into it. She shook her head, thoroughly nauseated as her face distorted in pain. She was agape for a few moments that seemed like eternity.

"Cassandra . . . I—it's not what . . . I swear I haven't touched her. I, em, please Cassandra, I can explain . . ."

Cassandra rushed at him and dealt him a violent slap. For some seconds afterwards, she remained confused and abashed as her eyes pierced through his with all the hatred in the world.

"You are filthy, Alexander. You are a filthy, disgusting, vile animal!" She groaned as her head continued swinging.

"Why? Why? Is this how to father a child? Why, Alexander?" she moaned, her eyes turning red, the venom in her increasing by the minute.

"Please, Cassandra, I can explain. I didn't mean to hurt her . . . I—"

"Tobi . . . Oluwatobi Majekodunmi. Why? Why? You dare betray your mother, Tobi? You dare betray your own mother?" Cassandra recited, moving slowly towards the sleeping girl. She slapped her hard on the cheek and stared in surprise as the girl lay limp on the bed. She looked from the girl to the man and vice versa.

"What . . . what did you do to her, you devil? You . . . you drugged her. You drugged my baby!" Cassandra wailed, raging at him with outstretched fist.

"Please Sandra . . . it's . . . honestly I . . . it was a mistake," Alexander stuttered, falling on his knees beside her; shielding his head from her vicious blows.

"You inglorious phoney! I gave you my love! Gave you my trust! Gave you my money! And this . . ." Cassandra gasped and crumbled to the floor, wailing uncontrollably. "God . . . I trusted you, Alexander. Why would you betray me this way? You . . . you beast! Pedophile!" she screeched, rushing at him like an enraged lion. With all her available strength, she tore at his head, clenched his right ear with her incisor and tore hard into it until the piece of flesh fell off. Alexander roared and fought back, cursing and spitting fire as he grabbed the dismembered ear. He roared again and grabbed the woman by the neck, ready to kill.

The timely intervention of the household staff saved the situation. Akpan had heard screaming from the corridor as he came towards the bedroom with his mistress's suitcase. He immediately called the housekeeper, who was following closely with the hand luggage. Both of them stood outside the master bedroom door, contemplating what to do. Instinctively, Akpan pressed his ear against the door to eavesdrop. When the scream-ing and roaring became disturbing, he flung the door open, just in time to push Alexander away from strangling his mistress, who was already choking. Minutes later, the case was reported to the police, and Cassandra ensured that Alexander was put behind bars. For months, she and her daughter were in shock over the incident.

Thereafter, she swore to deal with men at arm's length. As for Tobi, she suffered major depression for many months. Although she was fortunate not to have been physically abused, her psyche was terribly battered. Her mother painstakingly nursed her to normalcy, and for the first time since her daugh-ter was born, Cassandra wished she could summon courage to confess the real story of the girl's paternity. After all, if Tobi had known her father, she wouldn't have fallen prey to Alexander's whims. Now she, Cassandra, blamed herself for leaving her daughter vulnerable.

As the days rolled by, her guilt feelings continued, especially the guilt of hiding Tobi's paternal identity. How on earth was she to make the girl understand that the man—her father, was probably still alive? The problem was she had no inkling where or how to start tracing the tyrant—her ex-husband, whom she'd sworn to make an eternal enemy. Was Tobi's sentiment going to change things? That was a question to which Cassandra could not find an immediate answer. Fortunately, time gradually erased the bitter memories of Alexander. Mother and daughter were soon engrossed in other things.

CHAPTER ELEVEN

Alexander's months in prison were harsh and painful, filled with bitter experience and lonely moments when he wished the ground could just open up and swallow him. Death for him was more desirable than his present predicament. The agony of losing his ear was torturous, not to talk of the anguish and many pangs he suffered watching it rot away and—horrors! Having to eat it was the worst part. Recounting the episode was nightmarish and nauseating, yet the memory of it remained vivid, fresh as the morning breeze. Who would have warned him that Cassandra was a lioness and unpredictably carnivorous? That was the way he now qualified the woman who was responsible for his present distress.

The prison cell was horrible, filthy as a pigsty, with very little room for ventilation. There were about seven inmates in all, mostly hardened criminals convicted for various offenses. The oldest of them was a ruthless felon serving a life sentence for murder. He was bent on oppressing his fellow inmates, particularly Alexander in whom he'd taken special interest. He it was that commanded Alexander to eat the putrid ear that was discovered in his pocket days after his arrival.

It was a terrible experience for Alexander. Even the prison warders were indifferent to his plight when he reported the incident. As far as they were concerned, all convicts were the same irrespective of their offenses. Having been sentenced to a seven-year jail term for attempted rape, he had no grounds for complaint.

Days stretched into weeks and weeks into months. For Alexander, each dawn was like going on a journey to hell. Further assaults and harassment were always in store for him, the previous appearing to be preliminary and pre-emptive to more dehumanizing molestation from his fellow inmates. Meal times were torturous because he often had to feed on a mixture of food and human defecation. That was the climax. He took ill, and when his health condition deteriorated considerably, he was transferred to the prison clinic.

His condition was so critical that when eventually he started recovering, his case was reviewed and by a stroke of luck, a few weeks later he was declared a free man. It was like a dream. He couldn't believe it. Even as he walked out of chains, he had to jolt himself several times to be sure it was real. Yes, it was, and he was ecstatic. If there was ever a time in his life he felt like celebrating, it was that blissful moment when he turned his back to the prison walls.

Incidentally, his earlier resentment and craving for revenge appeared to have vanished with his recent freedom. He'd never felt more relieved and grateful to escape a hellish experience. He swore to avoid any possible contact with Cassandra, as the mere thought of reenacting their last episode was tormenting enough.

The woman had taught him a lesson to remember for life, and his only regret was that he was back to square one—broke and homeless, with no money and a very gloomy future. Paid employment was certainly not a very welcome idea. Where would he start from anyway? His track records weren't too promising and starting afresh as a fledgling schoolteacher was certainly not amongst his immediate ambitions. Just as he was contemplating on which direction to take, luck shone on him.

"My oh my! Who am I seeing?" Dele exclaimed, pulling his automobile to a halt beside Alexander, who had been waiting to catch a bus at the boisterous Ojuelegba bus stop of Lagos.

"Dele? I don't believe my eyes!" Alexander yelped in excitement the moment he sighted him.

The duo had met during Alexander's hype days with Cassandra. Dele was at the time dating Madam Simisola—Cassandra's best friend. Recently though, the woman dumped him for a more attractive leech. Despite their age difference of about fifteen years, Alexander and Dele were very congenial.

They had loved frivoling away, particularly with wealthy women who could provide them with adequate financial security. Dele in particular had a phenomenal reputation for dating older women. As a matter of fact, Madam Simisola, his erstwhile sugar mummy, was his mother's age.

"I hope my eyes are not betraying me," Dele shouted, poking his head through the window.

"Men, I'm glad to see you!" Alexander retorted in excitement.

"Hop in," Dele squealed, throwing open the door for his friend. "From where did you drop?" he continued effervescently as Alexander hopped into the seat beside him.

"My man, I've been to hell and back. Didn't you hear the gist?" Alexander quizzed as they drove past the boisterous scenery.

It was getting to nightfall, and the city was already agog with night crawlers as the duo arrived at the front of a popular nightclub along Adeniran Ogunsanya, Surulere. Dele hadn't any definite itinerary so they settled to drinks at a quiet corner of the club, which was still quite empty at the time they arrived.

"I've been languishing in jail," Alexander began as soon as they settled with booze and cigarettes.

"You're kidding me," Dele replied with surprise. "I thought you moved to Abuja with Cassandra."

"Abuja? Does Cassandra live in Abuja?" Alexander queried, looking quite perplexed.

"Haven't you heard? The woman is becoming a power player in Aso Rock politics," Dele announced, inhaling a cloud of smoke. "Don't tell me you're not aware?" he continued, watching Alexander with a bit of perplexity.

"I say I've been languishing in jail. You think I'm joking? I just got released."

"You can't be serious. What happened?"

"That bitch Cassandra. Can't you see my ear?" he queried, suddenly feeling self-conscious. "The bitch did this to me and still got me incarcerated," he announced with hate.

"I noticed your ear. I . . . I'm surprised. I mean, why would she resort to such callousness?"

"Cassandra is a tiger," Alexander stated, before going on to recount in detail the encounter that led to his predicament.

"I'm sorry, pal," Dele said, tapping him on the shoulder. "It's part of life's harsh realities. It's not your fault that you got enamored to her pretty daughter, is it?" he put in jokingly.

"You never change. Bad boy Dele," Alexander said, managing a smile.

"Men, I could have done the same if I were in your shoes. That babe Tobi is dangerously beautiful, deliciously irresistible . . . even the pope would give up celibacy for her sake," he put in, roaring with laughter.

Alexander followed suit with roaring laughter; they both jumped out of their seats and hugged each other playfully, before clasping hands and taking their seats.

"I thought I was the only one that saw something special in that girl . . . boy oh boy, you should have seen her anatomy . . . hey! I was on cloud nine when that witch of a woman interrupted and killed my joy."

"Boy, Cassandra messed up big-time. I can imagine your trauma. That Tobi girl is a deadly beauty. It's been a long time I had a secret crush on her," Dele confessed.

"You? You too?" Alexander asked, reeling with laughter.

"Better believe it, but I couldn't venture near her. Not with the likes of that ugly hag Simisola watching with keen eyes," he continued, referring to his ex-date.

"That reminds me, how's your relationship going with that Lagos big girl?" Alexander asked.

"Did I have a relationship going with her?" Dele asked with derision. "We were just using each other, and when we got fed up, we quit. Besides, she got herself another boy. I feel sorry for the idiot. He'll be in for a shocker soon because Simisola can never stay committed. My dear, the woman is a nymphomaniac. She's never satisfied. Assuming she were beautiful, I wouldn't have minded, but man, she was a dog, dirty, flabby, disgusting . . . the thought of her nauseates me," he put in, looking repulsed.

"So all the liposuction, vagina reconstruction, and breast enlargement she did made no difference?" Alexander probed.

"My dear, plastic surgery cannot turn a pig into a princess nor the beast to beauty. That is the problem with old women who think they can be forever young," he quipped.

"Anyway, you had nothing to lose. At least she was paying your bills," Alexander chipped in.

"Precisely, so who was I to complain? I made some cool bucks off the bitch. I even have a place of my own now—I bought a house in Ikeja," Dele announced, lighting another cigarette.

"You don't say. Men, I'm happy for you. That bitch Cassandra threw me out with absolutely nothing to fall back on," Alexander said regretfully, exhaling a cloud of smoke.

"You can move in with me until you sort yourself out," Dele offered, to Alexander's astonishment.

"Move in with you?" Alexander was not sure he had heard him correctly.

"Yeah, why not? You can even stay with me for as long as you wish," Dele assured.

"Men, I appreciate it. Thanks, my man, you are a friend indeed," Alexander said with relief. With a decent roof over his head, surely, the future did not look bleak after all.

CHAPTER TWELVE

Luck shone on the ex-nun. Not only was she successful with the General Certificate examination and the Joint Admission Matriculation Board examination, she'd equally gained admission to study psychology—full-time, at the University of Lagos.

In order to make ends meet, she continued to work part-time, mostly on the evening and weekend shifts at the fast-foods outlet where she gradually rose to a managerial position. Night and day, she toiled tirelessly to combine academic work with her paid job. Her dreams continued to motivate her, to drive her visionary quest for excellence.

Despite her many commitments, she found time to organize seminars, all bordering on gender-related issues, particularly the abuse of femininity and children in the society. Subsequently, her awareness campaigns became popular on campus and in the state, where she soon became the recipient of several merit awards. Upon graduation, she received a state scholarship to proceed immediately for a master's degree in psychology. At this point, she felt it was time to quit her job and change her vocation.

She then took up employment as an assistant lecturer while pursuing her postgraduate studies in the same institution. She continued with her campaigns, and her students particularly found her both enigmatic and intriguing. Her lectures were always delivered with precision, pragmatism, and expertise. One thing, however, remained her softest spot—her sentiments. Mercy could wear people's problems. She was empathetic and ever willing to share people's concerns. Her greatest weakness was her compassion. When people cried, she cried with them. When they hurt, she hurt with them. When they were hungry, she was ready to starve. To her, the essence of life was sharing and caring, and recognizing that the fellow next to you is human, just like you are.

It was therefore not surprising when she decided to initiate private counseling classes where she could offer personalized service as her own modest contribution to the well-being of others. The response was amazing, simply incredible, as students, lecturers, and the masses trooped in to unburden their hearts before her. Her listening ear, her patient disposition, her innate wisdom and exceptional empathy endeared her greatly to her clientele. She was always eager to hear them out, to sympathize, advise and encourage them in the right path. She became passionately engrossed in her work. So much so that she hardly had a personal life or even a meaningful emotional relationship.

Several proposals poured in, but she was never interested. Not that she considered herself "Miss High and Mighty," no, she just never met the right kind of guy. Who on earth could be her right kind of guy? What were her criteria anyway? She probably didn't even know or possibly never gave it serious thought. She only knew, for instance, that she detested profanity, lechery, and egotism. Unfortunately, most men who came her way often demonstrated all or more of those characteristics.

Could it be that all men were licentious, chauvinistic creatures? Or perhaps she was just downright fastidious? Her busy schedules did not help matters either, as she hadn't even time enough to critically analyze the issue—until that fateful day. It was indeed a fateful day, when her head of department, a venerable professor, invited her over for what he had labeled a serious talk. As soon as she stepped into his office, his usual sober face animated. It was as though a wind of life breezed through him.

"Welcome, Mercy, I'm glad you made it. What do I offer you?"

"Nothing, thank you sir."

"I must commend your hard work and proficiency in this department," he began.

"Thank you sir."

"You also happen to be the best postgraduate student of psychology this year. May I seize this opportunity to congratulate you?"

Mercy let out delighted laughter before speaking, "I didn't realize the results were out."

"Well, this is top secret. I happen to have privileged information, my dear. The results will be published shortly. I am very proud of you."

"Thank you sir . . . and thank God for showing me mercy."

"I like that. Mercy has become the beneficiary of divine mercy," he recited poetically.

Mercy smiled and kept her gaze on him as he continued. Although inherently demure, she was a confident woman who understood the basic dynamics of communication. She was particularly good with listening attentively.

"I called you here today for a very important personal discussion." He paused briefly before proceeding: "I lost my wife about three years ago. I am sure you are aware."

"I am, sir, accept my sympathy."

"No . . . no, I don't want sympathy anymore. I want something different."

"I'm listening, sir," Mercy offered, embarrassed by his lingering gaze.

"It appears you don't have a boyfriend."

Mercy was completely nonplussed and at a loss for words.

"We could make a good pair, you know," the man continued, not minding her discomfiture.

"With due respect to you, sir, I find this line of discussion highly unethical and embarrassing."

"Come on girl, you're mature. You should be thinking of settling down to marriage. Will you marry me?"

"Sir, with due respect, I beg to take my leave."

"You haven't said anything to my proposal."

"I am not interested. I am neither seeking male attention nor marriage. I am quite contented with my single status."

"You're wrong. Every woman needs a man. Menopause is already looming around the corner. You haven't got much time."

"Thanks for the information, and for your proposal," she snapped, getting up to leave.

"Or are you queer?" the middle-aged professor quipped, stopping her in her tracks. "You are too damn serious, Mercy, too officious, prim and proper, too prudish, priggish, unladylike, stern, dry, and unromantic . . . but I guess that is your unique selling point. You are quite unlike most Lagos girls who scramble for male attention. Yes . . . you are dignified, decorous, demure, and I must add, enchanting and mysterious. My dear, you need a man, a man like me to appreciate your urbane qualities," he rambled, as she interposed.

"Professor, you surprise me. Well, thanks for your ambivalent words of insult and praise. I am not interested in an amorous relationship with you."

"Aha! I didn't mean to be ambivalent. Succinctly put, you have stolen my heart, and for want of better adjectives in my mental lexicon to describe you, I probably did not aptly delineate between my real feelings and speculations. You see, in the etymology of words, sometimes an oxymoron becomes inevitable, particularly when attempting to qualify intriguing subjects like you," he said, as sweat dripped from his forehead to his nose.

"Your vocabulary is no doubt impressive . . . but please, sir, I am not interested. Thanks for your proposition, but no thanks. I must be on my way, please."

"Not so soon! You dare not walk out on a revered professor of my status. With degrees from the world's best: Oxford, Stanford, and Harvard, no woman dares turn me down," he barked.

"Well, let me have the honor to ring it in your ears again that I am not interested in office romance. Sir, a respectable professor like you should be able to take no for an answer."

"You are silly! I actually thought for a minute that you have some common sense. What I'm offering you is what many ladies are dying to have. I can count on my fingertips at least a dozen ladies who came here, pleading with me for an amorous relationship. But I gave it all up, waiting for this moment. Now I'm becoming convinced that you are not the woman I thought you were. You . . . you are probably a lousy lesbian, a silly pervert, a pretentious charlatan!"

Mercy was agape as she observed the man with revulsion before receding, a chilly air engulfing the room as he stared after her brazenly.

The ex-nun was dispirited as she sat sobbing in her office, musing over her discussion with the professor. His insinuation was not only defamatory, but also blasphemous in her ears. If the fact that she was forty-one and unmarried suggested homosexuality, then life at the convent was certainly more honorable and ennobled. There, they had no marital concerns. Nobody dared harass them; nobody dared challenge them. Certainly, a woman could be chaste, single, and fulfilled. After all, good marriages were constantly on the decline, and she didn't need to join the train just to fulfill all righteousness.

As for children, she already had them in abundance. From Africa to India and indeed other parts of the globe, she had donated her widow's mite to the upkeep and sponsorship of starving and deprived children. Mercy had indeed given hope to numerous orphans, to deprived children, needy youths, and abused women in her immediate and larger society. That to her, was a motherly responsibility. The inner peace she enjoyed was akin to the joy of motherhood, and she had never missed not being married and without biological offspring.

Suddenly, she wished there was somebody to talk to. Somebody who could understand and appreciate her life and passion. Mother Araba! She suddenly felt like seeing her, like talking to her. She would definitely understand. She also remembered Sister Esi, her beloved friend and confidant. Perhaps it was a big mistake, her leaving the cloister for secular life. There were so many norms and ethos, and she was a nonconformist. Or wasn't she?

CHAPTER THIRTEEN

It was the year 2000, the new millennium and a beautiful evening in August. Birds were twittering, the sun setting, and the cool breeze of the night was filled with the sweet fragrance of the Queen of the Night flower. From beneath the mango tree overlooking the fishpond of his expansive multimillion-naira home, Nick watched the twilight.

The mansion, which was situated at the Ikeja Government Reserved Area of Lagos, sat atop a breathtaking mass of land. From the main entrance, a boulevard with resplendent palms ushered visitors into the magnificent world of the Tiscos. Yes, the Tisco family was renowned for their immense wealth and royalty.

Nick's late father, Otunba Michael Kolawole Tisco, was believed to have been worth a fortune at his time of death. He had bequeathed his entire wealth to his heir apparent and only offspring—Nick Kolawole Tisco, Jr. Yet, the vastness of his inheritance and the grandeur of power could not fill the abyss and hollow in Nick's life. He was lonely, empty, and totally unfulfilled. As far as he was concerned, life ceased existing the moment she breathed her last. Yes, she was Elizabeth Tisco—the only woman he'd ever loved.

Day in, day out, he dreamt of her. He meditated on her. He dedicated his time to her evergreen memories. He could have remained glued to the spot meditating today but for the fact that he needed to start preparation for the annual ceremony.

Slowly and steadily, the handsome six-footer dragged his lanky frame off the ground. The neatly mowed lawn on which he lay smelt fresh, and he remembered like yesterday the treasured moments they'd spent there together. Many years had gone by, yet it was like yesterday when the arm of cruelty dealt him the hardest blow ever. "I should have gone with her; I should have transited with her to paradise. At least we could have been together; savoring the sweetness of our bond—our love, which even death could not quell," he thought, before soliloquizing:

"Oh why did you leave me, Elizabeth? What did I do to earn this punishment of your abandonment?"

The aches of the past years remained fresh and brutal. The ache was so intense and consuming and even worse as the days rolled by. Time was not in his favor . . . time could not erase his grief. If anything, his lonely heart kept wearing and tearing with every passing year.

At last and out of his usual line of reverie, he made up his mind to leave the lonely spot. From a distance, he could see his mother trimming the row of hedged flowers adorning the rear of the boy's quarters. The woman recently made a habit of tending the compound's horticulture, claiming it kept her idle mind occupied and her aging bones alert and invigorated.

Spontaneously, Nick mounted his stallion and rode in her direction. Amongst his several skills, horse riding was his favorite—his only regret being that she wasn't there to share the triumph of his mastery. They'd both looked forward to it during his training days.

"You're here, son; I was getting quite worried about you," Brenda Tisco remarked the moment her son appeared in the driveway.

"Mother, I'll be needing a bouquet of roses. You know very well it's Elizabeth's tenth anniversary requiem this week," he said, looking blank and distant, ignoring her comment.

Brenda Tisco wore an icy expression. The mere mention of the woman's name was repugnant in her ears.

"I'll be inside," Nick announced, unperturbed by her mien as he made to leave.

"Nick," she called.

"Yes, Mother?" he responded, stopping in his tracks.

"Don't you think you are taking this too far?"

"What do you mean?"

"I mean about Elizabeth. She's long dead and buried. You must face that reality."

"Her spirit lives on, Mother, her spirit cries out for vengeance. There's a killer out there that still hasn't been apprehended. The autopsy revealed she was poisoned, and up till date, I've not been able to avenge the blood of my innocent wife."

Brenda watched her adult son break into tears. As usual, painful memories of his late wife rendered him sloppy.

"You can't continue like this, Nick," she said in a curt and incisive tone. "If she truly loved you, she will rest in peace . . . in her grave."

"She is resting in peace, but I am not resting until I see justice."

"Your passion is abnormal. Can't you see? She's tormenting you."

"Stop it, Mother! Don't ever say anything against my wife," he warned, his voice fraught with grief.

"Your late wife. She is dead, and nothing can bring her back to life. I wonder if she bewitched you."

"Enough! I have . . . heard enough! You don't even care that she was murdered. You don't care about my happiness, do you?"

"Oh please, son, your happiness is mine; and you can only find it if you face the future and leave the past. You are not getting younger; I am not getting any younger either. I need a grandson. I need to see your children, my grandchildren."

"Oh yes! Your selfish reasons are always priority!"

"For goodness sake, Nick, you're forty-four. At your age you should have been done with childbearing."

"You want me to jump out, grab any woman, have her bear children, your so-called grandchildren. But that isn't my idea of family. Family has to be founded on love, and my only love is gone. Mother, my dreams of family ended with the demise of Elizabeth."

"Never! Never!" Brenda screamed, her shrilling voice resounding in the still environment. "She couldn't bear you a child. You could never have a family with her."

"Many thanks to you for pressuring her. Many thanks to your cynicism and efforts at wrecking our marriage."

"Shut up Nick! If your father were alive today, things would have been different. He wouldn't have allowed you to marry that gold digger in the first place. He wouldn't have let you drag our name in the mud. Elizabeth was barren. It's not my fault she got frustrated."

"You were the cause of her frustration," Nick yelled, cupping his face with his hands.

"Rubbish! Certainly I couldn't have also been responsible for her barrenness."

Stop it, Mother! She wasn't barren."

"Oh, she wasn't?"

"You never gave her a chance. If you had, she would have given me a baby."

"No, no way, Nick. I wonder why you choose to be blind to her faults."

"She did nothing wrong. She only loved me, and she got hurt for that."

"Love? Did you say love? You don't know the meaning of love. She never loved you. She loved your money, she loved your wealth, she loved your name. Our name!"

"Oh for God's sake, cut that off! You are the one who doesn't know what love is. Perhaps you never truly loved my father."

Brenda watched him in shock. "Nick, Nick, you dare say such horrible things to me because of that witch? I loved your father. I loved him with every inch of my being," she proclaimed, sobbing as she crumbled to the ground.

"Tell your tale to the marines. Announce it on radio if you please."

"I swear that woman will never see peace even in death. Elizabeth! Elizabeth!" Brenda yelled in a thunderous voice, distorting the peace of the idyllic environment.

"You are pathetic mother; I am sorry for you. You are venomous and malevolent. Nothing short of a sadist and killjoy," her son shrieked.

"Nick, believe me, Elizabeth doesn't deserve your affection. I have reason to believe she committed suicide," Brenda argued in between tears.

"Elizabeth could never kill anyone, let alone herself," he defended, eyes flushed in deep animosity.

"You've been brainwashed, son; you've been completely brainwashed."

"Mother, you are wicked. You are cruel and hardened. You don't even care that she died. Now I'm beginning to wonder why you convinced the police to stop investigations into her death."

"I was trying to protect you," Brenda yelled. "You were in pain, and I didn't want to prolong your grief. You would have been devastated to hear she committed suicide."

"Never! You have never been one to care for my feelings. You took advantage of my pain and confusion. I shouldn't have listened to you. I should have gone to the ends of the earth to arrest the killer," Nick moaned amidst heartfelt anguish.

"Awake from your dream, Nick. Face reality. Elizabeth was barren so she killed herself."

"She did not! Never! Elizabeth would never resort to suicide. She couldn't have! She didn't!" Nick retorted in frenzy, jolting his mother, sending cold shivers down her reins. He let out a regretful sigh and took a long hateful look at her before declaring, "You have an evil heart, ma'am."

With that, he stormed off on his stallion, leaving behind a steaming cloud of unease. Brenda sprang to her feet and followed him, running as fast as her feet could carry.

For the next couple of days, she was miserable. She just could not understand her son. His obsession with his late wife was something she felt called for serious thinking . . . thinking very deeply. Perhaps the time had come for her to intervene. She needed to think and act fast, before the situation got out of hand. Nick's bigotry and obsession was one that needed a combination of astute and witty tackling, and she, Brenda, would stop at nothing to suppress his unflinching passion for the deceased.

CHAPTER FOURTEEN

Finally, after several weeks of planning, she came up with a ploy on getting her obstinate son hooked. Mabel Wonder King, the elegant daughter and heir apparent to the Irish shipping baron, was a woman of irresistible charm. Mabel had a reputation for winning the admiration of sophisticated, discerning males. Many Lagos big boys, the movers and shakers of the society, the crème de la crème, were dying to date her. They couldn't resist her ethereal beauty. Not only that, she was one lady endowed not only with beauty, but with brains. Certainly, with her high profile antecedents, Nick would finally fall in love . . . and get Elizabeth out of his miserably depressed mind . . .

Clad in a studded, wine-colored, off-the-shoulder, body-hugging gown and a matching silk sash, the aristocratic lady made a graceful entry into the Tisco's exquisite home, led by the chief butler. Mother and son were already seated for dinner when she arrived. While Brenda's face animated on seeing her, Nick maintained a placid expression, merely nodding his head to acknowledge her presence.

"Welcome, my dear, I've been expecting you," Brenda announced, rising to peck their guest on both cheeks.

"Nick, meet Mabel Wonder King. Mabel, my son Nick. Before his father died, we all called him Kolawole Jr. But since the demise of his father, my son prefers to be called Nick, which is his middle name."

Nick again acknowledged the guest with a nod, while she in turn flashed him a smile, revealing her immaculate dentition.

"Do join us for dinner, please," Brenda offered, carefully concealing her apprehension.

Despite the hostess's efforts at making light conversation, there was an unusual chill as the trio ate their meal. They seemed preoccupied with their individual thoughts until Brenda decided to break the ice.

"So, my dear, how is Ireland?" she began.

"Not fun at this time. Winter's set in fully, and the whole place is snowed."

"But you're used to the climate there?"

"Not quite. Matter of fact, I often find solace in the tropics at this time of the year."

"Really?"

"Yes, and the timing is perfect 'cos I visit annually in my grandmother's honor."

"That's true, your father's mother is Nigerian."

"Precisely, although her mother is Caucasian."

"Your family pedigree is very diverse," Brenda chipped in.

"Oh yes, and it's spreading wider. Recently, my father adopted an Indian son."

"Your father's philanthropy is amazing. I often wonder how he finds time to combine fosterage and parenting with his business obligations."

At this point, Brenda looked at her son expectantly for a comment. "That brings the number of his adopted children to six?" she added, ignoring her son's apparent aloofness.

"Absolutely, you certainly are current on that."

"I manage to keep my ears to the ground, especially when your father voluntarily divulges the information himself. Did I tell you that Mabel's father and I were in high school together?" she asked, looking in the direction of her son. "That was way back in England, many decades ago."

Instinctively, Mabel turned to face Nick. "You haven't said much all evening, Nick. Are you okay?"

"Well, em . . . yes. I guess I'm okay," he offered, managing a smile.

"Nick can be taciturn at times," his mother explained. "Maybe with you around, he could cheer up a little."

"Mother! I'm fine, please," Nick exclaimed curtly.

"I don't know about that. Anyhow, you two should get to know each other better," Brenda stated flatly, rising to her feet as she excused herself from the table.

Nick looked on in bewilderment, staring after her.

"So, Nick, are you always like this?" the attractive stranger probed, the moment the hostess was out of earshot.

"Like how?"

"Melancholic and taciturn. You look very distant and sullen."

"Really? I didn't realize it was that glaring."

"You wanna talk about it?"

"No, I'm just fine."

"Well then, I feel like unwinding. What are you doing for the rest of the evening?"

"Me? Well . . . I really don't have plans," he replied, feeling rather giddy alone in her company.

"How about us visiting a nightclub somewhere? I could do with a bit of relaxation," she offered.

"I . . . Mabel . . ." he stuttered.

"Yes?"

"It's been ages since I last visited a nightclub. I've lost touch with social life."

"Never mind, I know a place we can go to," she said, watching him expectantly. "It is called Night Crawlers. It is also in Ikeja, just about fifteen-minute's drive from here. Shall we?"

Nick looked at the attractive hazel-eye half-caste. For the first time, he took a close look at her and observed that she was a real stunner. Her skin shone, fair and spotless, with her long ponytail cascading on her elegant shoulder. She was a rarity of beauty, the type of lady described as a mermaid by those who believed in the mystical existence of unusually attractive female creatures. Only that this one did not step out of the bar beach or sea world, she walked into his abode as flesh and blood, with no fins or physical ancestry to the water world. Surely he couldn't refuse such an offer.

"Your wish is my command," he said, noticing her elation as she rose to her feet and Nick led the way into the adjoining living room. He excused himself and returned shortly, dressed in a pair of denims, turtleneck, and a stunning black-leather jacket. He also wore a pair of dark glasses that came in handy to conceal his nervousness. Mabel was holding a framed picture when Nick returned.

"Who's she?"

He took the photograph and stared at it fondly before replying, "My late wife Elizabeth."

"Oh."

"It was actually on her account that I started using my middle name, Nick. She thought it was posh, preferable to my Yoruba name Kolawole," he explained. "Evidently, my mother's memory has failed to capture that bit of history," he added.

Mabel shrugged and cast him an inquiring look. She wanted to comment but couldn't find the right words.

"Shall we?" he asked, placing the picture in its usual position.

"You still love her?"

Nick wasn't sure if it was a question or a statement. Nonetheless, he replied.

"That is personal and confidential."

"Sorry for probing," she quickly put in.

"That's okay. Can we leave now?"

"Sure."

She followed behind him as he led the way out to the main entrance. Brenda smiled satisfied from behind the curtains as she watched them drive out in the sleek Mercedes Benz convertible. The duo spent several hours fraternizing at the club. They danced, dined and chatted. Mabel did most of the talking, making Nick laugh intermittently at her witty anecdotes.

They spent the next couple of days getting acquainted. Mabel was having the time of her life. She thoroughly enjoyed the company of the chivalrous dude, while Nick in turn found himself drawn to the fascinating extrovert. She had no airs, and he felt very warm and relaxed in her company. She also had a great sense of humor, and he found himself often laughing and appreciating her inexhaustible repertoire of jokes. However, he couldn't properly define his feelings for her. Attraction? Fondness? Or what? Mabel seemed to be floating on a different pedestal. She could almost swear she was in love. The guy was a gentleman to the core, and he knew how to treat a woman right without being pushy or abusive.

By the third week into their relationship, however, she began to worry. Having an exciting platonic relationship was one thing, but having a meaningful future in the relationship was another, and that to her, was cardinal to her emotions.

"Nick," she called one afternoon as they picnicked by the swimming pool, eating the spicy chicken suya purchased from the Ikeja Country Club by Nick's mother.

"Yes, Mabel," he responded.

"I'll be returning to Ireland next week, from there to the United Kingdom. You know I shuttle between the two countries, seeing to my father's IT business."

"I know."

"I . . . we've had such a great time together," she stuttered.

"Absolutely, I've enjoyed every bit of your company," he affirmed.

"You've never told me how you feel about me, Nick."

A surprised expression engulfed his face as she spoke. "Don't take it that I'm pushing you. I just need to guard my emotions. Do you love me, Nick?"

The man certainly wasn't prepared for the million-dollar question. "Do I love her?" he wondered, reflecting on the past few weeks. Mabel had certainly reawakened something in him. To start with, he was a much livelier person since the day she walked into his life.

"Do you love me, Nick?" she reiterated, cutting through his thoughts.

"Listen, Mabel, I find you very interesting and irresistibly attractive. You've brought a great deal of laughter into my life. I appreciate the good times we've had together, and I know I'm gonna miss you, but . . ."

"But what? You . . . you don't love me?" she asked, looking disappointed and hurt. "You don't love me, do you? You love yourself. You love her . . . your late wife Elizabeth," she uttered, forcing back the tears.

"Mabel, please calm down."

"I'm trying hard to understand why you don't have an atom of compassion," she blurted out, breaking into tears afresh.

Nick offered her a handkerchief that she gratefully accepted, dabbing her eyes with it.

"I don't know what to say, Mabel. Honestly, you've been such great company, and I think you deserve better than what I can offer."

"Oh Nick, why are you so dispassionate? Why can't you forget a dead woman, for goodness sake? Your mother has told me how obsessed you are with her. She's dead, Nick; awake to the reality!"

"That's the problem . . . I can't help myself."

Mabel's crying intensified as she listened to his cool voice. She was hurting badly.

"I'm sorry, Mabel, I really am sorry," Nick said in a gentle tone.

"I appreciate your passion, Nick. I appreciate the hurt you feel having lost a loved one. But that's not enough reason to give up on loving. Give yourself another chance. Life is all about moving on. I like you a lot. I really do otherwise, I wouldn't be here with you."

"Mabel, please," Nick interrupted, turning away from her gaze. "It's not that I don't like you. I do. Matter of fact, I think you're very attractive and desirable. The problem is there's no place in my heart for emotions. My emotions lie in the cemetery where my love is buried. Elizabeth is the only woman I've ever loved. My emotions ceased to exist the day she died."

"Please . . . please spare me further pain," Mabel stuttered, rising to her feet. "I've never been more humiliated in my life. I've never been rejected this way . . . for a dead woman!"

She cried, her voice rising with emotion. "I am sorry for you, Nick. I am sorry that a fine man like you would waste away like this. She can never be reanimated. Elizabeth can never come back to you. Can't you understand?"

101

Nick was up on his feet. He tried to calm her but couldn't find just the right words. Mabel was upset, perhaps heartbroken and devastated. But how on earth could he make her understand? She would never comprehend his life and passion. She would never understand the strength and power of love—the love he had shared with Elizabeth.

After a long uneasy silence, she requested to be dropped off. They walked back to the house and in a matter of minutes headed in the direction of her granny's. When the automobile finally halted in front of the Victorian-style duplex on Queen's Drive in Ikoyi, Nick took Mabel's hand and squeezed it gently, before saying:

"Good-bye, Mabel."

She stared at him for a few seconds before alighting from the car and walking straight into the house without a word or backward glance.

CHAPTER FIFTEEN

It was a sunny afternoon at the city's metropolitan basketball pitch, as various amateur players struggled to get the ball in the net. One man particularly stood out in the crowd. His maneuvering was so smooth and swift that in a three-minute spate he had scored a dozen times. Suddenly the game was over, chanting filled the air as the players dispersed, and Dele heroically found his way through the crowd, amidst cheers from fans and observers.

"That was good," Alexander complimented, shaking his pal's hand the moment they were out of the boisterous crowd. "Indeed, another Michael Jordan is born."

"Thanks, my man, but between Jordan and I, there's no comparison. I am just a local champion, a one-eyed hero in the midst of blind folks," Dele replied in excitement.

"I am serious. You could be a good match for the Chicago Bulls."

"Cut off the flattery, buddy," Dele said, letting out delirious laughter before adding, "anyway, nothing wrong with me enjoying the ovation while it lasts."

"On a serious note, I think you should start thinking of professional tournaments," Alexander put in.

"One thing at a time. For now, I'm quite contented with my team; if for anything, we get to keep fit and while away time."

"I guess so, but you could build a career in basketball," Alexander enthused.

"Not in this country."

"Don't be such a cynic. Be positive, you never know what could happen next in the world of sports."

"Football maybe, but basketball? Not in the foreseeable future."

"I give up," Alexander said, raising his hands in mock defeat.

"Good, now let's talk about more exciting things," Dele said, as they entered his sleek Toyota Land Cruiser.

"Such as women?" Alexander asked, lighting a cigarette for his friend. The homogenous duo burst out laughing.

"My man, I don't have energy for women tonight. I need to rest my bum," Dele said, exhaling a cloud of smoke. "The only thing on my mind now is fresh fish pepper soup."

"You're a genius. I could do with a steaming bowl myself," Alexander chipped in.

"In that case, let me call Moji immediately to start the cooking. She has the day off today," Dele stated.

Dele immediately called his sister Moji with his cellular phone, instructing her to prepare the dish. The guys continued chatting; their conversation dominated by lewd accounts of their numerous escapades with women. Alexander had become a permanent squatter in Dele's residence since his release from prison. He felt at home and comfortable living there, since Dele appreciated his company a great deal. They had become more like inseparable twins. Their lifestyle was similar, their lust for women insatiable, and their conquests pretty much alike. They simply were birds of the same feather, flocking together.

A few hours later, they were at the dining table, savoring the sumptuous fresh fish pepper soup prepared by Dele's sister. She was an expert in cooking delicious spicy catfish. The three of them sat at the table, with the men hungrily consuming the delicacy while Moji appeared contented watching them eat.

"Delicious," Alexander commented, digging into the fish head with his fingers, sucking every drop of sauce, picking out the bones and nodding his head in appreciation of the delicious meal.

"What do you expect from a caterer?" Dele put in, following in Alexander's stride, digging deep and licking his fingers, making suckling sounds with obvious relish.

"Someday, you should open a pepper soup joint, Moji," Alexander suggested, scooping in a mouthful of fish.

"Ah . . . where do I get the money? I beg oh! I'm okay with my paid job," she replied.

"Moji, how can a fine babe like you be complaining about money? One of your boyfriends should be able to write off the bill."

Dele shot Alexander an angry look before saying, "Don't give her such ideas. The girls in my family are very decent and respectable."

"I hear you. She'll get married someday, won't she?"

"Marriage yes, but fooling around? No. My parents will kill her," Dele put in sternly.

"Brother Dele, please don't mind him. I know he's only joking," Moji chipped in.

"I take it that it was really a joke," Dele quipped.

"I've forgotten the kinship ties. Pardon me, pal; after all, who wouldn't protect his sister?" Alexander asked, shrugging as he observed the lingering frown on Dele's face.

They ate the rest of their meal in silence.

"I'm off to bed," Dele announced the moment he finished eating.

"Sleep tight, my man. I should be off to bed shortly too," Alexander voiced as the former receded to his bedroom.

Shortly after, Alexander Moyo tiptoed into Dele's room. Dele rarely locked his bedroom door, except he had a female guest sleeping over. The guy was already snoring out loud. No doubt, he was in dreamland, totally exhausted from his earlier sporting activity. His live-in friend observed him briefly before gently shutting the door behind. From the corridor, he could see Moji clearing the table and whistling to a popular tune playing on the radio. It was Lagbaja, the masked one, doing a rendition.

"Hello, darling," Alexander whispered, squeezing the plump lady from behind.

Moji startled and turned. "Ah, brother Alex, you scared me."

"I didn't mean to, sweetie," he said, breathing hard and letting go of her.

"I thought you were going to sleep," she said with inquiring eyes.

"I thought so too until the sleep vanished with thoughts of you."

"Brother Alex, hmm, you can flirt."

"Moji, you know I've always admired you."

"Please, oh, don't let my brother hear that."

"Dele is fast asleep, and please, for goodness sake, stop calling me brother Alex. Just call me Alex, or better still, Lexy."

"But in Yoruba land, we always respect our elders," she explained, grinning mischievously. "Calling you brother is a sign of respect."

"So I'm now an elder, eh? Tell me, do I look old enough to be your father?"

"No . . . no . . . but . . ."

"Moji, act like a mature woman. Age shouldn't be a barrier between us. To start with, I am not your brother. That brother stuff as far as I am concerned is an outdated tradition. I'm a modern man, you know, cool and up to the minute."

"Okay, Lexy, what do you want?"

"Better. It is you I want, baby," he responded, gently clasping her hands.

"Look, brother Alex, I don't have time for boyfriend matters now. I want to get married."

"I've told you to stop addressing me as brother. I'm not your brother, okay? How old are you anyway?"

"Twenty-nine."

"You mean you are twenty-nine? Yet you're acting like a naive nineteen-year-old."

"Okay Lexy, I am asking again, what do you want from me?"

"If marriage is your contention, I will marry you."

"Are you joking or what?" she asked, letting out a prolonged laugh.

"I said I will marry you, and that is final. Does that make you feel better?"

"Hmm . . . anyway, *sha*, my husband will be very lucky," she said, grinning from ear to ear.

"I have no doubt about that; after all, the way to a man's heart is through his stomach." With that, he pulled her closely, caressing her neck until she broke off.

"Lexy, please, I can only take you seriously if you see my parents."

"What's this obsession about seeing your parents? I have given you my word, but it seems you still have reservations."

"I just have to be sure you are serious," she stated, standing akimbo.

"Look, I am a bona fide fellow, and my intentions to you are guileless," he proclaimed.

"I don't trust you . . . honestly I don't."

"Are you by any means suggesting that I am fake?"

"I'm not suggesting anything."

"Or perhaps I'm just a crazy philanderer," he sneered.

"All I am saying is, don't make promises you can't keep," Moji said, still standing akimbo.

"How on earth can I convince you? I've always adored you, and I know you like me too," he stated.

"Well . . ."

"Trust me, Moji . . . I wouldn't do anything to hurt you," he pressured.

"You won't do anything to hurt me, eh? Let me tell you, I Moji, will not, and I repeat, not take any man seriously until I see an engagement ring on my finger."

"Are you that desperate?"

"Desperate?" she quoted, sneering at him. "Between the two of us, who is more desperate?"

"Moji, relax . . . life is not all about marriage, you know."

"I didn't propose to you, did I? I am not a fool oh! I know your type, smooth talker, smooth rapper. I beg *ojare,* leave me alone. *Ejo, fi mi le.* Please leave me alone oh! You want to use and dump me, eh? *Emi ko,* it is not me oh. See, brother Alex, just respect yourself, eh; you are too old for these silly games."

"Are you insulting me or what?"

"Why are you not married at your age? *Oya,* answer me. I say why are you not married? *Agbaya!* Big for nothing!"

"Me married? Never! I relish my freedom too much for that bondage."

"You see, I said it. You want to use and dump me. I thought a few minutes ago you were proposing to me."

"Look . . . I am . . ."

"Better grow up and stop deceiving yourself, *oloshi,* stupid man! *Ode!* Stop disturbing me oh, or else I will report you to brother Dele."

With that, Moji hissed and continued clearing the table. Alexander watched her with distaste. He was inwardly vexed by her abusive words in the Yoruba language. She had called him useless, stupid, and foolish. He swallowed the insults, if only to gain advantage of the moment. He made quick mental calculations and continued . . .

"Come on, Moji, I can't believe you're playing hard to get. Look into my eyes and tell me you don't love me."

"*Na love I go Chop?* Can I eat love?" she asked in pidgin, thrusting her head forward indignantly.

"Moji, Moji, love of my life . . . can't you just trust me?" he asked, enveloping her from the side.

"Stop it," she warned, pushing his hands away. He persisted until she suddenly swung round and hit him hard in the face. "I said stop it! Can't you see I am not interested?" she shrieked, facing him with blazing eyes.

"You . . . you slapped me?" he stammered, feeling his chin. She'd hit him on the scar of his left ear that he lost, courtesy of Cassandra.

"Leave me alone oh, I am warning you!" Moji yelled.

"Stupid illiterate girl, local champion. You are not happy that I am chasing you. I'll teach you a lesson, brat!" Alexander swore, making towards her with menacing eyes.

"Leave me alone oh," she reiterated, confusedly stepping backwards in fear.

"I've told you I won't hurt you . . . I promise," he muttered as he grabbed her hands, drowning her scream with his fist on her mouth.

Moji used all the strength within her to hit him hard in the groin. Alexander fell to the floor, wriggling in pain, and she immediately raised an alarm.

"Brother Dele! Brother Dele oh!"

Dele jumped out of sleep in fright and came out of his room.

"What the hell is going on here?" he asked, shaking his head to be certain he wasn't dreaming.

"Brother Dele . . . your friend . . . he was trying . . ."

"Trying to do what?" Dele queried, observing the whimpering man, at the same time quelling his agitated sister.

"Look, pal, it's not what it seems," Alexander said, rising to his feet, managing to repress his pain. "We had a little argument, that's all."

"Moji, what happened?" Dele questioned.

"This man . . . he's not your friend . . . this Alex . . . he's a lunatic. He harassed me. He wanted to rape me . . ."

Dele held his shivering sister and cast the other fellow a long, hateful look.

"You . . . you . . . actually molested my sister? You . . . Alex? Oh my God, I don't believe it."

"He can't remain in this house. Brother . . . he's capable of . . ." Moji was saying when she was interrupted.

"Stop pretending! Were you not giving me a green light, begging me to marry you?" Alexander queried defensively.

"Hey! So you can lie like this? Me begging you to marry me? *Olorun maje!* God forbid bad thing. I can never marry a useless man like you," Moji retorted. "Just imagine pot calling kettle black," she shot back angrily.

"Women, women. They're all the same . . . capricious beings," Alexander voiced. "Just some minutes ago, she was giving me conditions, begging for an engagement ring. Now she's denying all feelings for me. *Na wa o*, it is unbelievable," he continued.

"It's true after all. You . . . you Alex . . . so you are man enough to attempt fooling around with my sister? You dare mess around with me?"

"Hey, my man, this shouldn't come between us . . . it's a small matter," Alexander was saying when Dele dealt him a hard blow in the face. Alexander felt his lower lip. It was bleeding.

"Listen, buddy, we can sort this out amicably," Alexander said, controlling himself in spite of his raging annoyance and desire to strike back.

"I should have known . . . I actually thought you were my friend. I was deceived . . . I pitied you . . . I trusted you . . . I should have known better than invite a maniac like you into my home. You are better off out in the streets!" Dele barked.

"Oh please, don't make a mountain out of a molehill. You only heard your sister's version of the story. Let me tell you mine."

"You old idiot!" Dele roared, charging at him with vehement indignation, thrusting violent punches on his adversary.

Alexander hit back at him and both fell on the floor, rending hard blows at each other. Moji screamed and ran out in despair. By the time help eventually came, both men were drained and bleeding profusely. If it wasn't for the neighbors whose intervention stopped the fight, one of them would have dropped dead that night.

CHAPTER SIXTEEN

It had become imperative for Brenda to invite the renowned psychologist over for a tête-à-tête in respect of her errant son. Nick was causing her a great deal of concern with his sequestered lifestyle and absurd passion; she was convinced it was about time he heard some home truths.

"Perhaps he would need some counseling and therapy," she thought, before the automatic glass door swung open and the spruced-up lady arrived.

"Brenda Tisco," she introduced, offering her hand.

"Mercy Treasure Dakova. Nice to meet you, ma'am."

They immediately settled to the business at hand.

"A friend of mine told me about you, and I knew it was important I invited you over for a chat."

"Well, I'm glad to be of service to you," Mercy responded, focusing her gaze on the diminutive seventy-five-year-old. Brenda Tisco, in spite of her smallish frame, was a lioness who commanded much respect. Very authoritative, she was still quite attractive, with a fair skin that showed no trace of wrinkles, despite her all-grey hair.

"My problem is peculiar, and I trust you will handle same with all seriousness and professionalism," Brenda stated, relaxing on her massage chair as Mercy took a comfortable position on the opposite leather settee.

"It is my business to offer you quality service, madam," Mercy responded confidently, taking in the exquisite view of the magnificent appointments.

The huge living room had a very high ceiling, glittering jumbo-size Arabian chandeliers, and a life-size television screen. Adorning the walls beside the flat screen television were two life-size pictures of the Amazon herself. Brenda Tisco was beautifully garbed in a black evening gown, wearing dangling diamond ear-rings, with her right wrist elegantly supporting her right jaw in a professional studio pose. In the second photograph, the matriarch of the Tisco family was gorgeously dressed in a rich traditional attire. She was dressed in a wine and gold colored *Aso Oke*, complete *Buba, Iro, Gele*, and *Iborun*. The elegant outfit; blouse, wrapper, head tie, and shoulder sash were specially woven for her, with a unique finishing that ensured that admirers and copycats would be unable to imitate the distinct design. She looked bigger in this photograph, which was difficult to determine whether it was a digital camera shot, a professional painting, or a perfect blend of both. Anyhow, it took a few seconds for Mercy to digest the intimidating view as she focused her gaze on her hostess who was saying something about a recommendation.

"I'm sorry, ma'am, I didn't get what you just said," Mercy put in, finally bringing her attention to the woman sitting oppo-site her.

"You said it is your business to offer me quality service, and I responded that I thought so, considering the recommendation I got before contacting you," Brenda stated, with inquiring eyes that spoke volumes.

Mercy immediately got the message and sat up attentively, with a determination to avoid further distractions. "Absolutely madam, please let me into your world, and by God, we'll tackle the issue."

Brenda sighed and paused briefly before proceeding. "I have a son in his forties. Let's say he is an overgrown, over-pampered kid. He is giving me a lot of concern over an obsession he has with a dead woman. The annoying thing is that I have made everything humanly possible, including fixing blind dates and connecting him with the most beautiful, glamorous, irresistible women I can think of. But no . . . Nick prefers a solitary life. A life that has caused me a decade of pain, anxiety, and stress. He is as hard as a rock, impenetrable, impervious, and dogmatic. He needs to crack, or else I will crack. I invited you over as a last resort. My son needs urgent help and counseling. Whatever it'll take, I want Nick reawakened to the reality of life."

"Your son, does he live here, madam?"

"Oh yes, but he's always locked in the bedchamber he used to share with her. Otherwise, he spends lonesome hours meditating and recapturing old memories."

"He must have loved her," Mercy put in.

"Rubbish! I do not believe in delusive passions which completely disrupt an individual's existence."

"What was your son's relationship with the woman?" Mercy enquired.

"She was his wife."

"I see. What killed her?" Mercy probed further.

"Strange . . . nobody knows what killed her. The autopsy showed that she was poisoned, but if you ask me, I am of the opinion that she got what she deserved."

"I beg your pardon?"

"I said she got what she deserved! I never approved of her," Brenda confessed venomously. "She was a gold digger. Just imagine the son of the late Otunba Michael Kolawole Tisco getting married to a riffraff with no history, no background, no pedigree. We are royalty, and royalty we shall remain!" she asserted derisively.

"The woman in question died mysteriously; did you console your son in his time of bereavement?" Mercy questioned.

Brenda was taken aback. She was numb for a while before responding. "No, I didn't."

"Why not, madam? Surely, you could have shown him some compassion. I would have thought that a mother should show sympathy, empathy, and concern for her grieving child."

Brenda was petrified.

"Are you here to criticize me? You have no right to pass judgments at me!" she snapped, throwing her guest an inimical look. "She was not the first person to die; after all, people die every day."

"You need some compassion, ma'am, some human feeling, especially when it has to do with your son. He is hurting. He's been hurting, and you aren't helping the situation."

"Enough, woman! You don't have a right to affront me!" Brenda warned, rising to her feet.

"My apology, but to put it lightly, you are partly responsible for your son's problem."

"How dare you!"

"I am concerned about a solution to your dilemma. You can change your attitude and help your son or remain indifferent, prolong the problem and live with it. The choice is yours."

Brenda watched in exasperation as the forthright woman rose to her feet.

"I will recommend counseling for you both. You have my number; don't hesitate to call when you are ready. Good day, madam!"

With that, Mercy made a brisk exit, leaving her hostess totally berated.

Meanwhile, Mercy's head was in a whirlwind as she stepped onto the state-of-the-art marble tiles lining the magnificent long corridor. This was one of those times in her counseling experience that she had to be blunt and unemotional. She must have heard footsteps behind because she turned suddenly to stare.

"Looking for someone?" Nick asked, standing before her akimbo.

"Well, *em* . . . I've been speaking with Mrs. Brenda Tisco," Mercy replied, surprisingly unnerved by the attractive stranger. "I'm Mercy Treasure Dakova," she offered.

"Call me Nick."

"Nice to meet you, Nick," she said smiling. "I was just on my way out," she continued, her head swirling in disarray.

"So I noticed. Let me see you to the door."

"Thank you."

"So, are you a friend of hers?" he probed as they stepped into the cool breeze of the night.

"Just an acquaintance. I only met her this evening."

"Hmm . . . what do you do for a living?" he probed further.

"Inquisitive, aren't you? Well, I am a counselor, a psychologist, to be precise."

"Really? I thought there was something unusual about you," Nick noted, nodding his head approvingly.

"I beg your pardon?" Mercy said, stopping in her tracks.

"Psychologists often meet with weirdoes, and I guess they often have this wall of resistance around them," he continued.

"I am in the dark. What's your point?" she questioned.

"That you look very deep and experienced. I mean in terms of human interaction. You are the sort of person that can literally empathize with people's plight."

"I take that to be a compliment," she said, smiling at the quizzical male.

"You look very familiar too," he added, staring at her in a probing manner.

"Really? Well, you never know; we may have met before. It's a small world after all," Mercy proffered.

"No . . . I mean we may have something in common . . . our past blending," he said, looking quite unsure of himself.

"Are you philosophical or what?" Mercy asked, rather puzzled by his line of reasoning.

"Call me a surrealist. I often see people beyond the physical. I look into their intellect, their soul," said Nick, regaining his composure.

"Now you are getting me confused. Can you unravel this puzzle, please?"

"You see, Mrs. . . ."

"Mercy, and please, I am a miss."

"Miss Mercy, right? I feel we should . . . I mean . . . never mind," he dismissed casually.

"You really are an unusual person," Mercy stated, wondering what on earth he had in mind.

"It's been nice meeting you, ma'am. Hope to see you some other time. Good-bye," he said with an air of finality.

"Good-bye," she responded, engaging the car engine as he returned into the house. She shook her head and shrugged before proceeding on her way.

CHAPTER SEVENTEEN

Barely a few weeks after his brawl with Dele, Alexander opted for paid employment—even if it was to work as a laundryman, a not too attractive opportunity for a socialite like him. With no relatives or friends to turn to, he had little choice at the moment. Having shelter, food, and a dependable source of income was top priority to his badly battered ego.

His boss was an extremely busy man whose business concerns cut across several African sub-regions. His home base, however, was Sango-Ota, somewhere on the boundary of Lagos and its neighboring Ogun State. The bulky chief not only had a brusque and dreary personality, he was also some sort of enigma, a weirdo, difficult to understand by his entire household. His frail, petite wife was permanently melancholic. She never smiled, never laughed and never had any moment of euphoria. She had no friends, no visitors, no vocation, and as a full-time housewife, she was home most of the time. Oftentimes she murmured and soliloquized, spending long hours just staring into space.

The household was always in a state of quietude except when the master's voice pierced through the stillness. Patrosa commanded great veneration and precision in everything.

"Adesuwa! Adesuwa!" his fierce voice called that morning as he stood before the breakfast table.

His wife was beside him in a moment. "Sir," she responded, shivering and looking downwards as he spoke.

"Have I told you before never to fry my sausages?"

"Yes sir, you said I should always grill them."

"So you chose to disobey my orders?"

"I'm sorry, sir, but the griller broke down yesterday, and the technician has been unable to fix it."

"Damn you and the technician! I keep enough money in your drawer so that you use your brain to make things work around here. I expect some initiative and not excuses."

"Forgive me, sir, it will never happen again," she promised, watching the scary fellow fall into his seat, yanking all the lids off the various food bowls set before him.

He ate in a hurry, like a bulldog, whilst she stood at a corner watching him consume several bowls of cereal, eggs, sandwiches, yogurt, and juice. The moment he finished his meal, Adesuwa picked a napkin and wiped his mouth, carried his briefcase, opened the door for him and led the way towards his limousine parked in the garage. From there, the chauffeur took over the master's briefcase, signifying the end of her morning duties to the man who married her and turned her into an elevated housemaid.

As she walked back into the house to continue in her routine doldrums, she wore a relieved but serious expression. Alexander, who had made a habit of eavesdropping on his employer's morning fits, receded into the laundry room the moment he sighted the mistress entering the house. The marriage between Ehosa Patrosa and Adesuwa was analogous to that of beauty and the beast. Alexander often wondered at their characteristic mismatch. The duo lived under the same roof but literally existed as strangers.

Adesuwa sank into the soft couch in the living room, finally relieved to have the tyrant out of the way. "Even if for just a few hours," she mused, stretching out and yawning. She must have dozed off because by the time her eyes caught a glimpse of the ancient clock hanging on the wall, it was already past noon. Instinctively, she jumped out of the seat and made straight into the kitchen, first to do the morning dishes and next to start preparing the master's meal, as he could breeze into the house anytime post meridian for his lunch.

"Good afternoon, madam."

Adesuwa was startled as she turned in the direction of the voice.

Alexander stood at the door, clad in his smart uniform, a bit of apprehension in his eyes as he watched the woman face him with a frown.

"I hope I didn't scare you, madam," he said, bowing politely at the sad yet visibly attractive woman.

"Any problem?" she asked, facing the intruder.

"I . . . I've finished the laundry, madam, and I was wondering if you'll be needing my assistance in the kitchen."

"Thank you, but I can manage quite well," she declined.

"I know you can manage, madam, but I feel odd about you doing the dishes, particularly when you have an able-bodied domestic staff like me around. Let me help out."

Suddenly he was by the sink, washing and rinsing before Adesuwa could even protest. It didn't take long before the whole place was sparkling and smelling fresh.

"Thank you," the woman offered before adding, "Don't bother helping me again. I can manage quite easily."

"No problem, ma'am, I'm at your service anytime. I'll be most honored being of service to you," Alexander put in gaily, bowing submissively.

The next day, Adesuwa couldn't refuse the humble, endearing and persuasive male's offer of some assistance again. Day after day, week after week, it continued and gradually became a habit for Alexander to assist her in the kitchen. It was quite relieving to get some help, and she in turn, rewarded his kindness with monetary gifts. Little by little, she started relaxing in his company until she found herself discussing her life and experience with the man.

"I grew up in a remote town somewhere on the outskirts of Benin City, here in Nigeria. Born into a family of nine children and very poor parents."

She let out a sigh before progressing, as Alexander knelt down in obeisance, giving rapt attention to her narration.

"My father was a peasant farmer who worked very hard to provide food for his family. I was the only girl in the midst of eight boys. I was also the first. My father was killed during a feud with one of the neighboring communities. That was when our real troubles began. I was just about eleven when I started fending for myself. Mother was too weak to sustain her children. Two of my brothers died from malnutrition. We were hungry, starving, dying. There was no help coming from anywhere because we lived in a very poor and hostile community. Even my father's brothers couldn't help. They could hardly even cater for their own families."

She paused and let out a regretful sigh before she proceeded.

"I don't know how we survived those years, but by the time I turned fifteen, I knew I needed a change in fortune. By this time, I had lost another two of my brothers—a set of twins, and then mother died. With four brothers and no parents, I had to pray for a miracle. That was when Chief Ehosa Patrosa came along. I was summoned to his house by a relative who sympathized with our family's plight. One look at me and Chief Ehosa Patrosa ordered I prepare for a long journey to the city with him, where I was to serve as a maid. By the time I turned twenty, chief took me back to the village, paid my dowry and made me his wife. It's been ten years since, and I really do not know why he chose to marry me; after all, I could have continued serving as his maid with no obligation."

Alexander watched her, a mixture of pity and distaste in his expression as she spoke.

"I am at least thankful to him for saving me from poverty. I may have died of starvation. He gave me food, gave me shelter, a new lease of life, but he hasn't given me joy."

"What happened to your surviving brothers?" Alexander questioned.

"Oh, I forgot to mention that chief recruited them into his workforce. One of them works with his company in Sierra Leone, the other in Ghana, and the other two serve as stewards in his hotel in Kenya."

"Your story is unusual, ma'am," said Alexander when she finished her narration. "I quite appreciate that chief has been of assistance to you, but since you are now his wife, he should treat you with some respect. You are a beautiful woman, and certainly you deserve some compassion."

119

"It's good to hear you say that, Alex, thank you," she voiced, smiling for the first time since he knew her. She suddenly looked animated and Alexander thought against his instinct to take her in his arms. Just then, the doorbell rang. In an instant, the laundryman vanished from the scene, and the mistress jumped to her feet as Chief Patrosa's bulky frame appeared at the door.

"Welcome, sir," she greeted, shutting the door after him.

"I presume my meal is set," he uttered, slumping into his customized adjustable leather seat.

"Yes sir," she responded with a bow.

"Take off my shoes," he ordered, and immediately she was by his feet, pulling off the extra-large shoes.

"Get my cigar!"

"Yes sir!" And off she went to get his cigar. She returned with it shortly.

Chief Ehosa Patrosa lit the cigar, puffed and relaxed his back.

"Come here," he commanded, lifting his feet. He slapped her on her butt, pushed her away, and Adesuwa stood with head bowed, waiting for the next order.

"Lick my feet."

"Sir?" She was not sure she'd heard him right.

"Go on and lick my feet, woman!" His voice was cold and intimidating. "As you can see, they're dirty and need cleaning up."

Adesuwa stooped and took a good look at the huge smelly feet. It appeared Ehosa Patrosa had spent the day swimming in mud or some stinking puddle that she could not identify.

"What are you waiting for, fool?" he barked, getting agitated by her delay.

"Chief, please, I . . ."

The man jumped out of his seat and with one hand, slapped her on the face. He scuttled away and returned with two sticks. With two hands, he lifted and placed the frail woman on a high stool, making them stand at par.

"You . . . you . . . dare disobey my orders?" he yelled and began to whip her.

"Sir . . . please forgive me. I didn't mean to disobey you . . .I . . ." she cried, wriggling in pain.

"Shut up!" The blazing voice cut through hers. Chief's eyes were fiery, and Adesuwa quivered as he spoke.

"It seems you've forgotten I am your savior."

"No . . . no sir, I haven't forgotten," she said, as he threw the sticks away and pulled her down to the floor.

A slapping pain on her back told her that his whipping had left incisions on her body. She wept inwardly, enduring the throbbing, fiery sensation with amazing courage.

"It seems you don't realize the reason for my marrying you," he screeched.

At this point, chief took a few steps backwards before continuing in a shrill tone.

"I gave you life, gave you hope, gave you a future, saved you from penury, destitution, gave you food, gave you shelter, and now you . . ." His bloodshot eyes widened as he spoke with deliberate emphasis on each word. "Patrosa . . . Patrosa will never condescend so lowly, other than for very strong reasons."

He paused, took a few steps back in her direction and then proceeded: "I am your master! Your ruler! I am your god!" His voice was resounding, firm, and absolute. "You must adore me, you must serve me, you must please me, you must obey me, you must extol me! Do I make myself clear?"

"Yes sir, I adore you. I worship you, I obey you, your wish is my command," she said, falling beside his feet in tears. "Forgive me, sir, I will never provoke you again."

"Never! Never! Never . . ." The room shook as Patrosa's thunderous voice echoed in the walls. He'd made himself clear, and certainly Adesuwa didn't need a prophetic confirmation.

She instinctively grabbed his right foot and started licking it. Little by little, the dirt vanished from his feet as her tongue and saliva did the washing. He watched her tortured expression with excitement as she swallowed the stinking filth. Suddenly she started puking. She could not contain the nausea. Patrosa in turn grabbed his sticks and angrily whipped her. He stormed away, cursing and swearing to deal ruthlessly with her. Meanwhile, she lay on the floor whimpering for the rest of the day. Her bitter moaning did not stop the whole night as she poured out a bucket full of tears, groaning and enduring the grief of physical and emotional abuse.

The following week, she was hospitalized for typhoid fever. She had a serious infection, which she was convinced was ingested from Patrosa's stinking feet. He did not care if she died in the hospital, so he didn't care to visit her. To him, the money he spent on her health insurance was more than enough generosity, and certainly, with good medical care, whatever her issue was would be addressed by the health practitioners.

CHAPTER EIGHTEEN

"Some people derive joy from sadism. They lack self-control and a sense of moral judgment. All they think about is how to use and abuse others. You must understand that by your human power, you cannot overcome sin. Even at the sound of my voice, there are some of you who are plotting evil against your neighbor. Something in you regularly leads you into iniquity. You must repent, or else the devil shall make mincemeat of your life. Premarital and extramarital sex will ruin you. You need the grace of God in your life. True love does not abuse, it protects. True love is of God. Jesus is knocking at the door of your heart. Repent and become born again . . ."

Alexander rolled out of bed and switched off the radio. He certainly did not reckon with the early Sunday morning sermon broadcast by Pastor Bimbo Odukoya. His mind was preoccupied with other things . . . her . . . Adesuwa. Now that the boss was out of the way on an official tour of his business around the continent, he could execute his plans. The ploy had been on for a while and reached a crescendo during her one-week stay at the hospital. There couldn't have been a better timing for him. Adesuwa had recovered fully from ill health and had resumed normal life in her home.

Alexander yawned and smelt his breadth. It stank of stale booze and fags. Dragging himself up from the bed, he sauntered into the bathroom to freshen up. In a matter of minutes, he was out, throwing on a clean cotton shirt and jeans, oiling his scalp, brushing his brows and neatly trimmed moustache before picking the neatly wrapped stuff from his drawer. It wasn't long before he entered the main house from his boy's quarters abode.

"Good day, madam."

The mistress of the house was humming what sounded like a dirge, her eyes riveted on the wall when he walked in.

"Can I help you?" she asked, an inquisitive expression on her face.

"I . . . I was just wondering if you needed my help around here," he stuttered.

"I quite appreciate your concern, but I'm fine. Chief traveled, and I'll be doing very little cooking in his absence."

"Okay madam, I just thought I should ask," he said, making to leave.

"Thank you, Alexander," she said, relaxing back in the chair.

"Do you need a drink, ma'am?" he asked suddenly, stopping in his tracks. "We've got some fresh oranges in the refrigerator."

"Very well, orange juice, please."

Alexander entered the kitchen, extracted some juice, poured the stuff into the drink and returned shortly to serve her.

She accepted the drink and forced a smile.

"Thank you, Alex, if I do need your help again, I'll call you."

"Certainly madam," he said, smiling back before taking his leave.

He didn't go far, as he returned shortly to find the woman asleep, induced by the narcotics. Gently, he lifted her off the sofa, straight into her cozy bedroom. He put her on the bed and slotted in a CD. Music filled the air as the licentious fellow undressed and gratified his lust with the woman. In a short while, it was over, and he lay beside her on the bed, thoroughly satiated. Before long, he got dressed and tiptoed out of the room.

It was several hours later before Adesuwa regained full consciousness amidst shock, discomposure, and disconcertment. Slowly and gradually, she replayed the earlier incidents of the day. After what seemed like a few minutes of delirium, she swallowed some sedatives, pulled on her clothes, opened her wardrobe, dug into a concealed compartment, pulled out a pistol and headed in the direction of the boy's quarters. She had acquired the pistol in anticipation of the day Patrosa's humiliation would be beyond her containment, then she would kill him and probably kill herself too.

Alexander was filling details of his depravity into his diary when the door flung open.

"Madam . . . you're here," he muttered, springing to his feet. He was a bit discomfited by the blank expression on her face.

"How are you, Alex?" Adesuwa asked, surveying the room with her eyes.

"I'm well . . . fine, thank you ma'am."

An indescribable smile enveloped her face, and for a split moment, Alexander thought she looked happy. Her smile lingered, and his earlier apprehension gave way to relaxation. He suddenly felt comfortable in her company.

"What kind of man are you, Alex?"

"What do you mean, ma'am?"

"I mean, how would you rate your masculinity?" she asked, taking a few steps forward. She propped up his head and felt his jaw with her soft palm. "Go on and tell me," she persuaded.

"Madam, I . . . I consider myself a virile, strong and attractive personality . . ."

He was interrupted with a slap, then another, and several others. He was out of shock in a moment, facing the seemingly frail female with impenitence.

"You dare to abuse me? In my own house! Under my roof! In my matrimonial home!" Her voice was harsh, her tone baleful.

"Take it easy, madam . . . I was only trying to help, taking into consideration your husband's negligence and scorn."

Adesuwa spat on his face and surged at him, hitting his stomach with all the available energy in her. She felt her pocket for the gun as the defiant abuser wriggled in pain and made to say something. His mien instantly changed to fear when he noticed the weapon.

"Don't do it, madam . . . please. I'll . . . I'll explain," he stuttered.

"You'll explain in hell!" she roared, firing a bullet into his right leg.

Alexander roared and fell on his knees in pain.

"P—please don't . . . don't kill me, please . . ."

"You bastard! You took advantage of me! You deserve complete extirpation! I will have the pleasure of sending you to the pit of hell where you belong!" Another bullet pierced through his second leg, and his screaming intensified. The door thrust open, and the security guard rushed in.

"Madam!" he screamed, viewing the scene with horror.

"Get out!" she barked, pointing the gun at the intruder.

The man hesitated for a while.

"I said get out!" she bellowed, threatening to pull the trigger. Both men watched in horror as she raised the gun closer to the security man's face.

Suddenly, tears started streaming down her eyes. She crumbled to the floor with the revolver clenched closely to her chest. In spite of the gunshots, Alexander managed to raise himself off the floor. The security man helped him out, while the woman remained helpless on the spot, in a pool of tears.

CHAPTER NINETEEN

Ever since the desecration, Adesuwa was in a state of extreme misery. What on earth was she to tell Patrosa about the disgraceful act! It was completely out of the question, hiding or cloaking the incident. Her conscience wouldn't let her be and knowing the chief for what he was, she was prepared for the very worst. She considered it better to die with the truth than live with the guilt. Having gone through much difficulty and emotional pain, the thought of joining her ancestors was a welcome relief; after all, hers wasn't particularly a glorious or even desirable existence. In fact, this was the perfect time and opportunity to end the many pangs that had become synonymous with her life. If only he'll be kind enough to spare her the agony of prolonged anguish. She definitely will prefer the quickest lethal method.

Ehosa Patrosa's thunderous voice thrust her back to the present. He'd finally returned home from his trip. Not quite long after he settled in, Adesuwa summoned courage and somehow initiated the discussion, recounting the experience, every detail she could possibly remember about how their laundryman drugged her and abused her femininity. As she'd expected, his reaction was swift; almost like a flash of thunder. Patrosa rushed at her with the roaring of a lion, eyes blazing, mouth spitting fire, raining curses, intensely provoked and ready to kill.

Then something happened—a twist in circumstance. Adesuwa gasped as she watched the colossus make a somersault, crashing onto the floor with a volcanic force, hands clenched to his chest. She came out of her momentary shock and raised an alarm.

Patrosa had a cardiac arrest and was rushed to the hospital. He was in a coma for seven days, all of which the doctors hadn't expected him to pull through. Adesuwa was at his bedside when he eventually opened his eyes.

"Doctor! Nurse! Please come . . ." she uttered, flustering excitedly as she rose to her feet.

"Adesuwa . . . stop . . . please," Patrosa muttered, stopping her in her tracks. "Don't call the doctor yet . . . wait . . . I have to talk to you."

"Sir, you must relax please. The doctor will be here soon," she said, kneeling beside the bed. "You've been in a coma for about a week now," she offered, her voice fraught with emotion.

"Adesuwa, I . . . I visited the other world."

She watched him in astonishment.

"I don't understand you, sir."

"I crossed over to the other side. The other side, where misery and pain are the order of the day. I met with Lucifer . . . he invited me to dinner. He embraced me. He told me I'd done a very good job . . . keeping a lot of people miserable . . . especially . . . especially you, Adesuwa. It was a horrible place. There was so much anguish . . . wailing and gnashing of teeth, so much pain. But Lucifer was laughing . . . he was laughing because he wasn't alone. He had many disciples, and he was earnestly searching for more." Patrosa paused briefly and started sobbing. Adesuwa stared at him in utmost surprise. Was this a dream or was her imagination running wild? Chief Patrosa crying? Impossible!

"I . . . am . . . please. Oh Adesuwa, can you forgive me? Can you forgive me for the pain I've caused you all these years? I humiliated and abused you, Adesuwa. I don't know how I did it, but I know why. It was because I was empty and lonely. I needed to exert authority. I needed to enslave another being because I was a product of slavery. Adesuwa, I watched my father endure humiliation because he was poor. He was treated like shit, scorned and ridiculed . . . and the worst part? My mother! My mother left him . . . for his master. My father's wife abandoned him for his master. That woman . . . she caused him pain and sent him to his untimely grave. My father died, but he left me a legacy: never trust women! If it's possible, treat them

like despicable animals. That's the reason . . . that's the reason
I tried enslaving you. Adesuwa, I wanted to avenge my father's
blood. I wanted to vent out my frustration and grief. I wanted
someone to pay for the sins of my mother. You were the victim.
You were the unfortunate victim, and I swear, Adesuwa, I had
worse things in store for you."

The narrative was shocking and revealing. Adesuwa watched
in dismay as the man unburdened his heart. By the time he finished, she was herself crying.

Only one thing I ask of you, Adesuwa . . ."

"Sir, I'm at your service anytime," she said, her tears streaming in torrents.

"Forgive me. Can you please forgive me?"

She nodded her head and watched him shut his eyes briefly.
He opened them after a few seconds.

"I want you to trace a woman by the name Cassandra. Sandra Majekodunmi. I haven't seen her for over twenty years. She
was my first wife. She was bitter when she left me. Ask her to
forgive me."

"Oh sir, I'm sure she would. For now, you must relax while
I call the doctor."

The doctor came in shortly to see the patient. After a few
minutes, Patrosa started gasping for breath and was placed on
life support as his condition became worse and critical, and he
fell into another coma. For several days, Adesuwa anxiously
watched over him. The doctors advised her to return home and
save herself further stress, but Adesuwa wouldn't budge. By the
seventh day and a stroke of fate, Patrosa opened his eyes.

"I have seen the light, Adesuwa," he declared, viewing her
with new eyes. "I have seen the light of the world. He blotted
away my sins . . . He's given me a new life. He has set me free .
. . I am free . . . free."

Patrosa's divine encounter left him a changed man. He
gradually regained full composure and was discharged from the
hospital with a clean bill of health and a reformed mind. He
became an evangelist, spreading the gospel of mercy and the
forgiveness of sins. The first person he begged for mercy was

Adesuwa. He was on two knees for hours, pleading for forgiveness from her. Adesuwa wept all through. She couldn't believe that the high and mighty Ehosa Patrosa was on his knees begging for her mercy. She took his utterances with a pinch of salt and inward scepticism.

Next on Patrosa's agenda was to find Cassandra Majekodunmi and plead for his first wife's forgiveness. Although his initial attempts at reconciling with Cassandra were difficult, he eventually had an audience with her, pleading and asking for her forgiveness for the agony he put her through during their short-lived marriage.

She reluctantly agreed to delete his name from her list of avowed enemies and even more amazingly, revealed her daughter's true biological ties. Father and daughter were shocked, to say the least. Suddenly from out of the blue, Tobi had a father and one who was extremely humble and compassionate, with no semblance to the picture she'd had in her mind all these years. Tobi Majekodunmi had borne her mother's maiden surname from birth, a deliberate attempt by Cassandra to obliterate his memory from her life. Adesuwa was the one to remain awe-stricken for many months to come. Had the one-time monster really changed for good? Well, time will tell . . .

CHAPTER TWENTY

Several months passed by before Brenda Tisco reconsidered her last discussion with the psychologist. Not that she wasn't ready for counseling, the fact remained she couldn't come to terms with Mercy's inference. How could she, Brenda, possibly be responsible for her son's predicament? She'd never felt more derided in her life, particularly since it was from a complete stranger. Despite that, she still felt the urge to contact the gallant advisor. At first, she was hesitant but finally braced for the drudgery. One dial and she got through to the woman's number.

"Brenda Tisco on the line. Can you make it to my place tonight?" she asked the moment the line went through.

"Nice to hear from you, madam," the counselor said before inquiring, "Have you made up your mind about counseling?"

"Obviously I have reached a decision, or else I wouldn't have called you," Brenda replied truculently.

"Have you broached the issue with your son, madam?" Mercy inquired further.

"What if I haven't? Just because you're a counselor doesn't mean you should joggle me."

"Listen, madam, I'm only trying to help . . ." Mercy was saying when the other voice cut in caustically.

"Obviously, what are counselors supposed to do?"

"There's no need for the sarcasm, madam. Anyhow, I'm at your service anytime."

"Do I presume you'll be here for seven tonight?"

"I'll be there for seven," Mercy affirmed before the line disengaged.

Brenda heaved a sigh of relief and relaxed her back on her rocking chair. She was glancing through *Success Digest Maga-*

zine, reading a home-front article by Esther Ojeagbase when her son walked in.

"Hello Mother."

"Son, I want you to meet someone tonight," Brenda stated, looking up at him.

"Another of your matchmaking meetings, I presume?"

"Nick!" she exclaimed with disapproval.

"Mother, I am not interested in your ploys anymore, and let me get one thing straight. If you ever bother me about women again, I'll be out of your life for good."

"Nick! Don't threaten me. I'm your mother, for heaven's sake."

"Let's consider this a closed chapter," he dismissed. "Now to other things, I am going on vacation. I'll be gone for at least three months. I'm handing over the business to you. The staff will now be fully responsible to you. Delegate authority as you please, withdraw money from the bank as you please and of course, do everything else, as you please. The general manager already has the full briefing on this, so liaise with him."

"Nick . . . Nick, please sit down," she entreated, in disarray.

Nick took a seat and crossed his legs, tapping his fingers in an unruffled manner.

"You can't take off like that," Brenda began. "I cannot cope without you. The business will suffer if you leave."

"I've got about a week to hand over to you, Mother . . . no cause for alarm."

"No . . . no, Nick. I've long retired from active work. I am not capable of running the business in your absence. It's yours; your father bequeathed it to you."

"Look, Mother, my mind is made up. You may wish to know that I care little for the business. I don't have an heir to take over, so I couldn't care less."

"Oh God! Oh no! Why is this happening to me? My son is turning his back on me. I don't have a husband. I don't have emotional support . . . why? why?"

"Hey Mother, cut off the sentiments. You don't care about anyone else but yourself. I've had enough of your apathy. I'm fed up with everything around here!"

"Please son, don't go away. Let's talk things over. I want us to be friends; I want to see a smile on your face; I want our home front to be peaceful. I need to know that you are happy."

"My mind is made up, and that's final. I'm only going on a holiday anyway," he retorted.

"Nick?"

"Yes, Mother."

"I love you," Brenda declared, in between sobs.

"I love you too, Mother," he replied bluntly.

"Please . . . let's talk things over. I . . . we both need to undergo counseling. A lot of things have gone sour between us. For about thirteen years now, our relationship has been strained."

"Yeah . . . thanks to your cynicism since the day Liz walked into my life."

"Please son, let's not recount bitter moments. Let's put the past behind. There's so much that the future holds for us . . ."

"Maybe . . . for you just maybe. But not for me, Mother. The future holds absolutely nothing for me."

"I'm sorry, Nick; I'm sorry you've suffered all these years. Forgive me, please forgive me."

"Forgive you for what?" he asked in an aggrieved tone. "Tell me, Mother, what am I to forgive? Is it the fact that you never gave Liz and I the chance to be happy together? Or is it the fact that you tormented and tortured her with your acrimony, belligerence, and contempt? Go on and tell me, Mother. Is it the fact that when she died you expressed no sympathy, no compassion, no consolation, no condolence, no regrets, no . . ." Nick stopped abruptly and faced her. "You talk about forgiveness? You want my forgiveness? No, Mother, there's so much that has gone sour. So much water has already gone under the bridge. I am in no position to forgive you."

"Please . . . don't say that. You must . . . you must forgive. You must forgive me for . . . I . . . I killed Elizabeth!"

Brenda slumped on the floor, hands on her chest, while Nick was agape, in shock. He fell on his knees beside her.

"No! Mother! Tell me you didn't. You couldn't have . . . no . . . you didn't . . . you couldn't . . . you didn't . . . you didn't!"

Nick crashed through the sliding door in frenzy, the shattering of glass rending the air, causing commotion in the usually serene compound. An ambulance arrived shortly to convey mother and son to the hospital. Brenda had suffered a major cardiac arrest and was in critical condition, while Nick sustained minor injuries from the glass cuts. He was, however, in a state of numbness for several days before he regained full control of himself.

After several days in a coma, Brenda regained consciousness to behold her son standing by her bedside. He'd been there for just a few minutes before she awoke.

"Nick . . . Nick, please forgive me," she uttered in a feeble tone.

Nick remained quiet, watching her with mixed emotions. Since her unexpected confession, all that he had in his head were images of his mother as a despicable murderer.

"I love you, Nick, that's why I did it. Perhaps . . . perhaps 1 was blind. Perhaps I was selfish . . . but I swear, it was all for you . . . all for my love for you, my son."

"You killed her," Nick stated flatly, watching her with antithetical feelings of pity and hate. There was a conflict of reason within him as he felt a flushing of emotions. "You didn't have to kill her," he added, stooping beside her, his eyes suffused with tears. "Look what you've done to us. Both of us have suffered untold misery since she died. Killing Elizabeth was the costliest mistake you ever made."

"I . . . I . . . I realize it now. It's too late, isn't it? I'm . . . please tell Elizabeth to forgive me."

"Oh Mother . . . Oh God," he groaned, watching her eyes go dim.

"Another person's pain doesn't guarantee my gain . . . a bitter lesson life has taught me," she whispered.

"Absolutely," Nick moaned, tears streaking down his face.

Brenda was in a coma for another seven days before she finally gave up the ghost. Her funeral was very brief and solemn, attended by few friends and sympathizers, including Mercy

Treasure Dakova. Suffice it to say that Mercy was shocked by Brenda Tisco's death.

"My sympathy," Mercy voiced, condoling the bereaved son of the Amazon at the end of the ceremony. Nick looked into the familiar face and managed a smile. They walked out of the cemetery together, towards the car park. "If you ever need someone to talk to, please don't hesitate to call," she added in a solemn tone.

"Thank you . . . Treasure," Nick replied with a sparkle in his sullen eyes.

Mercy looked at him in surprise. People hardly took notice, nor addressed her by her middle name. "Big deal," she thought, shrugging as he bade her farewell.

With all the other guests gone, including the Anglican bishop who officiated at the ceremony, Nick retraced his steps to his mother's tomb. He sat beside it and watched the serenity of the graveyard, catching a glimpse of several inscriptions on the surrounding burial chambers. It was apparent all beings had one thing in common—life and death, including Brenda Tisco, the formidable monarch who had just been committed to mother earth. His mind hovered and wandered into the past. In spite of all the unfortunate events, he knew within himself that his mother had loved him dearly . . . to an obsessive degree. If only she hadn't opposed his love for Elizabeth . . . if only she had appreciated the love they shared . . . if only she had foreseen the future, she wouldn't have . . .

"Oh Mother, why? I know you loved me. I know you cared . . . but why? Why take an innocent life, Mother?" Tears flowed from his eyes as he spoke.

"Look what you did to yourself. Look what you did to me . . . to us." He paused briefly and then continued. "You know I love you, Mother. I've always loved you. Elizabeth was in no way a threat to you. You have always been my mother; but you should have given me a chance to live my own life, to love and be loved in return by the woman of my choice. I'm sorry it had to end this way. I'm truly sorry."

After a long emotional outcry, Nick pulled himself together, cast a long glance at his mother's tomb and started receding from the scene. Ironically, Elizabeth's tomb was just a few meters away. Both women were laid to rest at the Sanctimony Court Cemetery, a private burial ground preserved for the elites, located along Lekki Expressway, Lagos. Slowly and steadily, he arrived and took a comfortable position beside her tomb.

"Elizabeth . . . it's been years since you left me. Life hasn't been the same without you. You know how much I loved you, Elizabeth. I'm sorry you had to go." Some tears escaped his eyes before he proceeded. "My mother . . . she killed you." Again, tears started flowing.

"She said she's sorry, Liz. She said you should forgive her. Please Elizabeth, forgive mama. She's gone. She's gone the way of every mortal, but please let her rest in peace . . . and so must you, Liz. Rest in perfect peace, my love."

The tears kept flowing. Nick Kolawole Tisco wept uncontrollably for several hours. The pain in his heart was intense. The burden of years needed therapeutic expression, and weeping appeared to be the practical way to express his grief. The more the tears flowed, the more the pain condensed. He cried until there were no more tears coming. Slowly and solemnly, he placed a wreath beside the tomb. "Good-bye, Elizabeth Tisco. Good-bye, my fallen love. Good-bye forever . . . rest in perfect peace."

As he made his way out of the tranquil environment, Nick could literally feel a surge of relief. A burden was suddenly lifted off him, the burden he'd shouldered for years, vainly and vaguely searching for Elizabeth's killer. The riddle had been solved, the mystery unraveled. Now it was over . . . the anxiety of years gone by. It was time for another phase, another era, marking the beginning of a totally new experience in his somewhat eventful and calamitous life.

CHAPTER TWENTY-ONE

"**L**adies and gentlemen, welcome on stage Mercy Treasure Dakova," the master of ceremony announced. "Mercy is the voice of the African woman, crying for emancipation. She represents the future of womanhood . . . the courageous advocate of change," he continued.

There was a standing ovation as Mercy gracefully made her way from the audience to mount the rostrum in the jam-packed auditorium to deliver a lecture before the large crowd comprised mainly of the intelligentsia of the Lagos social circuit. The event was being held at the banquet conference hall of the National Arts Theatre, Iganmu, Lagos. The hall had been specially decorated in pink and lilac satin with glittering lights creatively spotting the stage, roof, and entrance.

"Good evening, ladies and gentlemen." Her voice was assertive and confident. "Welcome to this epoch-making event, the first Pan African Conference on Abused Women. So much has been said about the role of women in development and nation building, yet very little consideration has been given to those downtrodden and desecrated victims of circumstance. Of significance is the fact that women have always played a vital role in the evolution and nurturing of mankind and humanity as a whole. To start with, every man was born of a woman. Except, of course, if you were a test-tube baby, but even then, the female ova and the male spermatozoa gave you life. If we must go back to history, in the beginning God made them male and female. He formed the woman from the man's rib, not from his foot, not from his head, but from his side, so that she could be a companion, partner in progress, and a co-heir to the heritage of God.

Ladies and gentlemen, the oppression of the female folk in our world calls for great concern. Sexual harassment, molestation, rape, prostitution, female circumcision, domestic violence, child marriage, forced marriage, polygamy, disinheritance of widows, and women trafficking are all pointers to the fact that there needs to be a reawakening, re-evaluation, restoration, and reinvigoration of our standards, values and above all, the virtue and dignity of womanhood. There should be stringent punitive measures adopted for the perpetrators of these illicit, unbecoming, sordid, base, and ignoble acts. Need I emphasize that men and women alike are responsible for the proliferation of this obnoxious occurrence?

To the men, I appeal to your conscience and sense of judgment. Every woman that is a victim could be your sister, your wife, your friend, or even your beloved daughter. For the women, let us realize that God created us for the purification of mankind. We are helpers of humanity, builders of glorious destinies. Our calling as women is honorable. We are agents of societal development. And if you have been a victim, take heart in the realization that there is coming a day of judgment, a day of reckoning, retribution, justification, and vindication. The African woman must come out of the doldrums. It is our time to arise!"

There was contention in the hall as the eloquent lady made a brisk exit from the stage. Her speech engendered controversy in the audience. While some commended her ardency and terseness, others criticized her guts and audacity. Somewhere in the audience, an impressed listener was sticking out his head in a bid to locate the articulate female. Just at the point of her being mobbed by excited journalists, fans, and critics, he made his way through the crowd to rescue her.

"Let's get out of here fast!" he said, pulling her as fast as their feet could go. Mercy gaped at Nick. He was the last person she expected to see.

"That was a remarkable speech you gave. Mind if we go out for a drink somewhere?" he continued, as they made their way out of the boisterous environment.

"Nick Tisco. I didn't realize you were in the audience," Mercy said, finally finding her voice.

"Surprised? Well I heard the advert on the radio, saw the newspaper publication and decided to avail myself the opportunity of listening to you."

"I wasn't expecting such a large turnout, I must confess," she stated, gasping excitedly.

"What do you expect of a renowned psychologist? Very few people can stir such enthusiasm in their listeners."

"Really?" I thought I caused commotion."

"A laudable commotion, yes. Get ready for fame and media attention . . . don't say I didn't warn you," he said excitedly.

"I'm flattered," said Mercy, delighted that at least one person appreciated her efforts.

"Be my guest to dinner, please; we could drive out in my car and come back for yours later," he suggested as they approached the parking lot. She nodded in the affirmative.

They settled for a choice restaurant at the seafront and ordered an eastern Nigerian delicacy. Mercy relaxed as the cool lagoon breeze freshened the environment, making her feel at home in the company of the dashing dude. For the first time in her adult life, she took time to observe that Nick was an exceptionally good-looking man. He was six feet tall, dark, and handsome. He had a smooth face and a clean shave, except for a thin, well-trimmed moustache. His hair was a low cut with streaks of grey dotting his front middle hair region.

They relished their meal, especially the spicy Isi Ewu, specially prepared goat head with local herbs and palm oil, which they ate amidst laughter and delight from the rib-cracking jokes made by a popular comedian performing live at the open-air arena.

"You make me feel alive, Treasure," Nick said, nodding rhythmically to the classical tune playing in the background. "I'm glad I met you again. I remember telling you that you are very peculiar. There's something magical about you."

Mercy swallowed hard and concentrated on her meal. She suddenly became taciturn, feeling rather uneasy and self-conscious.

"It's a beautiful night . . . one that holds lots of promises," Nick stated, watching her expression. "It's a privilege knowing you, Mercy. I wonder if you realize just how endowed you are," he said, scooping in every detail of her dark spotless face, which looked as innocent as a naïve sixteen-year-old.

Mercy was a beautiful lady, but her prim nature concealed her dazzle. She wore a neat bob, which was her trademark hairdo. She also wore no makeup, except for a colorless lip gloss. The ex-nun looked at him with starry eyes. If only he could perceive her inner turmoil, he'd have spared her further abashment. She shifted her gaze from him to the skies. She spotted a few stars, very distant, but at least the twinkle was a good distraction, if only to spare her from his probing eyes.

"Having fun?" he asked, watching her keenly.

"I'm . . . yes, I'm enjoying myself," she replied, managing a smile.

"Treasure, will you be my treasure?"

Mercy stared at him completely nonplussed. There was an unusual excitement in Nick's tone. He seemed to have suddenly discovered himself. She, contrariwise, was bewildered.

"As I reminisce over my life, I wonder at the irony of circumstance," Nick said, picking out a piece of the goat eye from the broth. Mercy remained numb as he spoke, simply nodding her head to show she was listening.

"You know, Treasure, I have been through harrowing times. Until recently, my life was in a state of ennui. Nothing meant anything to me. I was lifeless as far as I remember," he narrated.

"Really?" she asked, finding her voice.

"My mother made an unbelievable confession before she died. She killed my wife. Can you imagine it? My own mother, my flesh and blood, has been the source of my pain all these years."

"That is shocking," Mercy said with a quiver. "It's almost unbelievable. I mean, why would she? How could she? It's hard to imagine. I wonder why she did it?" she spluttered, watching him closely.

"She was just raving possessive. As her only offspring, she was obsessed with me, wanting to dominate and rule my life as though I didn't have a brain. I still can't fully comprehend her motive."

"Life is full of surprises . . . this one is just so ludicrous," Mercy put in.

"That is why I said I wonder at the irony of circumstance. I was in endless emotional quagmire, not knowing that my beloved mother was responsible for my pain."

"I hope you have forgiven her. I know it's difficult, but you must . . . forget the past and look into the future," Mercy stated, gulping some water to clear her throat. She felt some dryness within and wasn't sure whether it was a result of insufficient saliva in her mouth or a result of the inner tension she was experiencing.

"Do I have a choice? She's dead, and I can't continue for the rest of my life to hold it against her. Besides, she's my mother. Nothing can change that."

"I am impressed. Not many people have a heart like yours," Mercy put in.

"Thank you. I also believe you have a wonderful heart. That is why I want you to be my treasure."

Mercy gulped the remaining content of her glass and refilled with more water. The turn of their discussion was definitely unnerving.

"You have rekindled something in me. Call it the fire of compassion . . . the conflagration of companionship. I believe I'm . . . I . . . *em* . . . will you spend the rest of your life with me, please?"

She wasn't sure what her reaction should be. Was she to jump and proclaim: "Hurray! I've found my Mr. Right." Or perhaps she should simply smile and say, "I will, Nick; I've been waiting for you all my life."

"Tell me, Treasure, do you feel anything for me?" he asked, interfering with her thoughts.

"I . . . think you are a nice person, nice company too," she said, breathing so hard that she could feel the thumping of her heart. In fact, it appeared her heart was pounding and threatening to explode.

"Is that all?" he queried, staring at her straight in the eyes.

"Well, you are also deeply compassionate," she added.

"What do you mean?"

"Let's start with your interminable love for your late wife."

Nick was aghast. "How much do you know about me and Elizabeth?" he queried.

"Enough to know that your life hasn't been the same without her," Mercy asserted. "Nick, your mother told me about her. I know you loved her very much."

Nick was unable to respond immediately. He gazed wistfully into the dark, pondered for a while, and then began: "Elizabeth was one in a million women. Kind and gentle, tenderhearted, inexplicably trusting, she loved me for who I was. She believed in me . . . she motivated me . . . she entranced and gratified me in every way possible. It was like a dream . . . my life with her."

"I believe you, Nick; you both shared something very special. Elizabeth was every inch what you described, and even more. She couldn't bear to lose you. She desperately wanted to give you a child, an heir. That was the reason she came to our foundation for adoption."

Nick was agape for a moment. "Elizabeth? Elizabeth Tisco? Did you say she was at your foundation for adoption?"

"Yes. She was at the National Foundation for Young Mothers and Kids, Tamale, Ghana. She was to adopt a baby when death snatched her away."

"What are you talking about? Honestly, you're not making sense," Nick flustered.

"You see, Nick, I met Elizabeth in person when I was serving as a nun in Ghana. We only met once, but she made remarkable impact on me. Very passionate, determined, and markedly beautiful, her death awakened something in me . . . a zest for exhalation. I knew I had a calling outside of the convent, so I opted out."

"Why? You never told me you knew Elizabeth . . . Treasure, how come you never told me?"

At this point, Nick broke down. "Elizabeth went through so much trouble to give me a child? Oh God! She must have suffered," he moaned.

142

"She did suffer a lot of emotional distress," Mercy affirmed, watching the man turn sloppy.

Despite his attempt to contain his sentiments, tears flowed freely from his eyes.

"I'm sorry Nick . . . maybe I shouldn't have blabbed."

"No . . . please, I appreciate the information. Don't mind the tears. I'm not always like this, honestly."

"I understand. Perhaps we should leave now," she proposed in a soothing tone.

"No . . . I mean, not now please. But tell me, Treasure, you mean you were actually a nun?"

"Yes, I was. For about fifteen years."

"It sounds strange. I mean, you in a nunnery. I didn't realize that nuns could quit at will."

"Well, I had to quit when I lost touch with the vision and felt a stronger calling outside the convent. It was a really tough decision for me, but I'm convinced that I am fulfilling my purpose today."

Nick gazed fixatedly at her. The more she spoke, the more he was convinced that part of her purpose was to be his woman . . . forever. Something about the lady struck a chord in his heart. Was he falling in love or just being downright sentimentally silly? Rather than rationalize his feelings, he began to form mental images of life with her as his treasure. This would be the first time since the demise of Elizabeth that Nick would feel an emotional pull.

"Will you marry me, Treasure?" he asked suddenly, urgently.

Mercy stared at him with wonder.

"Marry you?" she questioned. "I'm not sure you know what you're asking. Just listen to yourself, Nick. I can assure you the last thing you need now is a relationship, let alone marriage. What you need is healing . . . emotional healing from God. He is the comforter and the tranquilizer."

"Okay ma'am, I'm willing to let God heal me . . . but I need to be sure you care for me."

"Of course, I care for you Nick . . . perhaps not the way you're insinuating. What I feel for you is compassion, pure agape love. I cannot replace Elizabeth. Nobody can, and you know it."

"Don't say that, please. I am not looking for another Elizabeth. God bless her soul; she's gone forever. What matters to me now is you. I care about you. I . . . I . . . I love you, Treasure," he pronounced.

Mercy burst out laughing. She stared at him in utter disbelief.

"You? Love me? Impossible! How can you love someone you hardly know? Listen, Nick, no need to adopt an escapist ideal just because of your present distress. Our paths in life are quite different. I appreciate us being friends, but that's just about it."

"Don't break my heart, please . . . what I feel for you is real. Believe me, Treasure, I've found real treasure in you. Please spend the rest of your life with me," he pleaded, falling on his knees beside her. "I love you . . . I do . . . if only you could see my heart. All these years, I've been aloof, but with you, it's different. The past is past, and I'm ready to launch into the future. If only you'll give me a chance," he continued.

"What do you understand by the word love, Nick?" Mercy probed.

"Love is an unconditional commitment to an imperfect being. Albeit not tangible or quantifiable, it is the adoring of the soul of another," he postulated.

"I like your definition, but surely, love is reciprocal," she argued.

Gently, Nick lifted her jaw with his hand, eluding her summation. "Look into my eyes, Treasure, and tell me you don't feel a tickle in your heart for me. Trust me, that is the seed of love. You only need to nurture that soft spot and allow true love to blossom. Something tells me ours could be a love built in heaven. I believe we are destined to be; let's not blow this chance."

Mercy watched him with open mouth, unable to speak or even think clearly.

"Please, Treasure, marry me," Nick proposed again in a voice laden with emotion.

"You don't know me, Nick. I . . . I'm not sure I'm the right candidate for marriage," Mercy stuttered.

"Don't ever put yourself down, my love," he put in.

"You don't even know me. You know nothing about my past. I don't want you to get hurt or disappointed someday," she uttered soberly.

"Everybody has a past. We are all products of a sinful world," Nick put in.

"Some pasts stink! Some people have been through shameful and dehumanizing experiences," she added.

"I don't understand you. What is it about your past anyway? Did you kill someone?"

"No," she replied, managing a smile.

"Were you a hooker, a drug addict, or what?" he probed further.

"No," she replied, managing another smile.

"So what is it?"

"I don't have parents," she stated flatly.

"I beg your pardon?"

"I said, I don't have parents, Nick. I don't have family. I don't have anyone to call my own. I grew up in an orphanage. Tell me, Nick, am I the sort of person you'd want for a wife?"

Nick was unable to reply immediately. This was certainly a night of surprises.

"Considering our cultural affinity for the extended family system, am I the sort of person you want for a wife, Nick?" Mercy reiterated, interrupting his train of conflicting thoughts.

"I . . . I guess I never thought in that line. I mean, about your background. But . . . that's no problem. It's just that I'm surprised. You've done pretty well in life. It's incredible, amazing that despite your background, you've turned out to be a remarkable success. I admire your valor. You are a rare gem, Treasure, and I love you even more now. Please marry me. I am still on my knees," he entreated.

Mercy watched him openmouthed, her emotions going haywire.

"I'm sorry I don't have a ring with me . . . I actually didn't plan this . . . it's all happening like a scripted drama, and this is beyond my natural instincts," he explained.

"I . . . I'm sorry, Nick. I'm sorry I have to disappoint you," she said finally, rising to her feet. "I can't believe we actually had this conversation. I am embarrassed!" she put in. "I can never be your wife!"

"Never say never, Treasure, especially when my intentions are without guile," Nick said.

"I can never be Elizabeth Tisco. Our paths in life are quite different. As a counselor, I am committed to the emotional healing of my clients. Our lives are poles apart . . . I must go now," Mercy interposed firmly."

With that, she was out of sight. Nick stared after her in surprise, unable to speak. Gradually, when he harnessed his thoughts, he dashed after her. But it was too late. She was gone.

The hollow in Nick's heart was deeper than before. Ever since the death of his mother, he'd never felt such emptiness. The earlier relief he experienced with his mother's confession appeared to have vanished and in its place lay a deep vacuum. The mending bits of his life were again torn apart. This time, the cause of his pain was Treasure. Mercy Treasure, who had bluntly rejected his love.

"Why should I be transported to a hollow zone just when I think I have found joy?" he wondered. As if in answer to his present concerns, the voice of a preacher came clear on radio. It was the new Salvation FM station proclaiming the Good News.

"Somebody out there is hurting. Somebody out there feels pain and emptiness. The good news is that God Almighty is the only true remedy for your pain. He is the Lord who feels your emptiness. He offers a valid solution today. Stop looking for human comfort. Stop looking for solace in another mortal. Your strength, your friends, even your family can fail you, but God never fails. He never fades. Give Him a chance today. Call upon

Him to take charge of your life. He is the immortal Lord, the invisible one, the one who never fails. Submit to His Lordship and be delivered from the power of Satan. Why not invite Him right now into your life?"

As the preacher's voice blared loud and clear, Nick fell on his knees in sorrow. "Yes Lord, I feel miserable, I feel sorrowful. My life is worthless! Take away this wrenching pain from me. Help me overcome the pangs of life. The trials and many uncertainties of earthly existence are driving me nuts. I know that in heaven, there will be no tears, no aches, no pains. It will be all bliss. Lord help me, deliver me!" he cried, groaning and releasing the tears of frustration unreservedly. Nick wept like a baby. He wept like he'd never done before, except at Elizabeth's tomb weeks ago. The difference, however, was that this time, he wasn't crying to man, he was crying to God, the Supreme Being, the Creator of the universe, the Omnipotent, Omnipresent, and Omniscient one. Gradually, magically, his pain started melting. The tension was dissolving, vanishing like vapor in the wind. When he opened his eyes, he felt relieved. He felt renewed, he felt refreshed. It was a new experience for him as he rose to his feet in ecstasy. He couldn't believe the joy in his heart. It was so dramatic, the transformation of his soul. From depression, he was now floating on a new pedestal of peace and hope.

One, two, three weeks went by, and Nick decided to make the call.

"Hello, Treasure, Nick Tisco on the line," he announced the moment the line went through.

"Nick!" Mercy gasped from her end. "I don't believe it. How have you been?" she asked, unable to contain her excitement. She'd actually had him in mind for some time.

"I'm doing great, Treasure. I've been meaning to speak to you. I've been eager to tell you that you were right. I've found the Lord, or should I say, the Lord found me."

Mercy swallowed hard and listened intensely.

"Oh Treasure, my life has changed. I've been healed of every pain and every ache. I'm a happy man, Treasure. I'm a new creature in Christ . . ."

"Congratulations Nick!" Mercy replied in excitement. "Congratulations, my friend, you have made a wise decision; the greatest decision any man can make is receiving true salvation. Congratulations!" she screamed in ecstasy. She was genuinely happy for him.

"Thanks, Treasure," he replied, then paused for a while.

"Are you there, Nick?" Mercy asked.

"*Em,* yes. I was just wondering . . ."

"Wondering about what?" she queried.

"Can I pick you up for dinner tonight? I mean, if it's convenient for you, of course," he stuttered.

"I would love that, Nick. You can pick me up from my office. I presume you still have the business card I gave you?"

"Absolutely, I know your office. I was there a week ago; I wanted to surprise you, but I didn't have the courage to see you face to face, so I simply turned back," he confessed.

"Oh my God, are you serious?"

"Oh yes, as serious as serious can be. I'll pick you up at seven. Is that okay?"

"Seven is fine," Mercy replied, smiling contentedly before they said their good-byes and the line disengaged.

At exactly seven o'clock, Nick was at her door. Mercy was set for their date as she locked her door firmly and followed him to his car. They agreed that Nick would bring her back to the office to pick up her car and go home afterwards.

Their drive to the restaurant was smooth. The traffic was light, and they engaged in a lively chat about the goings-on at work. Mercy was as usual, very busy with her numerous programs, whilst Nick, who oversaw his family business, narrated how boring his routine was as the CEO of his company. As soon as they settled to dinner, Mercy began with a different subject matter.

"So tell me, Nick, how did it happen? I mean, about your transformation . . . your salvation experience."

"You won't believe it. That day after you left me at the restaurant, I went back home depressed. I was so unhappy and miserable. That was quite understandable, considering that I'm human. However, I realized after a radio broadcast that my frustrations needed divine intervention. There and then in my bedroom, I invited Jesus into my life. I asked Him to forgive me my sins. I determined never again to wallow in self-pity. I don't have any regrets. That decision has changed my life."

"I am proud of you, Nick," Mercy said, her gaze focused on him. "You are a wise man. You are a strong man. Congratulations again."

"Thanks, Treasure. And what about you? When did you make that decision?" he asked.

"Many many years ago. It happened just before I went to the convent. My life was a wreck; I was physically, mentally, and emotionally unclean. I needed God to clean up my messed-up psyche, heal my pain, my hurt, my agony, and my frustrations."

"That makes us two of a kind," Nick put in. "Now tell me, what is the secret of your success?"

Mercy let out a delightful laugh before speaking. "You sound like you're interviewing the world's richest woman."

"You are right, Mercy. You are one of the world's richest women. Forget about quantifying wealth now in monetary terms. The fact is, you are mentally and spiritually wealthy; endowed with such great talent. Your impact and positive influence are phenomenal."

"Thanks Nick. I feel honored by the compliment," she said, her heart thumping hard with an inward tickle.

"I never really knew what poverty was," Nick continued. "I've never lacked anything materially since the day I was born. I would say I was born with a silver spoon. Yet, I feel humbled just looking at you and realizing that every man has the opportunity to make it in life, despite the inequalities of our backgrounds."

"I agree with you. By God, every human being has the potential to succeed," Mercy affirmed.

"You are truly amazing. I mean, you've been through harrowing times, yet you turned out so good," Nick continued.

"True," Mercy said, fiddling with her glass of juice. "I have been through very rough times. If it wasn't for sheer determination and of course, the grace of God, I would have been six feet under ground and eternally condemned. There were times in my life I felt lost, lonely, rejected, hopeless. But I looked beyond my immediate circumstances. I believed and still believe that it's never over until it's over. I had a strong will to live. My dreams were always driving me on. I was focused. I was determined to change my sad story. I was an orphan, Nick, but I didn't take it out on society. I had life, and that was enough evidence that God had a purpose for me. I wasn't looking for pity; I didn't want sympathy. I wanted to be me, the person that God created in His image and likeness. I wanted to make a difference, so I left my past behind and faced the present and my future."

She paused for a while, sighed and continued.

"It hurts so much to see children abandoned by their bio-logical parents. It hurts me even more when these children turn around to become miscreants and blame society for their predicament. Tell me, Nick, for how long can one be bitter with life? The important thing is to move on, to look beyond our shortcomings and count our blessings. Like I said before, the gift of life is enough evidence that every human being has a purpose for living."

Nick listened with rapt attention. He listened with eager-ness, with tenderness, and then he said: "You are an incredible woman, Treasure. The world needs to hear your message of hope, to learn from your experience."

"Absolutely," she said almost in a whisper. "That's why I've dedicated my life and time to the service of humanity. My great-est joy is to see hope in a situation of hopelessness, to see joy in place of sorrow, to see light in place of darkness. But I must say that one of the greatest problems of man is his inability to look beyond adversity. Man must realize that adversity often precedes promotion. Every negative situation in our lives can be converted to a positive one if only we have the right attitude of optimism, faith, and hope in God."

"I'm thrilled," Nick announced. "Absolutely thrilled," he put in, gazing at her fixatedly. "Treasure, please make me your partner in this crusade."

Mercy looked at him with inquiring eyes.

"What I mean is that I want to spend the rest of my life committed to the cause of humanity. I have been too bored with work, and I think I am beginning to see why. Beyond working for sustenance, one must make a difference in order to enjoy self-actualization. I think I need to make a positive impact too; otherwise, I may never be fulfilled. Please make me your partner . . . I want to invest quality time and quality resources to the success of your crusades. I believe that good visions like yours need the commitment and support of discerning corporate organizations and good-spirited individuals. Some of us are called to be a part of other people's noble visions. What's the essence of living if I can't affect my generation positively in my own little way?" he asked.

Mercy watched as he felt his inner jacket pocket. He brought out a checkbook and began writing. "Here. This is just for a start. I want you to use the mass media to spread your crusade to the ends of the earth. Tell people to stop looking back to their past, but rather to face the future squarely."

Mercy looked at the check and gasped. "One hundred and fifty million naira?" she asked, quite certain that her eyes were deceiving her. "It can't be. Is this one hundred and fifty million naira you're giving me? That's approximately one million dollars," she exclaimed, handing him the check in disbelief. Nick did not take the check from her, so she dropped it on the table.

"Yes, Treasure. That's because I want you to spread the good news. I want your campaigns for the women, children, and humanity to reach every nook and cranny of this land. If you are not comfortable with the check, let me have your bank details, and it can be paid directly into your account."

"I don't believe it!" Mercy exclaimed. "Do you know what one hundred and fifty million naira is?" she asked in confusion.

"Please, Treasure. That's the least I can do. It's no big deal really, and I tell you it gives me joy knowing I can contribute my little quota."

Mercy sighed and cogitated for a while.

"I can't accept this, Nick. You're giving this money on impulse. You may regret it tomorrow. Please, I can't have it. I really appreciate the gesture, but I can't. It's just too much."

"How big is your dream, Treasure? Tell me, how big is it? It's my money, remember? And I'm the one giving it. I feel delighted giving it. I feel honored giving it. Please, for God's sake, don't refuse."

Mercy rose to her feet. "You are always so full of surprises, Nick, but this one, I just can't handle it. I'm sorry."

Nick was on his feet immediately. "Do you despise me this much?" he asked, looking at her straight in the eyes. "No strings attached, Treasure. No strings attached, but I want you to have it, please."

"No . . . I can't, I'm sorry."

Nick watched in defeat, made to say something and suddenly blurted out, "Okay Treasure, I flopped. I meant no harm," he said in exasperation. "I was only trying to help. You don't have to accept the money really, but please don't go yet."

Mercy nodded her head, handed the check over to him and retraced her steps to her seat. They ate the rest of their meal in silence, each preoccupied with their private thoughts.

"Treasure," Nick called when they finished eating. Mercy raised her head to meet his eyes.

"I don't know how to say this, but . . . I . . . don't get me wrong; honestly, my intentions are genuine. There's something about you that belongs to me, Treasure, and that's your heart," he said, gently taking her hands. "Something tells me that we are destined to be. We are meant for each other, Treasure."

Mercy opened her mouth to say something but couldn't utter a word.

"I've tried hard to quell the feeling, but I can't help it." He paused suddenly, sighed and said almost in a whisper. "I love you, Treasure. I love you with my whole heart. Please give me a chance."

"Nick, please," Mercy said, turning away from his gaze. "I . . . I'm not sure you know what you're asking."

"I'm as sure as I am about night and day. You are the woman I want to spend the rest of my life with."

"What makes you so sure, Nick? What makes you so sure that you're not just acting on impulse?" she queried, feeling rather uneasy.

"I know from the depth of my heart, and something tells me you feel the same way too. But you are afraid. You are terrified about the unknown. Please, Treasure, I love you, and I want to marry you. If you will accept my humble proposal, I promise I'll never fail you. I promise to treasure you forever. I promise ours will be a marriage made in heaven. Do you believe me, Treasure? Do you believe the sincerity of my heart? Can you entrust me with your golden heart?"

"Nick, I—" she was saying when he interposed.

"Don't refuse me, Treasure. Don't reject my love, which is for real."

"I'm afraid, Nick," she said quietly, looking into his eyes. "I'm afraid that you'll be disappointed. Marriage has never been on my list of priorities. It's never even been my ambition. I don't know what it feels like to be in love. Honestly, Nick, I don't know what it feels like to love a man," she said solemnly, her voice barely audible as Nick gazed into her eyes with affection and compassion.

"Love is like a grain of corn planted in the soil. When it's tended and watered, it germinates. It grows and sprouts with cubs of corn," he said, in response to her fears.

"Love is a dangerous game, Nick; besides, love is not a bed of roses," she put in.

"Just like life isn't a bed of roses. Even if it were, roses have thorns. I want us to be together in good times and in bad times. I want to share your joy, laughter, and tears in trying times. Love makes the difference in a wicked world, particularly when that love is founded in God," Nick proffered.

"You sound so convincing but . . . I . . . I am not sure . . . I mean, this isn't part of what I bargained for when our paths crossed," she said nervously.

"Calm down, Treasure. I know you don't hate me. I know you don't despise me either. I know you like me as a person. But I also know that I'm not mistaken about you and me," he said convincingly, planting a kiss on her right hand.

Mercy closed her eyes briefly. She thought it was a dream, only to awake to Nick by her side still eagerly awaiting her reply. Before she could set her thoughts together, he was down on his knees beside her. Without further ado, he slipped a diamond ring onto her finger. "I love you," he said gently, rising to his feet and resuming his seat. "We can arrange the wedding immediately," he continued, unaware of her internal war.

Something in Mercy told her Nick was serious. Something told her they were going to be more than just good friends. Eventually when he dropped her off at her office that night, she was enthralled and entranced by the ongoing. As she drove homewards from work, thoughts of his proposition filled her heart. She didn't return the ring Nick gave her, but she told him to give her two weeks to consider the proposal. It was the longest two weeks of her life. She communed with God, the original lover of her soul, seeking His face concerning her and Nick. She got her Maker's approval, and an inexplicable inner peace followed. She thereafter called and spoke at length with her mentor, Mother Araba. After severe questioning, the reverend mother gave her consent and blessings.

Exactly six weeks later, Mercy and Nick were declared husband and wife. They exchanged their "I do" at a private ceremony witnessed by a few friends and associates.

CHAPTER TWENTY-TWO

It was the dawn of dusk and a cool evening preceding the late evening rains. For weeks, it had been raining cats and dogs every night before eleven. Bilkisu had just arrived home from work where she eked out a living full-time as an auxiliary nurse. It had been a very tiring day at work, particularly as it was a Friday and the backlog of the week's activities weighed down on her. The thought of returning to work early the following day to lead irritable pregnant women in their antenatal class was very depressing. She wasn't looking forward to it, and she was eager to gather all the strength she could in preparation for tomorrow's hurdle.

As soon as she entered her shanty room located in the heart of Mushin, Lagos, she became apprehensive. One thing she certainly didn't need at the moment was further stress, and that to her, was exactly what Alexander symbolized. She'd been accommodating him for the past three months and already was fed-up, sick and tired of him.

Her instinct was to send him packing instantly, but on second thought, she decided to keep her cool—if only for old time's sake. Who would have believed that a few years ago the going was good between them? It may not have been that good, but it certainly was better than what it was now. Imagine a struggling lady like her bearing the burden of a helpless invalid. To worsen matters, there was no hope in sight for him. His badly battered legs were decaying, despite her efforts at nursing him to normalcy.

She surveyed the room with her eyes, indisputably at her wit's end. First and foremost, she had to tell him some hard truths. Next, she'll definitely revisit his terms and conditions for squatting with her.

"Hey mister," she began in a harsh irritated voice the moment she shut the door behind her.

Alexander, who was taking a nap, jolted at the sound of her voice. "Welcome, Bilki," he said, sitting up on the dilapidated six-spring bed.

"What do you take me for?" Bilki asked, standing before him with frosty eyes.

"I don't understand," Alexander replied.

She jolted his filthy bandaged legs off the bed. "You will understand soon!" she yelled, her eyes glaring with annoyance.

"That hurt," Alexander cried, holding his hurting legs with both hands.

"Idiot! Let them hurt you," she retorted, poking him on the head and screeching, "I'm fed up! I'm sick and tired of you! I didn't waste my years in nursing school to be burdened by a pest like you. My promising career in banking ended prematurely, no thanks to your turning me into an emotional wreck. Look, Alex, you are a parasite! An unwelcome leech! And I advise you jump into the street and get yourself a job!" she raved.

"Please Bilki, be patient. As soon as my legs get better, I will get a job."

"When? When will that be? For many months now you've been lying on that bed. You haven't left this room, let alone earn or contribute a dime. See what my generosity has earned me!" she lamented.

"Don't say that, Bilki. I swear someday I will repay your kindness."

"Someday, someday maybe in a thousand years. Just when do you think those paralyzed legs of yours will heal?"

"No . . . no Bilki, they aren't paralyzed. They will heal some-day, I know it."

"Shut up and listen! Your hopes cannot impress me. Get out now and find something doing. Beg for alms, whatever, just make sure you do something or else . . ."

"Please Bilki," he moaned, breaking into tears. "Be patient with me. I promise things will get better," he said, crying uncontrollably.

Bilki hissed and retorted, "Crocodile tears won't move me. After all, you are only reaping the fruits of your wickedness. Shameless animal!"

"Do you hate me this much?" Alexander moaned.

"Yes, I hate you! I hate you with all my heart!" Bilki screeched in delirium.

"But I love you, Bilki," he put in.

"Love? Did you say love?" she asked with bitterness. "You must be very stupid to say that. You must be a big fool to open your mouth and say you love me. Tell me, what kind of love goes chasing everything in skirts?"

"But Bilki remember, I only cheated on you twice. I'm a man, remember? It's natural for us to go experimenting."

Bilkisu's slap cut him short.

"Shut up! Fool! You still have the guts to tell me rubbish, eh? In fact, you are completely useless, Alexander Moyo."

"I'm sorry, Bilki. Please forgive my shortcomings," Alexander wailed. "I promise I will make up for the past. As soon as I get better, we can get married."

Bilki burst out laughing. She continued laughing for some time, watching him in ridicule.

"*Olorun maje!* God forbid bad thing. You are a dreamer, Alex. In fact, you are a clown. Me? Marry you? Over my dead body! I pity you; that's why you are still in my house today. I have a conscience, unlike you. But I tell you, my patience is fast running out."

Alexander watched in exasperation, made to say something and thought against it. Was nemesis gradually creeping up on him? Was he reaping the result of his vulgar life? Of all his mishaps, Adesuwa's hit him below the belt. Those gunshots rendered him near paralyzed, and now his only comfort, Bilki, was rejecting him. Who else could he turn to?

"Please, Bilki, have mercy on me," he cried, jolting out of his reverie. "It's not my fault that armed robbers shot me."

"Oh please, stop looking for more pity. The armed robbers should have killed you if they were armed robbers at all. Why didn't your employers help you? Why didn't you report the case to the police? Look, enough of your lies," she warned, before sinking into a chair.

She was terribly tired and exhausted. Nonetheless, she determined there and then to get back at him for the emotional wounds he had caused her. Within minutes, she undressed and changed into a transparent blue micro-mini dress and matching pair of dangling earrings. From underneath her clothes, her red-colored underwear was glaring. She coated her pretty face with heavy layers of brown powder, a thick cloud of pink eye shadow, with her lashes stiffened in thick mascara. Her lips were coated with bright pink lipstick, and she wore a pair of stiletto heels. She was about to pick up her handbag when he asked:

"Where are you going to, Bilki?"

"None of your business. Anyway, for your information, I'm out man hunting. That's my own way of saying thank you for being an unrepentant flirt."

"Bilki!" Alexander groaned. "Don't do this to yourself. You'll ruin your life."

"It is your own life that is ruined beyond repair," she retorted before picking up her bag and heading out.

Alexander watched her leave, a mixture of anxiety and worry on his face. It was late into the night when she eventually returned with a sturdy chap in tow. Alexander was awake when they both entered. Bilki's guest surveyed the room, obviously unimpressed by the surroundings. His gaze focused on Alexander, who he regarded with disdain.

"Never mind my sick brother," Bilki offered, signaling Alexander to excuse them.

He did, and immediately the two fell on the bed. From where Alexander was seated outside, he could hear their moaning as well as the constant jerking of the bed. Resentment and repugnance filled him as he sat helplessly, waiting for the door to open. The mosquitoes in the corridor were feasting on his body, and it took a great deal of effort chasing them away. It was also raining heavily, with occasional thundering. The corridor where he sat was drenched in water from the leaking roof of the unkempt building.

It was great relief when a few hours later, the fellow walked out. He looked at Alexander pitifully, dropped a few naira notes beside him and vanished from the vicinity.

"You can come in now," Bilki announced, poking her head through the door.

Alexander picked up the alms he received and quietly made his way back into the room. She was wearing her red bra and underpants, unashamedly counting a wad of naira notes when he entered. He watched her with distaste, made to say something, but the words wouldn't come out. Bilki hid her money away and fell into the bed, not sparing him a glance. Alexander swore and cursed under his breath.

CHAPTER TWENTY-THREE

Neither Nick nor Treasure was expecting the news their doctor dropped barely a few weeks after their marriage. Mercy was confirmed pregnant. The couple were thrilled and exhilarated by the report and immediately swung into earnest preparation for the unborn little tot. Upon her husband's insistence, the workaholic wife had to slow down on her activities. A large room was renovated and converted into a nursery tastefully furnished with ultramodern facilities for the auspicious embryo. Exactly nine months into their marriage, little Miss Tisco was born.

"I'm a father!" Nick announced, ecstatic at the sight of the newborn. Video and still camera shots of the baby were immediately taken. "You did it, Treasure! You've made me a dad! I'm now a father! Hurray! Spread the news, I'm a daddy!"

Still in his state of euphoria, the new dad sailed out of the delivery room all the way to the lobby of the ultramodern maternity ward of the five-star hospital. His entourage of associates and well-wishers were on hand to congratulate him. The following day, mother and child were ushered home amidst pomp and circumstance. Beautiful decorations adorned the landscaping, and the entire surroundings were lit with bright multicolored floodlights. An imposing billboard at the entrance read:

"WELCOME HOME DARLING TREASURE"
"WELCOME HOME PRECIOUS DAUGHTER"

Music filled the air as various live bands and artists enlivened the evening and played their inspirational music for the cheerful crowd. Food and drinks flowed in excess. At the end of the day, the guests were suffused and thoroughly satisfied. The new parents were indeed thankful to the Creator for their precious little gift. Eight days after the baby's birth, she was christened Precious Princess Ayomide Tisco.

Days soon rolled into weeks and weeks into months. It was exactly twelve months after their daughter was born that Mercy staged a re-launch into active service.

With her husband's support, she resigned from her employment at the university and opened a state-of-the-art counseling and therapeutic center: PRECIOUS CARE CENTRE. Her fame was spreading fast through the nooks and crannies of the country and the continent as a whole. She was up and about, giving lectures and hosting seminars on challenging topical issues relating to her field of endeavor and specialization. She became the media's favorite, frequently granting interviews, and with the recent addition of a doctorate certificate to enrich her resume, nothing could stop the glorious attainment of her dreams and goals. A dream to succeed, a dream to excel, a dream to imprint her name in the sands of time. That would certainly wipe away every memory—every pain—every stain—yes, it was going to obliterate completely that stigma from her past.

CHAPTER TWENTY-FOUR

All efforts to appease Bilkisu had proved futile. Alexander at her insistence had taken to street begging, not minding that his wounded legs still hurt very badly. Getting harassed by hoodlums and pilferers was nothing to compare with the derision and humiliation he suffered on a daily basis from Bilki. His ego and presumed dignity were bruised, and it was in his opinion, a blot on his self-acclaimed personality.

The worst was yet to come, and indeed it was a nightmare when after several harrowing months, he was informed that losing a limb was the only option to saving his life. The mere thought of amputation was enough agony for weeks, not that he had much of a choice. After all, his life was at stake. This new turn of events only created more apathy from Bilki. She threw him out of her apartment and warned him never to step into her house again.

Bilki was the girlfriend Alexander had dated in the same season as Cassandra. Being the Casanova that he was, he had a string of other girlfriends alongside. Bilki was then working in a bank as a customer care officer. She was a very attractive, intelligent, and smart lady—qualities that instantly swept Alexander off his feet. Their relationship began with Bilki committing her heart to Alexander, so much so that she thought they were headed for matrimony. However, her hopes were shattered when she began to notice Alexander's wayward ways. Along the line, the emotional turmoil took its toll on her, and she began to fumble at work. She was queried several times before finally getting her appointment terminated. Since then, her financial fortunes dwindled, and she had never really gotten herself organized enough to get another bank job. She decided to resort to her diploma in nursing, a profession she wasn't interested in but had obtained a certificate in years back, for want of better training options at that time. She thus recently got employed as an auxiliary nurse in a neighborhood clinic.

Her relationship with Alexander was already strained when he suddenly reappeared with battered legs, informing her that armed robbers attacked him. Bilki did not believe him, but out of pity decided to accommodate him. However, she had exhausted every bit of patience in him and seeing no future in her relationship with the wounded man, she took a decisive step to get him out of her life for good.

Alexander was heartbroken. He wept for days nonstop and finally had to face the harsh reality. His left leg was amputated at the Igbobi Orthopaedic Hospital, Lagos, from where he proceeded to start life under the Ojuelegba Bridge, as a hoodlum. The experience was nightmarish, more so for a handicap on crutches. Several times he was caught and beaten while pick pocketing. On one particular occasion, he almost lost his life when he was caught by OPC guys, a local vigilante group who were ready to apply jungle justice. They had in fact thrown a condemned vehicle's tire over his head and were ready to set him ablaze when suddenly, a band of tear-gas throwing policemen appeared. Everyone scurried off and dispersed. Alexander struggled and managed to escape. He later learned that a riot at the adjoining street had brought the police out. It was a lucky escape for him and a terrifying lesson learnt, so he decided to stay off stealing.

Eventually, he resorted to begging for alms. Starvation became the order of his day, as he had to struggle and compete with his able-bodied counterparts—mainly children who were school dropouts turned professional beggars who harassed motorists in traffic for alms. Gradually, Alexander Moyo metamorphosed into an acrimonious, malevolent being. As far as he was concerned, society had been mean to him, and he needed to requite in the same coin. The time had come to hatch a plan, but how? And who on earth was to be the sacrificial lamb?

CHAPTER TWENTY-FIVE

"Talking about attitudes, are you optimistic, or are you pessimistic? Are you sanguine, or are you melancholic? Are you alive, or merely existing? Dear friends and comrades, it may interest you to know that your attitude shall determine your altitude in life. Your thoughts are powerful enough to determine the outcome of your life. You need a worthwhile vision. Helen Keller, though blind, deaf, and dumb, said that real blindness is not the absence of physical sight, but the absence of vision. Now I ask, how do you perceive life? If your thoughts are predominantly miserable, don't be surprised if you wind up a miserable wreck. Your mind-set needs positive transformation and so does your speech. Speak positively into your life and destiny. Believe in yourself and your innate potentials . . . some of them latent, some of them patent. Begin to develop them, rediscover yourself. Pursue your legitimate passion, live purposefully. Disregard your misfortunes. Who knows? They could even be a springboard to your fortunes.

"To forge ahead in life, you must delineate between your past and present. Learn from your mistakes, change for the better. Get rid of arrogance and inordinate selfishness. Develop positive character and inspire others. Mind your company; learn from the wise and learn from good resource materials. Subject yourself to professional training and acquire relevant skills because it will give you the winning edge. Dear friends, once again I appeal to those of you who feel mistreated. Perhaps you've been molested and maybe, rejected. My crusade is all about giving yourself another chance. Forgive and forge ahead. Realize that hurting people hurt others, and those with a low self-image will always want to belittle you. Leave your adversaries behind and move forward! You can unlock your inner treasure through knowledge, determination, persistence, humility, and unwavering commitment to excellence. Above all, don't forget the God factor. You need a senior partner to carry you through the challenges of life. I believe in divine intervention. I believe you can make it. Now is the time to make that change. Thank you."

The following day, the speaker's crusade continued on network television. Various testimonies were recounted by those who had been affected by her remarkable mission.

"I had given up on life. I was miserable, frustrated, and dejected until I met Dr. Mercy Treasure Dakova Tisco. She touched my life in a special way. I regained my self-worth, my confidence, my being. You may not fully comprehend or appreciate my anecdote unless, of course, you've experienced battering from a barbarian with whom you are espoused. Mercy did it for me, and she could do it for you . . ."

"Mine was a case of self-rejection, dejection, and self-damnation. I grew up a very depressed kid. Felt nobody loved me, nobody cared. I went out of my way in search of love, but what did I get instead? I got beaten, I got bruised, got battered. Life was a wreck. Suicide seemed the only solution; after all, nobody was going to miss me; nobody will remember me. Poor miserable me! Then one day I heard a radio broadcast. Mercy Treasure Dakova Tisco told me I was somebody, not a nobody. She told me I could make it in life. I was at the crossroads. Which way to go? Back? Forth? I chose the latter. Thank God I did, 'cos I found love . . . true love. Love from above, love from God. Precious Care Centre truly showed they care . . ."

"I have been a longtime beneficiary of Aunty Mercy's philanthropy and recently the Precious Care Centre Endowment Fund. I was given up to die with my children. My husband was ravaged in the 1994 Rwanda genocide where over eight hundred thousand people were murdered in one hundred days! We became homeless refugees. For several years we lived from hand to mouth. Our miracle came when Mercy's crusade reached our camp. We got lucky . . . we got sponsorship . . . we got deliverance. Not me alone, but thousands of others along with me can testify to the philanthropy of this angel in human form. We could have been dead and buried, but we're alive today. My heart cry is for people to emulate this exceptional act of kindness . . . this act of clemency. Thank you, Precious Care . . . Thank you, Doctor Treasure . . ."

"Mine is a tale of hope in the midst of crises. My name is Karman Jang. I am from Plateau State. I was born the same day Nigeria gained her independence from the British colonialists, on October 1, 1960. Mine has been a life riddled with pain. I lost my entire family in the Kaduna religious crises. Totally confused and heartbroken, I returned to my roots in Jos. I began to pick up the broken pieces of my life when tragedy again struck in Jos. I watched in horror, another round of massacre—men, women and children in my neighborhood slaughtered, beheaded, dismembered, their houses burnt, lifeless bodies littered the streets. I don't really know how I escaped, but I remember smuggling into a truckload of tomatoes and potatoes heading to Lagos. That was how I migrated here to start a new life. Miraculously, the same week I arrived in Lagos, I saw a newspaper review on Mummy Mercy's activities. I traced her, and she became my helper, my mentor (breaking into tears), my backbone in a cruel world where people in the guise of ethnicity and religion maim, kill and destroy their fellow man. It's a cruel and unsafe world, and I wish every human being could have a heart of compassion like our Mother Mercy."

Then came the last testimony, a gentleman who boldly declared:

"I remember those days; I was a very bright kid. Went from kindergarten to primary, then to college and the university. I graduated with a first-class honors degree, had great expectations, great dreams, great ideas. I was a wizard in my field. I had one major passion—to build automobiles and jet planes, but instead I got jetted. I mean, I was literally thrown off track when my scholarship application for my master's degree program was rejected. I hated the government . . . hated society for denying me the opportunity to explode. I got disillusioned, worse still, couldn't get a job. The economic depression had affected almost every company I approached for employment. With my dreams in pocket, I took to the bottles. Then to crack, and then . . . I cracked. Couldn't cope 'cos I was broke. I'd reached the end of the road, when one day I met Doctor Treasure. She gave me treasure, empathy, hope, faith. I'm no longer bitter, but I am better. I'm stronger, experienced and equipped to face life's challenges and sometimes uncertainties. I had a second chance, and so can you. Thanks to Treasure, and thanks to the PCC—Precious Care Centre—they truly care."

The presenter's sign-off was next, as the program episode came to its conclusion. It was a ninety-minute syndicated television broadcast on the activities of Mercy Treasure Dakova Tisco's philanthropic activities.

Alexander sighed as the next show came on air. He'd been an ardent viewer of the network series from a public beer parlor where he often lavished the meager alms he made. Something about the subject juggled and puzzled him. Could be that something needed to be demystified. Something obscure, something blurred by time and distance.

"Mercy Treasure Dakova Tisco . . . her name sounded unfamiliar but . . . there must be a link . . . there must be a link," he soliloquized, reminiscing as he flipped through the pages of *Encomium Weekly* magazine, where she granted a detailed interview about her charity work.

Week after week, he kept track of her activities, her progress, her fame, her wealth, and grandeur. A complete dossier was all he needed, and sure enough, he wasn't giving up until something tangible manifested.

CHAPTER TWENTY-SIX

Distinguished men and women, mostly the crème de la crème of Lagos high society, mingled amid cocktails, choice wines, delicious finger foods, an exotic dinner, splendor and grandeur. An observer could easily discern that the ceremony, though grandiloquent, was certainly not a frivolous, baseless affair. Getting recognition at home for one's philanthropy was remarkable, but getting international recognition and honor for one's outstanding qualities and service certainly called for celebration. Mercy had been crowned "QUEEN OF EMPATHY" by the Consortium of World Charity Organizations.

Her awareness campaigns had spread around the globe with astonishing results attesting to her professionalism and expertise. An award ceremony was held in Washington, D.C., a few days ago, and on her return home, a surprise banquet was hosted by the diplomatic community in her honor. The events created sensational news headlines. Today's banquet had as the lead host the American ambassador to Nigeria. The venue was the residence of the consulate general of the United States Embassy, on Ikoyi Crescent in Ikoyi, Lagos.

Renowned journalists flew in from different continents to cover the celebrated, august event. Several captions were adopted to carry news on the glorious celebrity:

"TREASURE IN TREASURE"
"FROM GRASS TO GRACE"
"FROM THE CONVENT TO LIMELIGHT"
"SQUALOR TO SPLENDOR"
"HEART OF GOLD"
"QUEEN OF EMPATHY"
"WOMAN OF EXCELLENCE"
"AMAZING COMPASSION"

Alexander Moyo, as usual, was an avid follower of the train of events. His curiosity was ignited to the point of desperation. Something in him groaned for the recapitulation of an antiquated episode. The more he wondered, the more his perplexity. Slowly and gradually, he retraced the path of his callousness, her vulnerability. His cruelty, her helplessness. His iniquity, her defilement. His villainy, her injury. His advantage, her stain. Alas! His abstruse conception metamorphosed from an indistinct fantasy to a valid picture. The first move at striking his victim will be to have an audience with her. It was easy getting her office landline number from the internet and even easier getting through with just one dial.

"Good day, Precious Care Centre, may I help you?" A female voice came through from the other end.

"*Em,* I . . . I want to speak with Mercy . . . Mrs. Tisco."

"What about, please?" came the response.

"I need counseling," Alexander announced.

"What's the nature of your problem?" the voice inquired further.

"I said I want to speak with her myself," Alexander barked irritably.

"Easy, sir," the cool female voice responded, surprised at the caller's tone. "It's important that I know the nature of your problem to enable me to know which of our counselors can attend to you."

"I am not interested in another counselor. If I was, I wouldn't have bothered calling."

"I'm afraid Dr. Tisco is not available at the moment, but if you insist on seeing her, I could book you in for the twenty-ninth of next month."

"What? That's almost six weeks away!"

"I'm afraid that is when she'll be accessible. Presently, she's on tour. When she gets back, she'll attend to other appointments preceding yours."

"Are you saying she's so busy she can't even spare time for an emergency case?"

"I already explained to you, sir, she is on tour presently."

"Listen . . . I am at the brink of suicide. My whole life's been invaded with calamity, and I'm in dire need of counseling; otherwise, I'll kill myself."

"Suicide? Did you say you'll kill yourself?"

"You heard me right, I wanna die . . . I'm gonna kill myself," he responded histrionically.

The exasperated lady at the other end sighed, paused for a few moments, and looked through her diary before uttering: "Suicide is a crazy option, sir. I believe you're mature enough to know that killing yourself will not bring a solution to your problem. However, you may come in tomorrow. What's the name, please?"

"Alex . . . Alexander Moyo," he replied, smiling satisfactorily.

"Do come in and see the counselor by 11:00 a.m. tomorrow," she concluded, before the line disengaged.

Very early the following day, Alexander was up, having had a restless night in apprehension of the 11:00 a.m. appointment. If all his plans materialize, he'll be kissing poverty good-bye for good. No doubt, the buoyant counselor would budge, and no doubt, she was very capable of accommodating his modest request of a few million bucks. He laughed coarsely at the thought of becoming a millionaire. The first thing he'll do will be to decongest his bowels of all the low-quality food he had eaten in recent times. Thereafter, he'll refill with his favorite native dish of pounded yam and vegetable soup, enriched with periwinkle and assorted meat, including snails, cow leg, smoked and stock fish.

"Then, I'll drink myself to stupor, live forever in a five-star hotel, employ a chauffeur and drive around town in a limousine. I'll buy a Rolex wristwatch, wear dark sunshades, put a big cigar in my mouth and paint the town red. I will employ two drop-dead attractive mistresses who'll give me a massage twenty-four hours a day, three hundred and sixty-five days a year. Of course, that will be after I must have fixed an artificial limb to make me get around more easily."

He laughed intermittently as he soliloquized in anticipation of his projected fortunes. At exactly a few minutes to eleven, he arrived at the premises of the Precious Care Centre, where he was immediately ushered by the receptionist into an office.

"Good day, sir, I'm Agnes Bossa, and you must be Alexander."

"You are not Mercy!" Alexander exclaimed in agitation. "What the hell's going on here? You people take me for a fool, ay? Oh, it was a ploy to bring me over."

"Please sit down and let me explain," the former said in a calm voice. "Dr. Tisco is presently on tour and considering the urgency of your case, I believe we can discuss your problem, and you'll get the same good advice you'd have received from our director."

"Hell! You deceived me!" he cursed under his breath. "Listen, I don't care to see you or any other counselor for that matter. It's either Mercy or nobody!"

"I would have thought that with the prevailing circumstances you would understand," interposed the counselor.

"I'm not changing my mind, and I'm certainly not discussing my problem with you. I'll be back to see her. I don't care how long it takes."

With that, he stormed out of the room, leaving the woman totally consternated.

CHAPTER TWENTY-SEVEN

Life at the National Foundation for Young Mothers and Kids had taken a new dimension with their recent sponsorship from the Precious Care Centre. All the buildings were under renovation, upgraded with state-of-the-art facilities, as well as new quarters under construction for the orphans and resident nuns. Mercy was delighted to donate generously to the cloister where she'd received the tutorship and discipline she was presently enjoying in her present vocation. Mother Araba and the other sisters were glad to receive her. Sister Esi was ecstatic on seeing Mercy. She shed tears of joy and embraced her warmly.

"You promised not to forget us, and you didn't," Esi effused before taking time to fill her in on major happenings at the foundation since her exit.

Afterwards, Mother Araba had a lengthy discussion with Mercy, where Mercy filled her in with details of her experience, trials, and triumphs outside the convent.

"I'm happy for you, child," Mother Araba repeated several times in the course of their discussion. "Perhaps your decision to leave the convent was for the better. You have blossomed adorably. I'm proud of you, Mercy."

"Thank you, Mother," Mercy said, hugging the older woman for the umpteenth time since her arrival.

"I must confess there were times I yearned for the nunnery, times I wanted to come back. I thought I'd made a mistake. You know, Mother, life here is quite different from life out there. While the former is peaceful, patterned, and secure, the latter is rough and full of uncertainties. But when the going gets rough, the tough get going."

"Yes, that's the spirit, my child. Even here at the foundation, you know we do have our share of trials and tribulations.

Nonetheless, the Lord always strengthens His own. Thank you for remembering us, Mercy. Thank you for your generosity. God bless you."

"God bless you too, Mother," Mercy replied delightedly.

"Please send our love to your husband and child. Tell them you did us great honor and we proudly identify with your success."

"It's a privilege to be part of the foundation's honorable mission, Mother. That's the least we can do."

"You have done very well, Mercy; I'm glad you boldly walked by your heart's leading. Sometimes, we really should listen to our natural instincts, for somewhere within our deep convictions is the voice of God," Mother Araba said solemnly.

"Oh Mother! I am glad you see it that way. Honestly, I was expecting nothing short of condemnation and reproof from you."

"That should never be. Judgment remains a preserve of the Lord. I am certainly not in a position to condemn you; rather, I have learnt in all things that the Lord can work in diverse ways, and you are a testimony to that. Being a nun is not the ultimate; rather, serving God and pleasing Him take supremacy."

"Thank you, Mother, you are my mother indeed, and your endorsement means a lot to me."

"Ah, I am the one that is privileged to have a daughter like you, Mercy. I must confess, I was shocked to my marrow when you called to inform me about Nick's marriage proposal. You didn't have to, but the fact that you did shows that you still respect my opinion as your spiritual mother. That says a lot about you, Mercy. It shows you haven't forgotten your roots. You are not one of those that burn bridges and despise the hands that fed them. Fame and success haven't gotten into your head, and that is evidence that your best is yet to come."

"Oh Mother! Thank you for your kind words," Mercy said, falling on her knees and taking the reverend mother's hands. She kissed both hands amidst teardrops and pondered for a while before continuing:

"I bless the day I met you, Mother. My life in seclusion would forever hold cherished memories for me."

"And you would forever be an indelible part of the foundation's history," the reverend mother pronounced, just as Mercy rose to her feet.

They chatted a while longer before Mother Araba led her to the rest of the team, waiting to bid her farewell.

A few hours later, Mercy was aboard the Ghana Airways flight back to Nigeria. News of her visit and accomplishments in Ghana were already rife nationwide. Major newspapers carried detailed accounts of her philanthropy there, and as usual, the machinator was an avid trailer of events.

"Shit! Shit!" he cursed, making mental calculations of her estimated expenses, as reported in the news.

Time wasn't exactly on his side, he figured, considering that the woman could blow all her money on charity and there'll be little or nothing left for him.

"Damn! Damn!" he swore, lighting a cigarette. After what seemed like several minutes of raving, he sank onto the dusty floor, exhausted, frantic, and fiery. He needed to act fast, and very smartly too. This time, he was prepared to take the bull by the horns.

CHAPTER TWENTY-EIGHT

The following day, very early in the morning, he was at the premises of the Precious Care Centre. Mercy had hardly settled to work when her door was flung open to her utmost astonishment.

"I tried to stop him, but he wouldn't listen," her secretary cried. Mercy looked at the resolute intruder, a bit of inquisition in her expression. He had barged in, dressed in rags and holding his crutches, with bloodshot eyes that sent her a danger signal. His foul body smell filled the air-conditioned room as he opened his mouth to reveal yellow, discolored teeth that stank of marijuana, cigarettes, stale food, and lingering bad breath.

"Finally we meet . . . Mercy Treasure Dakova Tisco," Alexander drawled in a voice fraught with sarcasm.

"I don't assume we've met before?" Mercy responded, a tinge of perplexity on her face.

"Oh yes we have. Think back. Juggle your mind."

She signaled to her secretary to excuse them before turning to face the man.

"Do sit down, please," she offered, still wearing a perplexed expression. "How and where did we meet?" she queried, looking him straight in the face.

"Does the name Alexander Moyo ring a bell?"

"Well, not exactly."

"Go on and crack your memory. Look deeply into your past."

Mercy watched him, rather perturbed by his lingering presence. She was startled when his harsh voice cut through her riotous thoughts.

"Well then, surely the name Dada Salako, my original name, rings a bell, or better still, your name, Dada Iseoluwa, the very name you dumped and very conveniently changed for a more prestigious name . . . Mercy Treasure Dakova Tisco."

Mercy looked on confusedly, made to speak, but remained numb.

Alexander interrupted her thoughts in a voice that revealed absolute confidence and composure, "Tell me, Dada Iseoluwa, how come you turned your life around, changed your name and adopted a completely new identity? Dada, my very own name-sake, who chose the path of prudishness, refusing the advances of her debonair schoolteacher. What did she get in return? Alexander and his band of pals . . . eight of us had a field day, tearing through your youthful flesh, defiling and befouling her majesty virgin maid. Oh, how I relish that moment! I wish we could reenact the episode . . . re-dramatize it. Pity though, those poor pals went six feet underground. But Alexander remains . . . alive!"

Mercy was in shock. She opened her mouth to say something but couldn't utter a word. Darkness suddenly overshadowed her. She couldn't see clearly. Perhaps her senses were failing, or she was in the middle of a nightmare. Or maybe this was a scene from a Nollywood movie. A shrill laughter followed as he folded his arms and lit a cigarette, enjoying every bit of her misery.

"How ironical life can be. You've transformed, and so have I. You changed your name, and so did I. How ironical that after three decades, I should be back in your life." He paused, exhaled a cloud of smoke and then continued.

"It was very difficult recognizing you, I must confess. I couldn't even trace the resemblance, particularly since you've done away with your dreadlocks. You can see I did so too. But something told me I knew you from somewhere. Something in your eyes betrayed you. The emotions you display over and over again on TV, radio, the dailies. I knew there was more to you than meet the eyes."

More shrill laughter followed before he suddenly stopped laughing and quenched his cigarette stub.

"Dada Iseoluwa. Who would believe you were born wretched! A common orphan girl just like me, abandoned to fate. No father, no mother, but you've beaten all odds to become a superstar, a hero of the people. The compassionate nun turned crusader. You sure have always been ambitious, my dear."

Mercy let out a shrill cry, holding her hands on her head, sweating profusely.

"I'm only asking for five million naira. Five million naira and I'll keep my mouth shut."

Mercy was aghast as she listened with deep repugnance and venomous numbness. "Why? Why had the stigma resurfaced from the blue?" she wondered. Never in her wildest dreams did she imagine she'd see him again. Why was the stigma taunting her? She thought he was dead that day when she heard the news of the death of his cohorts. Why was he blackmailing her? If a prophet had predicted this day, let alone blackmail by the unscrupulous fellow who abused her, she would have sworn it could never be. But alas, her whole world seemed to be crumbling. Certainly the man didn't expect her to dance to his tunes, not after the way he assaulted her, along with those . . .

At that instance, a raging nausea swept through her system. She rushed into the adjoining restroom and vomited in torrents. Her head was swirling, her vomit filled the WC bowl, and as she flushed it, she felt another round of nausea. Again, the vomit filled the toilet bowl, and the waste looked like dirt and filth from yesteryears, all coming together to be eliminated from her system. Mercy rinsed her mouth with water and rushed back into her office. Alexander was already seated, sipping a can of Diet Coke that he got from her refrigerator. Without thinking, she yanked the almost empty can from his hand and threw it into a trash can.

"You are taking too long to reply, darling," his voice rang unashamed.

"Am I in the middle of a dream or something?" she wondered.

"When do I pick up the money?" he asked, jolting her out of introspection. It was no dream after all.

Bitter memories continued to fill her senses, the acid taste encroaching on her sanity. Suddenly she started screaming, her piercing voice resounding in the noise-proof walls. She went lunatic for a moment. The pain, the agony, the pang of her affliction stared her in the face. The healing sore was opened afresh. Her heart ached, her spirit crushed, her mind somersaulted and erupted. It appeared she was at the end of the road.

"Hey lady, it's only five million naira I'm asking for," Alexander said, watching with pleasure as she underwent psychotic catastrophe.

"You are vile and disgusting. You are pathetic and rotten. You are doomed for the asylum of execrated creatures. You will pay for your sins," she blurted out, shivering and quivering, shuddering at what can best be described as the absurdity of circumstance.

Alexander's roaring laughter cut her short.

"Come on, five million naira is no big deal. Just give me the money, and I'll be out of here. Or would you prefer the world knowing the little secret of how you were deflowered? How you went into hiding . . . in the convent to cover your shame? How you disguised and assumed a whole new personality? Tell me, Mercy Treasure Dakova Tisco, how will you like your original identity and infamy revealed to the world? It will make a best-seller, you know; it will surely make news headlines. And it will definitely be the most fascinating twenty-first-century tale, captioned 'from grace to grass.'"

"You are a dirty rotten scoundrel!" Mercy screamed.

Alexander roared with laughter before he quipped: "Have you seen the movie? *Dirty Rotten Scoundrel* . . . ha, ha, ha . . . ! I could do a better act than Steve Martin," he mocked.

"You lousy joker, you are doomed for atrocious disaster," she screeched.

"I have nothing to lose, bitch!" he spat, quite unnerved by her speech. "You are the loser. Consider your daughter's life, which could be at stake. Your husband's too, not to talk of a career which took you several years to build. This blockbuster scandal could ruin your life just like that," he blurted, snapping his fingers dramatically. "I have nothing to lose . . . absolutely nothing!" he boasted with an air of finality.

"My God, my God! Why? Why is this happening to me?" Mercy groaned. "Dada Salako . . . you're dead . . . no, you're still alive. You . . . you're here," she stuttered and wailed.

"Ah . . . you thought I was dead?" he asked, wearing a wry smile. "Sorry to disappoint you. I am alive, and our paths were destined to cross again. Dada, my namesake, do you know we are one of a kind? The two of us have so much in common, except that you are pious . . . you played too hard to get. I wanted to make you a real woman, but you refused. I'm a man, and a man must gratify the desires of the animal in him."

"Stop it! Stop it please!" Mercy yelped in utter distress. "All men are not reprobate. All men are not lowly animals. There's still a remnant of men who know what it means to be human. They know what it is to love and respect womanhood. I am sorry for you. I am sorry that you are lost in depravity!" she screeched.

"Be sorry for yourself, my dear, because I have nothing to be sorry for. At the very worst I'll end up in jail, but you? You have everything at stake."

"Tell me why? Why are you driven by evil? Why are you doing this to me?" Mercy asked in between sobs.

"You . . . you dare ask me why? This is *W-H-Y!*" His voice screeched like a thunderbolt as he gesticulated with hate, one hand feeling his disfigured ear, the other feeling his amputated leg.

"I hate you! I hate women! I despise the very essence of femininity. Women are evil. They're cruel. From the beginning of creation, women have been evil. They are the greatest source of pain to man. Eve deceived Adam in Eden. That bitch! She made him eat the forbidden fruit. Then my mother . . ." At this point, he paused briefly and began to weep.

"My mother . . . the woman who gave me life. She abandoned me, she threw me away. She wanted me to die . . . but I survived. I survived through the orphanage where I was raised. I grew up a lonely child. I suffered hunger, nakedness, and rejection. Nobody loved me. My mama didn't love me; that's why she rejected me. Do I have any reason not to be bitter? No!

179

No! I have no reason for not hating the world! Women are evil. They're cruel. They are only good for sex. Yes! That's the only reason they were created, to satisfy the animalistic craving in man!"

"Stop it! Stop blaspheming!" Mercy stuttered, sobbing quietly into her handkerchief. "Not all women are evil. The Virgin Mary was the mother of Jesus. She was a good woman, and God used her. Yes, the woman had her role to play in the fall of man, but God also used her to restore humanity."

"Rubbish! Women don't deserve any respect. I can never love a woman. Never! Never! Never!" he screamed, his heart thumping at an incredibly fast pace, his voice at a horrifying intensity. Suddenly, he was quiet for a few seconds, then he began again.

"I use women. I use them to gratify my fleshly drive for vengeance. Yes! I have to avenge for everything I've ever suffered at the hands of women. Look at my ear . . . a woman . . . that bitch Cassandra bit it off. See my leg . . . another daughter of Eve shot me. Adesuwa . . . that bitch. She shot me and made me have my limb amputated. Then it was time for Bilki . . . that common whore. She threw me out of her house when I needed her most. The bitch! Just like all women, she was cruel to me. Listen, Mercy, or whatever you call yourself . . . you are no different. You're just a woman! A common woman to be used by men like me!"

"You're wrong . . . I'm different," Mercy said coolly, surprisingly calm and quiet. Her tears had finally dried up. She looked at him fixedly and continued:

"You suffered early rejection . . . and so did I. My mother equally abandoned me. You've been hurt by women. We have all been hurt. So why take it out on an innocent orphan girl? You . . . you abused me sexually. What did I do to deserve your brutality? What in heaven did I do to deserve callousness and cruelty from you? In your quest for vengeance, you went too far. You went for the wrong victim. You vent your frustration with warped obsession. You misfired. God the Almighty says we should leave vengeance to Him. What do you think would become of the world if everyone embarked on self-revenge? No . . . no. You don't have any excuse for treading the path of evil. We all have the freedom to make our choices—good or bad."

Alexander watched her scornfully, cynically, his face twisted in irritation as she paused momentarily and continued.

"Dada Salako Alexander Moyo. You chose the path of evil. You chose to ruin yourself. You rejected the love which God so freely gives humanity. Look at you . . . wretched, wrecked, and ruined. You ruined your life . . ."

"Enough! Enough! No woman can ever evoke my sympathy. Not even you Dada Iseoluwa. The only feeling I have for you is disgust and spite. I despise you! I relish every moment of the pain I've caused you. Your pain is my joy . . . your suffering my fulfillment. For every pain I've caused womanhood, I derive pleasure."

Mercy was numb. She watched Alexander with a shiver.

"You're inhuman," she managed to say when she pulled herself together.

"Society made me so," he snarled, with coarse laughter following.

"For how long will you make excuses for yourself? For how long will you blame society for your misdemeanor? Can't you see you have a right to choose your path in life?" she questioned. "Man is a free mortal being with the freedom of choice. You need God in your life. You need the Lord to cleanse you from your wickedness . . . from your evil and unrighteousness. You need deliverance from your depravity. You . . . you can make that decision and repent. You can be delivered from the chains of misery. You can be set free by the blood of Jesus."

"Damn you! Save your sermon for someone else. I don't care a hoot about God. Where was He when my mother abandoned me? Where was He when Cassandra bit off my ear? Where was He when Adesuwa fired bullets into my legs? Where was your God when that prostitute Bilki threw me out without caring how I survived?"

"So you're blaming God? Is that it? Listen, God is not responsible for your misery."

"Like hell He isn't!" Alexander screamed.

"So it's no longer society but now God that you blame. I put it to you, Dada Salako, that you are responsible for your actions. You are to blame for allowing Satan to ruin you!" she retorted.

"Who created Satan? Wasn't it your so-called God?" Alexander queried.

"Don't blaspheme the name of God. Don't you dare refer to God as so-called. You are hardened and filled with pride. You are behaving like Lucifer, who ended up barred from the presence of God. Oh Alexander, make hay while the sun shines. Repent and make a detour. By God you can be transformed from a sinner to a saint. I want you to know that God is willing to forgive you for every iniquity you have ever committed."

"I said damn you and your God! I don't care if I spend eternity in hell. I curse the day I was born. I curse the day I was made a human being," Alexander screamed, cutting her short. "I should have been a dog. Yeah . . . I don't have human feelings. I don't want God . . . I don't want Jesus either. I reject your offer. Save your breath. Save your sermon for someone else," he concluded, sweating profusely, panting like an enraged python.

"You're pitiful. God help you. God have mercy on you," Mercy muttered with a quiver.

"Give me the damn money and let me get out of here, bitch! Five million naira and nothing less," he growled.

"You certainly are foolhardy," Mercy stated, observing him piteously. "From where do you think I'll get such money to give to you? Shouldn't you be concerned about languishing in jail? Are you so sick and demented that you can't even think right?" she queried.

"I swear, I'll keep you miserable for the rest of your life," he said slowly and deliberately, rising from the chair. "I'll make sure that everyone and I mean everyone gets to know about your stinking past. I'll make sure your husband and daughter suffer. Yes! I will wreck your life. I will cause your family eternal pain. And as for you? How about you experiencing that stigma from your past all over again? We will reenact that episode . . . only that this time, you stand a high risk of getting infected with some incurable STD like HIV. You might not be so lucky to survive. Remember, AIDS is real," he bragged unrepentantly.

"Get out!" Mercy screeched. "Get out before I call security."

"Still the same stubborn girl, eh? I'm impressed," he uttered, roaring laughter renting the air as he gazed into her eyes unashamedly, clearly manifesting his reckless churlish proclivity. "I can see you want history to repeat itself," he drawled, feeling his rough chin. "Go ahead, call security. Throw me out . . . I'm waiting. You think I'm afraid? You're mistaken. Go ahead, call the police commissioner. Invite your husband over. We could have a party here, and I will tell them what kind of rotten skeletons you've hidden all these years."

Mercy was exasperated. Her heart was thumping so hard she couldn't speak. Her mind was in distress . . . she was confused. Her whole life seemed to be crumbling before her. She was so confused and frightened that she couldn't even think straight. There were so many conflicting thoughts going on in her mind. So many that she became tired and exhausted. The thought of losing Nick was torturous. He was the only man she'd ever and would ever love. And now, should she damn the consequences and tell him about her painful past? Should she stake her daughter's life to the blackmailer? Should she stake her reputation and honor for the scandal that this would likely generate?

"The money . . . I haven't got time," Alexander called, interrupting her thoughts.

Perhaps the duress of the moment, coupled with her inner turmoil, took its toll on her. Like a lamb led to the slaughter, Mercy unlocked her drawer, pulled out some mint bundles and placed them on the table. Alexander's eyes feasted rapaciously on the money.

"Two hundred and fifty thousand Naira? That's far below what I demanded."

"Take the money and leave," she said quietly.

"Don't be in such a hurry, ma'am," Alexander cut in.

"Get out!" Mercy screamed, exasperated by the happening.

"Cool your temper, lady. We are still negotiating, right? Produce something substantial, and I'm out of here in a jiffy."

"Oh shut up and get out before I call the police," she threatened, quite surprised at her response.

"Bluffs. Why bluff? Remember it's your reputation at stake here. Besides, I asked for five million naira, not two hundred and fifty thousand naira."

"Listen mister, I will not have you press me further." She was intercepted by his brazen roar, followed by a violent thrust at her table.

"I could be reckless, woman! Don't dare me. You know what I'm capable of doing."

She quivered and watched him, alarmed and frightened as she pulled open another drawer. Without thinking, she emptied its contents on her table. Alexander counted the money. It was another two hundred and fifty thousand naira.

"Thank you darling, this would do for now," he announced, throwing the money into a black nylon bag and within minutes, vanishing.

Her first instinct was to alert the police, but on second thought, she decided against it. Should she intimate her husband on the nightmarish event, as well as detail him on her tainted past? How would he react to the news that his treasure was sexually battered by a band of no-good layabouts, including her ex-schoolteacher, who was the gang leader? Not to talk of the humiliation before the public who held her in high esteem. Not that it was her fault she got raped, the fact remained that nobody had the slightest inkling of that stain in her past. The stigma she'd been haunted by suddenly stared her boldly in the face.

CHAPTER TWENTY-NINE

Days rolled by, so did her anxiety. Blood pressure was constantly on the increase for her, and for the first time ever, it appeared the courageous female had reached a roadblock. Despite her anguish and many sleepless nights, she was able to conceal her troubles for a while. Nick, however, started observing her demeanor.

"What's troubling you, Treasure?" he asked over breakfast one morning.

"Me? Nothing," she quickly dismissed.

"I know you too well, Treasure. There is a problem."

"It's probably stress that's telling on me. I think I need a break," she offered.

"Precisely. Take a few days off work and just relax, okay?"

"Right. I think I'll do just that," she replied.

Soon after Nick left the dining room, the phone rang. A cold feeling swept through her body as soon as she picked the receiver of her residential landline. His voice was unmistakable—distinct, coarse, and very desperate.

"The money . . . you still have a greater part of the ransom to pay."

Mercy suddenly felt giddy. Was this really happening to her?

"When do I get the money?" he queried, breathing hard into the receiver. She could almost feel his hard breath beside her.

"I . . . that's not possible," she found herself replying, in spite of the gritting of her dentition.

"How much have you got?" he demanded.

"I don't have more money for you, please."

"Don't be silly, woman! I know you've got money. Your foundation is a very rich one."

"The center's funds are managed by the governing council," she stated, surprised at her calmness.

"Rubbish! In that case, your husband is rich enough to foot the bill," he proffered.

"I . . . can't. I mean, how do I explain to him?"

"There'll be no need for explanation if the lid gets blown off the can. If you do not cooperate with me, I'll be left with little choice." With that, the line went dead.

The following day, she was at her office very early to clear her table. It was obvious she needed a break and time to sort out her emotional impasse. She'd made up her mind there and then to confess to her husband. The timing, however, was going to be a problem; and how on earth was she to broach the subject?

"Well, time will tell," she figured, just as the door thrust open and in came Nick, hands behind him as he entered the office.

"Sorry to barge in, darling. I decided to surprise you," he announced, smiling gaily.

"Hi, I wasn't expecting you," she replied, observing his amused expression.

"Fancy having a career woman for a wife. It's our wedding anniversary today, and I know you've forgotten," he reeled off, before presenting a bouquet of fresh, luxuriant roses to her.

"Oh my God! It completely escaped my memory. Happy anniversary, darling," she said as they reached out for a warm embrace and Nick planted several kisses on her face.

"They're beautiful," she stated, inhaling the flowers.

"I'm glad you like them. So when are you starting your leave?" he asked effervescently.

"Matter of fact, I was just clearing my table. I should proceed fully by tomorrow."

"Splendid. In that case, we can go on a short vacation together. I've been long overdue for leave myself," he chipped in.

"Nick," Mercy called in a subdued tone.

"Yes darling."

"I have something to tell you."

"I'm all ears," he replied expectantly.

"I . . . it's about my past."

"Yes?"

"Oh Nick, there are some things you don't know about me," she said, breaking into tears.

"What's the matter, Treasure?" he asked, perturbed by her sentiments.

"It happened when I was in college, in a boarding house years ago." She broke into fresh tears, started weeping and slumped into a chair.

Nick pulled her up. "It's okay, Treasure, you don't have to say anything now. I can see you're very upset." She nodded in the affirmative, and he added, "We can talk about it later, okay? Let me drive you home."

"I think I can manage. I'll be going home shortly though; remember I've got a seminar paper to deliver tonight," she explained.

Nick nodded, gave her a squeeze on the shoulder before leaving.

Shortly after, Mercy's table was cleared, and just as she rose to her feet to leave, her door flung open. She stared in shock at the intruder, made to say something but couldn't utter a word. Her flustered secretary who had come in behind the fellow looked on helplessly, muttering her apologies and explaining that Alexander had shoved her aside and forced his way in, claiming that Mercy was expecting him.

"I told you I'd be back," Alexander uttered, making himself comfortable on a chair. The secretary made a quiet exit when it was apparent the unwelcome guest was engaging in a private dialogue with her boss.

"We could strike a good deal, Mercy," he continued brazenly, lighting a cigarette. "I've been thinking a lot about you lately. I think I already told you that we have a lot in common. The two of us . . . you know what I mean?" He said, letting out a dry laughter before proceeding. "I was raised as an orphan, so were you. Our parents abandoned us to die. The world hates us. We need to requite. We need revenge . . . we can become partners . . ."

"No! Stop it please!" she intercepted, tears rolling down her eyes. "You're sick. You need help. Yes, I may have suffered early rejection, but that's no reason to be forever bitter. You . . . you have caused me years of sorrow, Alexander, but . . . I could, I choose to forgive you. Please get out now! Don't ever come back. If you do, I'll call the police."

His roaring laughter cut her short.

"I'm impressed. Still the same generous heart, ay? The saint who forgives all the way. Well, sorry to disappoint you, and you better awake from your delusion. Your past will always haunt you. I will always taunt you. No matter how hard you try, you'll forever remain the gutter kid with no family pedigree."

"No . . . you're mistaken. My past is past. I live in the present, in the now. I belong to the family of God. I am a happy woman surrounded by people who love me. I am sorry for you, Alexander. I am very sorry for you. You're blind . . . deceived . . . hardened . . . unrepentant. But . . . it's not too late to make a change. Oh please, Alexander, turn your life to God. He loves you. He wants to clean up your messed-up psyche. Turn a new leaf. Repent from your sins," she preached, still visibly shaken.

"The money . . . quickly . . . give me the money," he uttered, quenching his cigarette stub on the table. "I'm broke, and I need the money," he pressed desperately.

Her brief sermon had obviously fallen on deaf ears. With trembling hands, Mercy dialed a number on the intercom. The chief security officer was in her office in an instant. She gave strict instructions concerning the villain and warned that Alexander should never be allowed anywhere near the premises again.

"You'll regret this, I swear!" Alexander threatened as he grabbed his crutches angrily. "Prostitute! Whore! You'll be sorry! You'll regret this I swear!" he screeched, spitting and cursing as he was shown the way out.

She stared after him, shivering as his last words hung in the air. Her head was swirling when she eventually found her way out and homewards. She had detailed the assistant director of the Precious Care Centre to represent her at the earlier scheduled seminar.

CHAPTER THIRTY

It was exactly 7:00 p.m., the occasion being the annual summit on women's rights. As was expected, several lectures were delivered by various proficient speakers. The twenty thousand seat National Stadium auditorium was jammed with men and women of various races, class, religions, and ideologies. As soon as her name was announced, a rousing ovation ushered her onto the stage. All attention was on her; the spotlight beamed with distinct illumination.

Other than her firm, compassionate voice speaking for the lot of the people, one could literally hear a pin drop. Suddenly, there was roaring laughter. Heads turned around in confusion. Alexander was standing beside Mercy on stage. He grabbed the microphone and faced the puzzled crowd, while the confounded woman watched in horror.

"Distinguished ladies and gentlemen, pardon my intrusion as I recite some memorable memoirs from the archives of your so-called Queen Of Empathy. We date back a very long way . . . or don't we, Mercy?" he taunted before concentrating on the curious onlookers. "Perhaps after this lore, you shall be convinced that worms could be plastered with treasures. Not all that glitters is gold, so never judge a man by what you see. Look beyond the surface. There is more to a book than just the cover. Mercy Treasure Dakova Tisco is no saint after all. Her legendary benevolence is a facade . . . a veneer of piety! I wish to disabuse your minds and liberate your thinking. She is phony! Sham! Unreal! But I am a bona fide fellow, dear listeners, and it is my intention tonight to give you a true picture of the despicable, atrocious past, including her scandalous sex exploits of which I happened to have been a partaker. She was a whore! To the core! I will go on to give you a vivid description of her obliquities, after which you all will know

189

she doesn't deserve your honor and respect. You shall despise her beyond imagination; she shall be reproached, disgraced, eternally ostracized and immortally condemned!"

His voice gradually became faint as Mercy crumbled and passed out, amidst whisperings and pandemonium in the hall. By the time she finally regained consciousness, she lay helplessly in a very unfamiliar environment. Nick leaned over her as she opened her eyes.

"Nick," she called weakly.

He stared at her icily before jerking her up. "Tell me it isn't true, Mercy."

"Oh Nick, it's not what you think. He twisted the whole story," she moaned.

"How come you never told me you were a whore? How come you never mentioned your scandals? How come I was fooled into believing you were a decent woman?"

"Nick! Please let me explain."

"I'm listening, go on and narrate the details of your promiscuity!"

"Oh Nick, he abused me; they abused me. I was raped. I was going to tell you, believe me."

"What? What did you say?"

"They raped me. Eight of them . . ."

"No! N-o-o-o!" he screamed, gyrating as he stumbled out of the room.

Again, Mercy lost consciousness. By the time she revived, she was alone in the room. A nurse came in shortly.

"You're awake finally. Here, sign these."

She looked at the documents. They were divorce papers.

"Mr. Nick Tisco has ordered you sign these immediately," the nurse explained.

"Nurse . . . what's the meaning of this? Am I in the middle of a dream or what?"

"Don't ask me," came the frosty response from the broad-faced nurse, who added, "the whole world is aware of your maneuverings and ploys, including how you cajoled the unassuming widower into marrying you."

Mercy stared at her in disbelief.

"What are you talking about, nurse?"

"You dare ask me questions after the scandal's been blown?"

"What scandal are you talking about? The story was twisted, believe me," Mercy explained.

"You never stop acting, do you? Tell me, Mercy, how did you manage to seduce the handsome bloke and heir apparent of Otunba Michael Kolawole Tisco? I could do with a few tips, if only to gain Nick's attention now that you're estranged."

Mercy dealt her a hard slap in the face. The nurse was out of shock in a moment.

"You . . . you despicable whore! How dare you strike me?" the angry nurse spat.

"Any more insults from you, and you'll regret it," Mercy warned, pointing at her angrily.

The threat worked, because the angry nurse simply hissed and toppled out of the room. It seemed all hell was let loose and bent on wrecking the ex-reverend sister's life. As she made to leave the hospital premises, a newspaper headline caught her attention. Most of the dailies were shouting her name. Worse still, one of them was a disclaimer. According to the report, Nick had dissociated himself from her, and she was advised not to bother contacting him, except through his attorney.

"I am doomed! I am finished!" she wailed amidst contemptuous stares from passersby. The irony of life, the twist of fate and its pains thereof . . . but no! She wasn't giving up. The time had come for willful acts . . . the time had come for vengeance!

It wasn't difficult tracing him to his posh hideout where her hard-earned money was obviously at play. Gaining entry into the executive chalet was easy, as the door was unlocked. Alexander Moyo lay in the huge tub, soaked in scented foam bath, whistling to Fela Anikulapo Kuti's Zombie lyric, amidst splendor, opulence, and tranquillity. The bathroom door thrust open, and in came Mercy. She regarded the scoundrel with revulsion and repugnance while he looked on in surprise.

"We meet again," she stated throatily.

"Surprise! Surprise! To what do I owe this august visit, my zombie African queen?" he asked, disguising his earlier apprehension.

"To what do I owe your wrecking my life? You have been a thorn in my flesh for too long!" she screamed.

"Come on, Mercy, don't take it personal, take the bitter with the sweet, that's life. You know I've always admired you, only you played too hard to get."

"So you've always had the last laugh?" she put in.

"Not at all. Let's make up for the past; we can at least start by being friends. Come on in, darling, hop into the bath with me."

"You repulsive subhuman villain. Good-bye forever!"

The next thing he saw? A glittering dagger descending on him. His wailing went unheard as she dug into his head, chest, abdomen, every available part she could feel . . . until he slumped, fully immersed in a pool of thick red blood. She viewed the gruesome sight with utmost satisfaction before rinsing the weapon. It glittered the more as she held it up and brought it down slowly, making to stab herself. Suddenly there was screaming in the air. Nick shook her until she awoke. It was a dream after all. She was drenched in sweat and horror-stricken by the long, lurid encounter.

CHAPTER THIRTY-ONE

"Nick . . . you're here," she said, gradually regaining her senses.

"You must have had a very bad dream. You've been struggling in your sleep."

"Oh Nick . . . Oh Nick," she wailed, in a voice that unnerved him.

"What is it, Treasure?"

"I . . . where are we? What happened to me?" she queried.

"Don't you remember?"

"Not precisely. I can't remember where the dream began. It was so detailed, so real."

"You must have slept for very long then."

"Yes . . . it's our anniversary today, isn't it?" she asked.

"Sure it is."

"The annual summit . . . the seminar. I was humiliated. I was disgraced. It was ignominious," she reeled off. "You believed his lies . . . you didn't even give me a chance to explain."

"What are you talking about?" Nick questioned, watching her with surprise. "The seminar is still a few hours away. Come out of your dream, Treasure."

"You mean there's been no seminar?" she questioned, still visibly shaken.

"Oh come off it, Treasure, it's just four o'clock, and the seminar begins at six."

"Thank God," she said, heaving a sigh of relief. "But I remember you were at my office earlier and I told you I'll be coming home shortly," she continued.

"Precisely."

"That's it! I remember he came to my office shortly after you left. I ordered security to send him out. Then I came home thoroughly fatigued before slumping into the horrible dream. Oh Nick, it was so vivid. I stabbed the man to death. I was going to kill myself too."

"God forbid! It was just a dream, dear."

"Oh Nick, it was so real. The man in the dream . . . he raped me. He raped me several years ago when I was a teenager."

"Which man? You're not making sense," Nick said, watching her in dismay.

"I wanted to tell you everything. I was going to tell you in the office today. Believe me, Nick, I would have told you, but I was afraid. I was ashamed of that taint on my past. Forgive me, Nick, forgive me for not telling you earlier. My shame . . . my stain . . . my grief . . . I was used . . . I was abused."

"Calm down, Treasure," Nick said, trying to make sense of her confession, at the same time, pacifying the aggrieved woman. "Who abused you?" he asked when she appeared to have quieted.

"Dada Salako. That's his name. He was my schoolteacher. He harassed me. He raped me. Can't you understand?" She took a deep breath and started narrating. "It all began when I was in my fifth form in secondary school. Dada Salako, now known as Alexander Moyo, was my tutor. He was wanton and lecherous and made several sex advances that I bluntly refused. Honestly Nick, I wasn't interested in a male-female relationship, let alone with my tutor. I made it quite clear that all I wanted was to graduate from school and proceed to a higher institution of learning. I desperately wanted to change my lot in life and make an impact in my generation. I was brilliant, and the prospect of getting a scholarship into the university was very bright, coupled with the support I was getting from the orphanage where I was raised.

"That fateful day, I received an anonymous letter summoning me to a house in our teacher's quarters. I hadn't the slightest inkling that it was a setup. Nick, I still remember vividly how I hurriedly set out for my tragic journey into destiny. It was raining heavily that night, but I beat the rain and found my way to the house. The place was deserted when I arrived, except for a jalopy parked outside. The door was open, so I entered. The living room was empty, with no sign of life. Just as I began wondering if I had missed my way, a door opened behind me and I heard a voice. It was Dada. I startled and started panicking and before I knew what was happening, I was surrounded by a gang. I asked what they wanted, and Dada Salako ordered me to remove my clothes. I was frightened and started screaming. In the twinkling of an eye, he pounced on me. I fought hard but in vain. One after the other, they defiled me. How I managed to survive the ordeal, I don't remember.

"I was hospitalized and in shock for days. Whilst in hospital, I heard in the news that a jalopy with several men had crashed the night of my ordeal and there were no survivors. I thought he had died with them because I never saw him again. However, I felt unclean, befouled, and unholy. I needed to purge myself of the impurity. There was no way I could continue in school. My mind was in turmoil, and all I could think of was running away and escaping the stigma of that hateful experience.

"The opportunity came calling after I attended a female fellowship organized by one reverend sister. She talked about the honor and virtue of selfless service to God and a life of self-denial. She talked passionately about a life free of worldly cares, one that would be Christ oriented and God focused. I was convinced about my calling as a reverend sister. That was how my journey to the nunnery began. I served in Nigeria for only a few weeks before I was sent to Ghana with some missionary nuns for training. Thereafter, I became a full-fledged nun.

"Nick, I was in Ghana for fifteen years when I felt restored enough to face life outside the convent. I felt I'd spent enough years in seclusion, and the stigma from my past was almost completely obliterated. I returned home to pick up my life from where it had stopped. And then suddenly, from out of the blue, Alexander Moyo, the rebranded Dada Salako, reappears to haunt me, to blackmail me."

Nick was aghast as he listened to the full narration of her distasteful past experience. Mercy further narrated the reappearance and up-to-the-minute encounters with Alexander Moyo, her fears, and the stigma's blackmail. The ransom, his threats, and the horrible dream, everything fell in place like a dramatic series.

"It sounds ludicrous," Nick stated, watching her with a frown. "How did you survive? I mean, such an ordeal can hardly go without the infliction of physical and mental injury. A teenager, raped by a band of hoodlums . . . you, that teenager? It's ridiculous."

"Nick, I was wounded. It was a miracle I even survived because by the time I found my way to the dormitory, I could hardly walk. I collapsed and was rushed to the school clinic from where I was transferred to a teaching hospital. The doctors were convinced I was assaulted, but I refused to tell them the truth. I was so ashamed, I chose to remain mute. I didn't want the world to laugh at me. I couldn't confide in anyone, not even my best friend, Mairo, who showed a lot of concern. By the time I returned to school, I became withdrawn. I was depressed, confused, mentally sick and bitter with life. I couldn't concentrate on my studies. I often hallucinated, and every male became a potential rapist in my eyes. I was almost losing my mind when that opportunity came calling. That fellowship I attended was timely, as it gave me hope for a future. I gave my life to Christ, and that made the difference."

She paused, swallowed hard and continued:

"God made the difference in my life, Nick. He saved me. He delivered me. He healed me of every ache and every stain. By the time I was set to leave for the convent, I went for adult baptism and changed my name. It has been a long journey to emotional healing, but somewhere in my subconscious, the stigma still taunted my mind from time to time. Oh Nick, forgive me. I couldn't summon courage to tell you all this. I wanted my embarrassing past to remain buried. My real name is Dada. Dada Iseoluwa. That was the name I was given. I had natural dreadlocks; that's why they named me Dada at the orphanage. But I insisted my hair be shaved before I began my journey to the convent. I hated my old self, and I wanted a new identity. The irony of it all is that he was my namesake . . . Dada. He also changed his name and apparently shaved his dreadlocks too. His new name is Alexander. Alexander Moyo. That's what he told me."

Nick was unable to speak. He was confused. There were so many questions he wanted to ask, so many things he needed to clarify. But he simply found himself gazing at her, awestricken and numb.

"Nick, I know I should have told you. I should have damned the consequences and let you into the details of my stinking past. I should have confessed to you. I'm sorry . . . so . . . so . . .rry," she stuttered. "I didn't mean to deceive you. Forgive me," she recited tearfully, falling beside him on her knees. "I'll understand if this means the end of our relationship. But please know that I never meant to deceive you. I was just afraid. Confessing to you would have been like opening a healing wound afresh," she confessed throatily, amidst regretful, heartfelt sorrow.

She continued crying, weeping, and Nick continued gaping, staring at her like a stranger from the moon.

"But Treasure, why? Why didn't you tell me? Why did you allow the felon to get away with the dastardly act? Why on earth will you allow him come back to blackmail you when you should be the one suing for justice? Why, Treasure? Why?" Nick asked in quick succession, looking quite hurt and dismayed.

"I don't know. I only know that I was ashamed. Being raped is not something anyone will want broadcast in court, let alone me. Oh Nick, you'll never understand. I didn't want to soil my reputation. I preferred for the ugly nightmare to remain buried in my past."

"No, Treasure . . . not when the beast comes threatening you. The past should be past, true, but justice must prevail: otherwise, evil will continue to thrive. He should pay dearly for his sins! Remember there could be other victims out there crying out for justice. They are hurting and sorrowing just like you. But how on earth can the law be enforced if there are no official reports by the victims? Rapists are killers, and they should face the full weight of the law. They should pay for their sins!" he screeched in distress.

"You're right, Nick . . . you're absolutely right," she responded in a croaky voice.

"The government and concerned agencies need to be aware of the heart cry of innocent victims of assault. The judiciary particularly needs to empathize with the agony of the victims. What if you'd contracted one of the deadly venereal diseases? What if your condition had deteriorated or degenerated to loss of life? What if you had ended up demented and confined to an asylum? But thank God. Thanks be to God, the greatest physician of all times. The One who knows where we hurt and where we sorrow . . . I'm glad you found Him, Treasure. I'm glad He saved and delivered you. I'm glad He wiped away your tears," Nick recited throatily before pausing for a while. "I'm sorry, Treasure. I'm so sorry you had to go through the nightmare all by yourself," he continued, pulling her up, embracing her, consoling her, comforting her. "Weep no more, my dear. Weep no more, for it's all over," he added compassionately.

He kissed her eye and tasted her salty tears. Mercy was unable to speak. As Nick spoke, her tears continued to flow. She couldn't believe her ears. Did Nick really have a heart of gold, or were her ears deceiving her?

"I empathize with your plight, Treasure. I can imagine the hell you've been through these years. I'm so sorry," Nick continued, quite aware of her inner turmoil.

Suddenly, Mercy broke down again on her knees beside him. She wept and wept until she finally found her voice and asked, "Nick, can you ever forgive me?"

"Please, Treasure, weep no more," Nick repeated, pulling her up. "It hurts me to see you devastated. I am a mere mortal just like you. You're the one that's been hurt, and I can only be thankful that you survived the trauma. There is absolutely nothing for me to forgive," he said, stroking her hair comfortingly.

"Oh Nick, but I should have told you," she argued in between sobs.

"Don't blame yourself, Treasure. The past is past. Now we should be concerned about getting that villain, that scoundrel, that arrogant criminal convicted."

"Thank you, Nick. Thank you for forgiving me, and for understanding," she said, torrents of tears flowing from her eyes. She fell on her knees beside him again, weeping uncontrollably.

"Oh Treasure, don't cry please," Nick said, falling on his knees beside her. "We are all products of the mercy of God. The nightmare is behind you now," he soothed, rising to his feet, pulling her up, reassuring her, comforting her.

Mercy couldn't stop the tears. Tears of yesteryears, tears of her present relief. The aches, the pains, the guilt and the fears all vanished in a moment. It was like starting life afresh. Purged and purified. Hers were tears of joy, and Nick was there to share them with her.

Meanwhile, it wasn't long before the villain heard his name blaring on radio. The police and anticrime agencies were after him. Nick had informed concerned authorities to get him apprehended. Various electronic media were contacted to aid the search. On his own part, he wasn't taking chances and immediately went into hiding. After several days, he decided to flee.

CHAPTER THIRTY-TWO

Days passed by, and he was still on the run. His name was intermittently announced on radio; even his description by the announcer was explicit. Only the previous night, he had a terrifying encounter with Lucifer. It was like a vision—but it must have been a dream, because by the time he awoke, his eyes were fully cleared, and he was sweating profusely. He remembered vividly how Lucifer had congratulated him for all the feats he'd accomplished so far, while encouraging him to continue unrelenting in his drive and journey to hell. As a loyal disciple, a special crown was awaiting him, as well as a special seat of authority in the kingdom of darkness. Time was not exactly on his hands, so he had little time to ponder over the dream. All he could think of was escaping his adversaries.

The Seme border of Badagry, Lagos, was certainly the cheapest and most convenient route for him. Without further delay he was out on the street, flagging down a taxicab and heading towards the border. As the vehicle drove on, he clenched onto his bag of money, the money he wittily collected from his victim of many years. Silently, he hoped there'd be no interference by the police. Luck was with him for a while, until suddenly, he felt a chill and noticed the driver staring at him in the rearview mirror. It appeared the radio announcer was bent on revealing his identity as he went on blaring:

"Alexander Moyo, wanted immediately by the police in connection with fraudulent extortion of five hundred thousand naira. Anybody with useful information should contact the nearest police station. A handsome reward awaits anyone with useful tips. Alexander Moyo, dark-skinned man with one ear and one leg, urgently wanted by the police. Anyone with useful information should please contact the nearest police station or the Precious

Care Centre security department. Alexander Moyo is a reckless criminal. He moves around with crutches. Anyone with useful tips that could lead to his arrest should contact the police immediately. You might be his next victim. Alexander Moyo . . . he might be the man sitting next to you. Alexander Moyo . . .."

"*Oga*, what is your name?" the driver questioned, watching Alexander keenly through the mirror. "You look like the man the radio *dey* talk about," he said in pidgin.

Alexander screamed and ordered the vehicle to stop. The frightened driver halted and watched the man throw open the door, making an effort to dive out with his bag of money. But alas! The bag got hooked on a stray piece of metal on the door of the dilapidated cab. The body of the vehicle was so worn out that the door wiring and metals used for its construction were all exposed. Nonetheless, Alexander dived out—unfortunately, he miscalculated. He was knocked down by an oncoming motorbike. Sympathizers gathered round, and people were shouting and talking at the top of their voices, mainly semi-literate folks who witnessed the accident.

"*Okada don* kill person oh!" one sympathizer shouted.

"E no go better for you oh! *Okada* driver, God go punish you!" another voice put in.

"E be like say the man still *dey* alive!" another onlooker exclaimed.

The taxi driver who had observed the dramatic turn of events and parked his car on the roadside, stepped out and made his way towards the victim. Or villain? It was a juxtaposed oxymoron.

Meanwhile, the bike rider who hit him had sped off in fright to avoid the possible repercussions of the accident. The angry comments by the crowd who berated his driving had put fear into him, and even though he had initially stopped to show concern, he made quick mental calculations and escaped. He could hear the faint voices of some observers arguing in his favor, exonerating him from wrongdoing as they blamed the accident victim for jumping into the road without looking.

Chukwudi, the cab driver, with the help of some sympathizers carried Alexander back to the old taxicab. He lay helplessly in the car, groaning in pain. He had sustained some injuries on his head and right hand, which was bleeding profusely. His crutches were placed in the boot of the vehicle to give him enough legroom where he was positioned inside.

The radio was still on; it was Eko FM, and the news on Alexander Moyo was again repeated. This time around, Chukwudi quickly used his GSM phone to store the contact number pronounced on the broadcast. He dialed the number and told the recipient that he had with him the subject of the news broadcast. He was immediately given directions to the office location of the Precious Care Centre.

Whilst Alexander was wriggling in pain in the car, Chukwudi heard cheers of "God bless you" by onlookers who found his rescue of the victim from the accident scene quite magnanimous. As he ignited the engine and began heading towards the Ikorodu road, which he intended linking to the Precious Care Centre destination in Maryland, Ikeja, he sighted the bike rider who had caused the accident. The man was looking ruffled and riding at top speed when Chukwudi sighted him. Their eyes met for a brief second when the cab passed the bike. Since the taxi driver had other plans, he simply zoomed off as though he didn't know about the rider's escape. As for the bike rider, he was relieved that he escaped from the scene, as he feared that some violent observers could have taken the laws into their hands to lynch or manhandle him, as many were wont to doing in such circumstances.

The traffic was light this afternoon. It was about twelve noon. Except for a brief traffic jam at the intersection leading to Ikeja, Maryland, and Ojota, movement to his destination was almost nonstop for the driver. While in the traffic, various magazine vendors brought their products for him to purchase. Chukwudi took a quick glance before turning away. Soon, the yellow light flicked and then the green, and off he zoomed until he arrived at the imposing headquarters of PCC.

The Precious Care Centre had an inpatient hospital opened to the public. It also served as the organization's staff clinic, as well as a medical center for beneficiaries of their counseling, rehabilitation, and related services.

On arrival at the premises, Chukwudi parked his vehicle and headed briskly to the reception area to inform them about Alexander's physical condition. On hearing that he was an accident victim, a medical team was immediately dispatched to convey him on a stretcher to the emergency ward of the health center.

Dr. Isa Ishaku, a consultant traumatologist, was on call with Dr. Adaku Ozoka, a young female doctor who had just finished her housemanship with the Nnamdi Azikiwe University Teaching Hospital, Nnewi. She recently started at the center for the compulsory National Youth Service Corps, her important service to her fatherland.

Doctor Ishaku, a graduate of medicine from the University of Jos, Plateau State, with vast experience in the field of healthcare, mainly in northern Nigeria, had been with the Precious Care Medical Centre for about six months. He immediately swung into action with his team. The victim, who was by this time unconscious, had lost considerable blood and urgently needed a blood transfusion.

Doctor Ishaka took the patient's blood sample and sent to the laboratory for grouping and cross matching. Other tests were also included in the laboratory investigation. He equally set an intravenous normal saline to build up the blood volume of the victim.

Within fifteen minutes, the results of the test results were out. Alexander's blood level was expectedly low, his blood group was O-negative, and he was HIV positive. An auxiliary nursing staffer of the medical center was immediately sent to the Ayinke House blood bank of Lagos University Teaching Hospital, LASUTH, Ikeja.

Incidentally, the nurse was Bilki, Alexander's ex-girlfriend, who had previously squatted him. She had recently resumed work at the Precious Care Centre, where her conditions of service were much better than her previous employer. Bilki was amongst the nurses who attended to Alexander when he was rushed into the emergency ward. When she saw him, she initially felt no sense of pity. As a matter of fact, if she had her way she would have strangled him! The bitter taste of their relationship gone sour was still in her. She was still mad at him for messing up her banking career, where she was much more comfortable financially. Matter of fact, his saving grace was the simple fact that the ethics of her present profession, which she respected, did not permit her to act in a mean way to any patient. Her mind wondered at the irony of life and how fate had brought them together again. Suddenly, she felt a wave of pity for him, shuddered at the irony of life, and focused on attending to him with the highest sense of duty, for which the Precious Care Centre was renowned.

Mercy arrived at her office with her husband Nick in tow. She was wearing a worried look as she stepped into the reception. There was so much going through her mind, particularly distasteful thoughts of Alexander Moyo. She had been alerted by her secretary that the guy was apprehended by a taxi driver, but she did not know about his accident and the fact that he lay unconscious in her medical center.

"Where is the bastard?" Nick barked, evidently agitated and prepared for a showdown with the fellow who had caused his Treasure prolonged heartache and pain. He was boiling on the inside and felt ready to deal brutally with the chap and teach him a hard lesson he would never forget for the rest of his life. This was perhaps the perfect opportunity to display his boxing prowess.

Over the years, Nick had been a keen follower of world boxing championships. When he watched the fight between Mike Tyson and Evander Holyfield on June 28, 1997, in which Tyson bit off a portion of Holyfield's ear, he began to take more interest in boxing.

In the last few years after the death of his first wife, Elizabeth, out of boredom he registered with a boxing coach who trained him thrice weekly. The semi-literate coach had even boasted that he was a one-time trainer of Bash Ali, the Nigerian-born boxer who went to the United States of America on a wrestling scholarship from Mildred Burke professional school of wrestling in September 1974. Bash never wrestled in the United States but changed to boxing, having his first professional bout on June 1, 1978, in Sacramento, California.

Nick was not really interested in details of the trainer's profile. All he was concerned about was pouring out the aggression from his lost love into an imaginary opponent, having several knockouts and forcing his opposer into permanent incapacitation. Yes, this Alexander guy certainly would be the first recipient of his physical aggression. He wondered why the women in his life had been victims of man's injustice to man: Elizabeth, victim of his late mother's contempt and murder, and Mercy, victim of Alexander Moyo's desecration and recently, extortion.

"Sir and madam, here's the driver that brought Mr. Alexander here," the receptionist cut into Nick's thoughts.

"Thank you very much," Mercy said as Chukwudi rose from his seat, bowed in respect and went on to narrate the proceedings of the day. Mercy and Nick were astonished by the story and even more amazed when the gentleman handed over a black bag to them. Inside was four hundred and fifty thousand naira, apparently the leftover money earlier extorted from the ex-nun.

Mercy was so impressed by Chukwudi's bravery and honesty that she immediately pledged to give him the entire sum to boost his business. However, that would be after he had made official statements to the police to aid their investigation and enable them to press criminal charges.

Meanwhile, the couple were informed that Alexander was hospitalized, so they made their way quickly to the clinic, leaving Chukwudi behind at reception.

"He came in here unconscious," Doctor Ishaku explained, as soon as they were through with pleasantries.

Mercy and Nick were numb as the doctor continued: "We have resuscitated and stabilized the patient, although he is still unconscious. Preliminary lab investigations were carried out, and the results are out. Someone has gone to Ayinke House to get some blood because we need to transfuse immediately to avoid a compromise in the body circulation."

"Is his condition that bad?" Mercy asked with perplexity.

Doctor Ishaku pulled out the laboratory result from the file on his table and proceeded: "His blood level is 10 percent, he is HIV positive, meaning his immune system is weak, and his blood group is O-negative, which means he can only receive blood from a fellow O-negative donor. I received a call from Bilki, the lady we sent to the blood bank, and there appears to be a delay in her getting the matching blood. I strongly recommend that we call for an emergency ambulance referral. Let us move him immediately to LASUTH. This will also avail us the opportunity to have other expert opinions."

Nick felt saliva welling up in his throat. The scenario unfolding was like a scene from an interesting movie. The twist of circumstance and impuissance of the patient was so unexpected. Suddenly, he felt a wave of triumph. Perhaps this was providence avenging his wife, Treasure, and a quicker way to sentence the villain to eternal damnation. It was better he died and rot in hell forever. Nemesis had finally caught up with him! Nick was still rejoicing inwardly when Mercy suddenly cut through his thoughts:

"Doctor, can I donate my blood, as an urgent remedy? I am also O-negative, and I am aware that O-negative blood group is a universal donor but can only receive from same O-negative. Since our blood group is compatible, please take some blood from me and let's save his life."

"Are you out of your mind, Mercy?" Nick interposed in a voice that startled her. This was the first time in their married life that he'd be calling her Mercy in real life. "Let the fellow die and rot in hell for all I care!" he yelled.

"*Em* . . . sir, I don't think that is the right thing to say in this circumstance," Dr. Ishaku put in.

"Like hell, keep your opinion to yourself! That guy is the most despicable creature that ever lived. He does not deserve any sympathy, least of all from my wife!"

"Please darling, I . . . I understand how you feel," Mercy began. "But the scripture says in Luke 6:35 and 36, 'But love your enemies, do good, and lend, hoping for nothing in return; and your reward will be great, and you will be sons of the most

High. For He is kind to the unthankful and evil. Therefore be merciful, just as your father also is merciful.'"

"You are not Jesus Christ of Nazareth, who came on earth to die for a bunch of wicked folks who despised and ridiculed him and sent him to the grave!" Nick retorted.

"Going to the grave was necessary for the redemption of mankind. Christ Jesus died and rose from the dead to save the worst villain, including Alexander Moyo."

"Please yourself," Nick said, rising to his feet in anger. "Does Christianity remove one's brain or common sense? I cannot stay here and listen to a sermon on how you intend donating your blood to that vile fellow! Can't you see he is evil? He does not deserve yours or anybody else's mercy!"

As Nick was talking, Dr Ishaku received a call informing him that Bilki had collected the blood and was already heading back to the office.

"*Em* . . . well, sir and madam, I don't think the issue of donating blood should create tension between you. Bilki is already heading back with the sample. But we need to move him out of here to the teaching hospital for further investigation."

Nick stopped in his tracks, calmed down and squeezed his wife on the shoulder. She sat down quietly, deep in thought. Her offering to donate blood to her adversary was not an attempt to act sanctimonious. In fact, she hated the idea; after all, she was human, with feelings and emotions. However, her life was not just about doing what she liked or loved to do, but behaving in a manner that the Creator will approve and be proud of. Hers was a life of total obedience to God.

"Doctor, do whatever is necessary to save the fellow," Nick said, throatily. "Also keep us updated on his progress report," he concluded, before pulling Mercy up gently from her seat.

"We have to go . . . Chukwudi the driver is still waiting," Nick stated.

With that, he led the way out, and Mercy followed him behind quietly. For the rest of the day, she was taciturn, saying very little, except for when they were at the Ikeja police station to make statements.

Nick wrote a check of five hundred thousand naira and gave it to Chukwudi in appreciation of his role in remanding Alexander. He also commended him for being a good Nigerian. The cash retrieved was tendered as an exhibit to the police, and the couple rode back home in silence, each engrossed in their individual thoughts. Mercy believed it was appropriate for Alexander to be properly treated, and hopefully recover. Thereafter, he will face the legal consequences of his actions. Nick was thinking in the same direction too. Neither of them spoke, but apparently, Nick had had a rethink on his earlier antagonistic position.

CHAPTER THIRTY-THREE

It wasn't long before the villain heard with utmost shock and disbelief his name and description blaring on radio. He hadn't expected Mercy would involve third parties, not after the way he had threatened her. All along, he'd been planning new strategies on how to extort more money from her. His plan thereafter was to relocate to another country. Although he hadn't made up his mind which country to migrate to, his mind was set on any country outside the continent. The African shores, as far as he was concerned, had little or nothing more to offer him. Despite his disability, he was convinced the western world would offer respite for him if he eventually found his way there.

He would seek asylum from a rich and liberal nation, perhaps Canada. He wanted to spend his remaining years in splendor, but that could only be possible if he had enough money. Mercy was certainly his only tool for realizing this dream—and now? The police were after him? Impossible! Impossible? Well, so he thought until the announcement continued on radio. All major stations were hooked up and bent on revealing the identity of the blackmailer.

"Alexander Moyo wanted immediately by the police in connection with fraud and felony. Alexander Moyo is dark skinned, wears a moustache, probably in his late fifties or early sixties, has an unmistakable disability with one leg and one ear, uses crutches, his head clean-shaven. Alexander is ruthless and dangerous. You could be his next victim, so fish him out now! Any useful information about him will be highly appreciated. A handsome reward awaits you . . ."

"No-nooo!" Alexander screamed, crushing the radio set with his hands. He used all his energy to destroy the electronic set, raving at it like a possessed animal. In a desperate bid to find respite, he shut his eyes . . . but respite wouldn't come. Instead, a detailed picture of his track records suffused his senses. It was like replaying a dirty home video. From the reckless life he lived as a schoolteacher harassing his students, his mind wandered to that day he led the band of hoodlums to assault his teenage namesake.

He remembered vividly how he went on self-exile to Ghana, his sojourn at the Institute for French Education, Accra, his several escapades and relationship with Dorothy, which ended suddenly with the report by Adorkor, his student. He remembered the impending scandal that forced him to terminate his stay in Ghana and return home. Next was his foiled attempt to sexually molest Oluwatobi Majekodunmi, Cassandra's daughter. Thereafter came his fight with his erstwhile friend Dele over Alexander's attempt to seduce his sister Moji. The picture of his depravity and vile abuse of his ex-boss's wife Adesuwa flashed through his mind, his encounter with Bilki, et cetera. Rather than relish the thoughts of his reprobate lifestyle as he had often done, he yelped in torture as the reality of those events consumed his mind.

Suddenly he was in court with the women, all of them testifying strongly against him. There was hatred and bitterness in them all and a loud cry for vengeance. The judgment was pronounced, and he was found guilty, but even at that, his victims were not satisfied. They vented their anger and frustrations out on him. They yearned for him to suffer pain. They raised their voices in unison and declared "unrepentant beast! Animal! Brute! Vile rotten disgusting pig!" He started running, and they started chasing. They all chased after him, but he kept running until eventually he found himself descending an abyss. He continued descending until he ended in the bottom of the pit.

Then he heard voices . . . and what sounded like terrifying laughter. He turned round in fright and standing before him was Lucifer himself. "Welcome to my kingdom, my dear. You have done very well. You've accomplished many feats. You are a loyal disciple, and I'm happy to crown you with the seal of darkness . . . and blackness. You must continue your journey to hell. There will be wailing and gnashing of teeth. A party of anguish, a party of tears . . . a party of fire burning from everlasting to everlasting." Alexander screamed and made to run, but it was too late. He was already ablaze. As his body started burning, maggots appeared. They were gushing out of his eyes, and he made to scream but couldn't. Eventually he found his voice . . . and then his eyes opened. It was a dream after all. He was drenched, sweating profusely.

"He's all right now," a voice said as two men leaned over him.

Alexander was sure his eyes were deceiving him. Or was this a sequel to his earlier vision? Three gentlemen and a policeman were there with him in the room. He shook his head several times to gain full control of his senses. Then he remembered where he was. It was his room in the posh hotel at Surulere.

"Are you all right now?" another voice asked as he gaped at the intruders in utter confusion.

Apparently, his nightmare had been accompanied with screams and struggles. His roaring had attracted the hotel attendants to his door, and the manager ordered them to break in. They were surprised to see him struggling and wailing, barking like an enraged dog. Immediately, the in-house police security was called to help save the crazy situation. Not only were they disturbed by his violent display of madness, they were also concerned about the vandalism of their stereo set. Besides, he had some questions to answer about the mint bundles of naira notes lying on the dressing table.

"I will need a statement from you, sir," the policeman announced in a cool, calculated voice the moment Alexander appeared to have calmed down.

"It's her money. It's hers," Alexander blurted out, quivering, to the surprise of the onlookers.

"What are you talking about?" The policeman asked, looking rather puzzled.

"Give it to Mercy. Give it to Mercy Treasure Dakova Tisco," he continued in delirium. "She's haunting me . . . tell her to leave me!" he screamed, igniting curiosity in the policeman who inquired further.

Anuli Ausbeth-Ajagu

"How did you get the money?"

"I swear the money belongs to her. I stole it from her. The news is on radio. I destroyed the radio set," the blackmailer squealed in quick succession.

Suddenly, Lucifer and his cohorts appeared and started dancing around Alexander. He was invited to a banquet where the table was set with dark, stinking, horrible food that looked like rotten human intestines and defecation. The food was thrust down his throat, and he began suffocating, then puking and screaming, jerking until he jumped out of bed.

His eyes were finally open; he was fully conscious and in a split second, viewed his hospital room environment, where he had been lying down unconscious for six days. He'd had several nightmares, including extended nightmares in the nightmares.

A nurse came into the room to check on him. She wanted to refix the intravenous fluid line that was recently removed because of a swelling where it had been on the patient's hand. On seeing the patient on the floor fully conscious, she ran out in excitement to alert the doctor. Incidentally, Dr. Isa Ishaku of the Precious Care Medical Centre had just arrived to get feedback on the patient, whom he had transferred to the Lagos University Teaching Hospital shortly after the blood transfusion last week. Today would be exactly seven days since he first set eyes on the patient, whom he would be seeing conscious for the first time.

Alexander's physical condition improved. But his mind and mental condition degenerated. Day in, day out, he became more delirious. A consultant psychiatrist was invited to examine him, and after intensive holistic examination, he declared the patient raving mad. Alexander's case was irreparable. Sanity for him was irrecoverable. He would have to be taken to a sanatorium. Mercy and Nick had been informed about the villain's recovery from coma. They anxiously awaited further news of his health improvement to enable them to take him to court for his train of sins. That was never to be, because although Alexander was no longer unconscious, he was now an invalid, a raving lunatic, who was inadmissible in a court of law.

212

Alexander was thereafter confined to a mental home, where day in, day out, he roared and lived like a demented animal, thrusting his body on the floor, crushing his head against the walls, eating roaches and ants, feeding on his own excrement, exuding an aura of total ugliness and disgust. He was alone in his confinement. Nobody could go near him except for the steward who dropped food daily for him. Nobody wanted to associate with him. He became a plague, an outcast resigned to fate. Surprisingly though, he didn't die, at least not until after a few years of slow internal hemorrhaging.

CHAPTER THIRTY-FOUR

M ercy continued to wax stronger and greater, enjoying a life of unending bliss with Nick. He remained loving, generous, tender, and loyal. He was one in a million men. A man of strength, a man of character, a man who knew exactly what it was to love and respect a woman. Life couldn't be better for Treasure, Nick, and their beautiful daughter, Precious Princess. The Precious Care Centre also grew in leaps and bounds. It became the beacon of hope not only in Nigeria but in the entire African continent. It was the choice organization for grants from all over the world. The health center developed into a world-class hospital, attracting patronage from the western world.

The Precious Care Centre also floated a state-of-the-art orphanage. Mercy and Nick became adopted parents to several children, particularly abandoned kids who were too old for adoption as well as those who for some reason remained unadopted at the orphanage. The vision of owning an orphanage was conceived after Mercy had gone to visit the orphanage in Badagry, where she spent her early years. The place was unkempt, and the few children there were malnourished and sickly. She wept at the miserable condition of the home.

The current matron lamented about their lack of funding and told Mercy categorically that she wanted to shut down the place. It was at that point that Mercy decided that the Precious Care Centre could resuscitate and take over the management of the orphanage. With the paperwork done and appropriate government approval given, the PCC became the new owner of the orphanage, which was renamed, rebranded and soon became a world-class home for abandoned children.

In the course of the new management takeover, a file was handed over to Mercy by the old management team containing historical details about the orphanage. She spent weeks reading through the documents and stumbled on a shocking letter. The paper on which it was written looked rumpled, the date on it faded, but the main content, handwritten in blue ink, was unmistakable. The letter simply read:

"It has been thirty-five years since I gave up my children to your orphanage. The first was Dada, a handsome baby boy, whose tangled hair when I abandoned him at eighteen months reminds me so much of myself. His sister, also Dada, was born eight years later. A beautiful baby girl, she also had tangled hair and was dumped for you when she was nine months old. I would not have abandoned them beside the trashcan of your orphanage but for the fact I believed they will have a better life without me. My profession, high-class prostitution, will not allow me take care of these innocent children. Now I am terminally ill and soon going to my grave. I plead for forgiveness from my children. I don't know what became of them or if they even survived. My two Dadas, born ten years apart, should allow me go to the grave in peace. I am sorry . . .
Your regretful mother."

Mercy was in shock as she read the letter several times over. She then took time to look through other documents in the file. The one that confirmed her suspicion was the Child Naming Chart. Inside was the documentation of the first Dada, who was given the surname Salako by the former matron of the orphanage. His passport picture was stapled beside his name. Looking further into the document, Mercy saw her own name listed in the record several rows below. Her name was listed as Dada Iseoluwa. An asterisk was placed beside her name, and her passport picture looked like the split image of the older Dada, except that she wore a stud earring. Beside her name was a footnote: "Likely sister of the boy Dada Salako. Just for the records."

Mercy shook her head pitifully. "He was my brother . . . my flesh and blood," she soliloquized. She wondered at the surprising turn of fate. Alexander Moyo, who had passed on about two years ago, buried in the Yaba Cemetery in Lagos, was actually her biological brother. She sighed and fed Nick with the latest information. Nick Kolawole Tisco shuddered at the irony and unexpected twist. He was grateful that they both had no guilt feelings or regrets concerning the way Alexander was treated, particularly as regards the medical care he received at the Precious Medical Centre when he was in a coma. Nick was especially grateful that he allowed the natural course of justice, rather than taking laws into his hands. Indeed, it was a small world, full of mysteries, ironies, and lessons about life.

As part of its revolutionary effort in raising children, chains of schools were birthed by the Precious Care Centre. These were schools of international standards, where character molding of the children was as much priority as their intellectual excellence.

Interestingly, Chief Ehosa Patrosa and his wife, Adesuwa, became volunteers in the Precious Care Centre orphanage. They had heard of the noble mission of the center and met with the management to offer their services free of charge. Patrosa also endowed 20 percent of his business profits as a lifetime corporate grant in support of the center. Adesuwa was unable to bear biological children, so the couple adopted a set of twins, a boy and a girl, who brought unending joy and fulfillment to their union. Patrosa's only biological offspring, his daughter Tobi, maintained a cordial relationship with her father and his wife and doted over her adopted siblings. Her mother, Cassandra, continued to live life as a high-society woman. She continued dating her strings of men, some old, some young, whilst keeping rich lovers in high places to ensure she maintained her high-profile lifestyle. Her political career flourished, and she got elected as a member of the federal house of representatives, a ticket she clinched on account of being a mistress to her state governor, who ensured she got there by hook or crook.

All that mattered to Cassandra was being politically visible, making money, partying, wearing designer labels, investing in exclusive jewelry pieces, junketing around the world and gracing the covers of magazines as a society big girl. Her daughter Tobi was not impressed with her mother's way of life, particularly her relationship with men, and despite her words of caution to her mother, Cassandra did not change. As far as she was concerned, she was having fun and Tobi was too serious-minded for comfort. Their relationship became strained, as Tobi was heartbroken and ashamed of her mother's frivolous lifestyle. She, however, found solace in the comforting arms of her compassionate father, Patrosa, and her loving stepmother, Adesuwa.

One thing remained constant: Mercy forever appreciated her life and trials, her trials that eventually gave way to her calling, a calling that shot her to limelight. An innocent orphan girl, abandoned to fate, brutally abused, she had a reason to be bitter with life. She had a raison d'être to blame society for her plight, but despite all odds, she was resilient. She was hopeful, focused, patient, dogged, diligent, and persistent. She recognized the role of divine intervention, she realized the power of inner will. She rarely compromised value or integrity. She did not relent on doing good, neither did she repay evil for evil. She was compassionate, humble, and forgiving.

The challenges of life, rather than wreck her, brought out the treasure in her, showing that after darkness comes light. She was a living proof that adversity was opportunity in disguise and pain was a propelling force to birth purpose. Her challenging story became a source of inspiration to hurting souls. Now, she could look back and smile. Now, she was the one having the last laugh as peace absolutely enveloped her world. The Creator had avenged her. The stigma was gone . . . never to resurface again.

GLOSSARY

Agbaya—big for nothing, an abusive word in Yoruba language.

Aso Oke—a hand-loomed cloth woven by the Yoruba people of southwest Nigeria.

Buba—blouse in Yoruba pattern and language.

'Cos—short form of because.

Dey—a Nigerian pidgin word that means several things, depending on the usage. It could mean is, am, are, etc.

Don—a Nigerian pidgin word for has.

E—a Nigerian pidgin word for it.

Ejo fi mi le—please leave me alone, in Yoruba language.

Em—a Nigerian expression showing one either at a loss for words, or a near stutter.

Emi ko—not me, in Yoruba language.

Gele—head tie in Yoruba language.

Gonna—going to.

Iborun—shoulder sash in Yoruba language.

Iro—wrapper in Yoruba language.

Isi Ewu—spiced goat's head, an eastern Nigeria dish.

Kente—type of silk and cotton fabric made of interwoven cloth strips, native to the Akan people of Ghana and Ivory Coast.

Lagbaja—the brand name of a Nigerian masked musician. It also means somebody else, in Yoruba language.

Masala—a term used in south Asian cuisines, especially Indian cooking, to describe a mixture of spices and other ingredients—often garlic, ginger, onions and chili paste.

Na love I go Chop?—means "Can I eat love?" (a derogatory remark in Nigerian Pidgin)

Na wa o—I wonder, in Nigerian pidgin.

Nollywood—a coined name for the Nigerian movie industry.

Ode—fool in Yoruba language.

Oga—boss in Nigerian pidgin.

Ojare—let me be, in Yoruba language.

Okada—commercial motorcycle in Nigeria.

Olorun maje—God forbid, in Yoruba language.

Oloshi—means a stupid person in Yoruba language.

Oya—come on, in Yoruba language.

Sha—a slang word for anyway, in Yoruba language.

Suya –a kebab-like food originally from the Hausa people of northern Nigeria and Niger. It is made with skewered beef, chicken, or fish, and often served with ground pepper and onions.

Wanna—want to.

ABOUT THE AUTHOR

Anuli Chioma Ausbeth-Ajagu (nee Ufodike) is an indigene of Nnewi in Anambra State, Nigeria, West Africa. She is a human capacity developer, voice of influence, agent of change, mentor and mother figure to many. Anuli has a Bachelor of Arts degree in theatre arts, a post-graduate diploma in journalism, and master's degree in mass communication. She has equally attended numerous training programs and conferences in different continents of the world and is committed to lifelong personal development. A versatile communicator, she has written and published over five hundred articles in various media locally and internationally and has been published in several anthologies. She is also the author of several published books, including some gender-sensitive books like the drama *Nwanyibuife* (a woman is to be reckoned with), *Maiden* (an inspirational novel), *The King's Verdict* (a storybook).

She is the founder of Youth and Gender Network (YGN), a non-governmental organization committed to youth, girl child/women advocacy, health, education, empowerment, and development.

Mrs. Anuli Ausbeth-Ajagu is a creative mind, versatile in oral and written communication, a multi-tasking woman of impact. As a professional communicator, she has been a member of several professional groups, writers, public relations, and social development bodies. As a public speaker, she addresses diverse audiences, academic institutions, corporate, management, social, business, and religious groups.

CPSIA information can be obtained at www.ICGtesting.com
Printed in the USA
LVOW122017260312

274844LV00001B/23/P

9 781612 047928